WITHOUT FORESIGHT

WITHOUT FORESIGHT

REG RAWLINS, PSYCHIC INVESTIGATOR #12

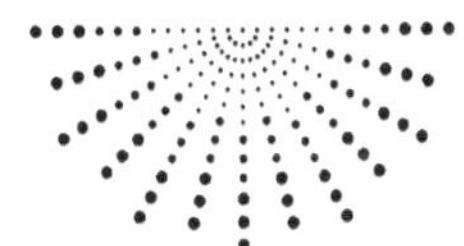

P.D. WORKMAN

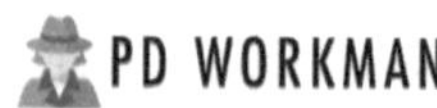

ISBN: 9781774681039 (IS Hardcover)
ISBN: 9781774681022 (IS Paperback)
ISBN: 9781774681046 (IS Large Print)
ISBN: 9781774684986 (KDP Paperback 2 ed)
ISBN: 9781774683170 (Lulu Paperback)
ISBN: 9781774681008 (Kindle)
ISBN: 9781774681015 (ePub)

A Fowl Play on Christmas Day (Christmas crossover story)

Lunar Lies

X Marks the Past

Spellbound Statues

Fur and Fury

Enchanted Mirror Maze

The Hidden Hoard of Drakuntsee (Coming Soon)

Breaking Unboundaries (Coming Soon)

Kenzie Kirsch Medical Thrillers

Unlawful Harvest

Doctored Death

Dosed to Death

Gentle Angel

Rushin' Death

Posed for Death

Death of a Corpse

Endowed with Death

Shattered to Death

Captured in Death

Currying Death

Healed to Death

Death's Charm

Discharged to Death (Coming Soon)

Following Death (Coming Soon)

AND MORE AT PDWORKMAN.COM

CHAPTER ONE

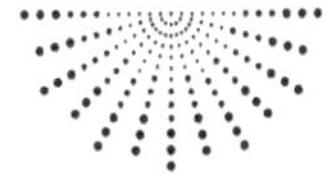

*R*eg looked with dismay at the broken eggshells and dried egg white and yolk that covered her door and doorstep. Who would egg her cottage? Teenagers? Someone who didn't like a psychic reading she had given them? Maybe it was a mistake, meant for one of her neighbors rather than her. It wasn't like she was involved in urban warfare with someone in the neighborhood; she couldn't imagine why she had been singled out for the honor.

Sarah returned from the big house with a bucket of soap and water and a scrub brush. She shook her head, lips pressed together grimly. "This is reprehensible," she said. "Vandalism. Who in Black Sands would do something like this?"

"I don't know. I can't understand it. Maybe it was a mistake," Reg floated the theory to see what Sarah thought of it.

Sarah scowled. "It was a mistake, all right. And you can bet that if I catch whoever did it, they're going to know how big a mistake it was."

"I meant… maybe it was meant for someone else. Not me."

"I don't know. I just know that it's here now, and it needs to be cleaned up."

"I'll do it." Reg tried to take the cleaning supplies from Sarah. "It's my door. You don't need to do that."

"It's your rental. It's my cottage. It's my responsibility as the property owner to keep it in good condition."

"Yes, but this isn't your fault."

"It isn't yours either." Sarah wet her scrub brush and started in on the door. Reg stood there, feeling helpless and guilty. She wished that Sarah would use magic to clean the egg off instead of manual labor. She didn't like the old woman having to do a job like that. Whatever Sarah said, Reg knew that the fault lay with her, and she should be the one to do the work to clean it up.

"Why don't you pick up the eggshells?" Sarah suggested.

"Okay. I can do that." Reg went back into the cottage to get a garbage bag. Starlight looked up from the patch of sunshine he was lounging in and made an inquiring sound.

"Someone threw eggs at the house," Reg told the tuxedo cat. "I can't believe it. I don't know why anyone would do that."

He cocked his head at an angle, looking puzzled. Reg tried to figure out how to explain it to him. Rather than using words, she opened her feelings to him. He sat up abruptly and looked toward the door. Reg nodded and sighed. She got the garbage bag and went back outside to help with the cleanup.

She painstakingly picked up all the eggshells she could find on the ground and doorstep. There was something on a large flat rock in the side garden, and she stopped to look at it.

"Sarah?"

Sarah put down her equipment and walked over to Reg, arching and rubbing her back. She looked down at the rock, where Reg had found several melted candles and markings, including a roughly painted figure that looked like a woman with a bird's body. Sarah picked up the candles one at a time and put them into Reg's garbage bag. She examined the markings and looked back at Reg.

"What does it mean?" Reg asked.

Sarah pointed to the bird woman. "It's a siren."

"A siren?" Reg puzzled over it. "But it's a bird. I thought that sirens were… more like mermaids."

"They are often represented in early art as birds." Sarah shrugged.

"Clearly, actual sirens cannot fly. It's metaphorical. Maybe because of their song. But they are not mermaids either. While they operate in the sea, they can't live and breathe underwater."

Reg stared down at the picture, trying to understand what it all meant. "So… does that mean that someone knows… about me? That my mother was part siren?" Reg couldn't bring herself to say that she herself was part siren or had siren instincts or powers. She was still trying to work that all out herself. But of course, that was what she meant.

Sarah nodded her agreement. "Someone knows about your heritage. And that is why you were targeted. These candles and that representation… and the other symbols… it is a spell of protection."

"Against me?"

"Against sirens. Yes. And the eggs… well, I guess their meaning is clear." Sarah shook her head. "Witches are peaceful. They live in harmony with nature and their communities." She looked back at Reg's door. "They don't engage in this kind of… hate."

But obviously, they had. They hadn't been satisfied with a spell to protect themselves from sirens; they had to take it further. They had to make a personal gesture against her too. To make sure Reg knew that they did not appreciate her presence in Black Sands.

"Should I… what should I do?"

Sarah raised her eyebrows in query.

"I mean… should I… is there something I can do? Should I just ignore it? Should I try to find out who did it and tell them to knock it off, or I'll turn them in to the cops or their coven? Should I… leave?"

"You can't leave," Sarah protested immediately. "No, that wouldn't be right. You can't let them force you out. Just ignore it; I'm sure that once people have vented their worry, it will die down. They'll see that nothing has changed, realize that you're not hunting here and not a danger to them."

Reg swallowed and nodded. She didn't like to think about how close she had come to doing harm due to her siren instincts being inadvertently triggered. The people in Black Sands were right to be worried. But she wasn't going to give in to those instincts. Corvin said that the more she resisted them, the easier it would become. And considering his own predatory nature, he probably had a pretty good idea what he was talking about.

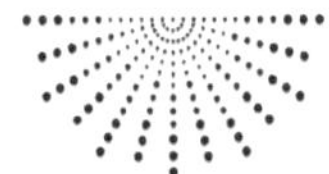

It took time to get everything cleaned up, and when Reg and Sarah finished and everything looked the way it should, Reg felt pride in their accomplishment. They had erased the mark against her name. She felt energized, as if the cleaning had been a catharsis. Getting rid of all the bad and starting fresh and clean. It felt good. Sarah too was smiling.

"There you go. All taken care of. That wasn't so bad after all, was it? Probably needed a good spring cleaning anyway."

Reg nodded. "Yeah. It feels… welcoming," she said, looking at the front door of her cottage.

"Yes, it does. Well, now we don't have to worry any more about that. How does your schedule look?"

Reg walked back into the cottage to look at her datebook on the kitchen island. Sarah probably had a better idea than she did how everything looked. She seemed to find more clients for Reg than she found for herself, and kept everything neatly organized.

She flipped through the next few days. "Pretty light. But that's okay. I could use a break. Things have been kind of crazy lately."

Sarah nodded. "Yes, things always seem to pick up around this time of year. May as well take your break while you can get it. And," she lowered her voice, even though there wasn't anyone else around to overhear them, "it isn't like you desperately need the money. You have what you need, even if you do go through a dry spell."

"It's not a dry spell. It's just… a break. I need it," Reg insisted.

"Okay. Yes, of course. Everyone needs time for rest and recovery."

Reg closed the book so that she wouldn't have to look at the mostly blank pages. Sarah was right. She was the only one who knew about the small chest of gems Reg had received from the fairies to compensate her for her services. It wouldn't do to tell other people about it and make herself a target. If she was the only one who knew about her wealth, she didn't have to worry about burglars breaking in to steal from her.

Even if she didn't have anyone else coming to her for readings or seances, she could live off of the gems.

"I'm just going to kick back and relax for a while," Reg told Sarah. She'd gotten up earlier than usual when Sarah had discovered the mess on the door. She would probably have a nap to catch up on the missed sleep. And to build up her strength after everything else that had happened recently.

"All right, dear. I'll see you later, then." Sarah bent down to pet Starlight, and then let herself out of the cottage.

* * *

Reg decided to go to The Crystal Bowl for supper. She didn't want the food Sarah had left in the fridge and she didn't want to order in. And she didn't cook much.

To be honest, she never cooked.

And she wasn't about to start. But The Crystal Bowl had been her go-to restaurant since that first day she had moved into Black Sands and had met Sarah there. Pleasant atmosphere, good food, plenty of other practitioners around who saw nothing strange about the psychic with her red hair in box braids and flamboyant fortune teller clothing. There were plenty of cloaks and capes and other odd fashions in evidence at The Crystal Bowl. Reg didn't stand out even with her eccentricities.

She sat down in a booth, not wanting to chat at the bar. She waved at Bill the barman and nodded to a few other people she knew casually.

Their reactions were a bit *off* from what they usually were. People looked puzzled by her wave instead of responding with a smile and wave of their own. They turned away from her and whispered together. Talking about Reg? She didn't like the feeling that everyone was watching her, waiting for her to do something.

A waiter approached Reg's table. He looked at her, then looked around for assistance from the other wait staff or his manager. No one stepped forward to help him or give him any instructions. It wasn't like he was new; he knew how to take an order. He frowned, then walked up to Reg's table.

"Uh… how are you today, Miss Rawlins?"

"Reg." She shrugged. "I'm fine. What's going on here? You look like you're waiting for a bomb to go off."

"Well…" He again looked around for help, and still no one else stepped forward to assist. "It's just that… we were wondering if you wouldn't be happier going somewhere else."

"Somewhere else?" Reg repeated blankly.

"Yes… maybe a different restaurant… or staying home tonight. Ordering in."

"No. I came here because this is where I want to eat." Reg looked at her hands, half expecting to see that she was changing color or into some other creature. What was wrong with Elliot? He'd never acted that way around her before. He was usually casual and pleasant, good-humored, exchanging jokes with her or telling her stories about everyone else's problems. "Why would I want to leave?"

"It's just… we don't serve your kind here."

"My kind? I've eaten here a hundred times before. What are you talking about? I'm a paying customer. You're not going to turn away paying customers!"

He looked increasingly uncomfortable. "That was before. When nobody knew about… you know."

"When nobody knew what?" Reg demanded. But, of course, she was already putting it together. The worried looks, the mention of "her kind." She'd been turned away from restaurants plenty of times in the past. Back then, "your kind" had meant a person they deemed homeless or unable to pay. But that wasn't the case in Black Sands.

"Miss Rawlins," he said in a low voice, ducking his head down and looking around as if he were afraid other people were going to hear her making a scene. She hadn't raised her voice. But she certainly could, if he were doing what she thought he was. "I'm sorry. It's nothing personal. The Crystal Bowl is for human practitioners of magic and the supernatural arts. We don't serve… other types here."

"You've always served me before and I've always paid my bill and never caused any trouble. So why is it a problem now? Nothing has changed. I'm still going to enjoy the meal and pay you afterward. If you're looking for a bigger tip…" She shrugged. "I'll do what I can. But I don't see why there should be any problem."

"I know… but it's policy. We can't have people in here… hunting. We can't take the chance of putting our other patrons at risk."

"That's crap. You let Corvin Hunter eat here, and you know he's a predator. You let Norma Jean eat here when she was in town, and her bloodline is more pure than mine. I've seen all kinds in here in the months that I've lived in Black Sands."

"I've been asked to pass the message on to you," Elliot said, raising his hands palms-out in a defensive gesture. "Don't shoot the messenger. I'm really sorry."

"You think I'm just going to start… attacking people? Really?"

"No." He looked down at his feet. "No, *I* know that…"

"You can go back and tell your manager that I'm not leaving. He or she can come out here and talk to my face. What are they doing sending a kid in here to try to get rid of me, anyway?"

Elliot looked relieved at this. He wasn't going to end up being Reg's next victim. "I'll go get you someone, Miss Rawlins."

He disappeared into the back hallway. Reg shook her head. He hadn't even served her a drink. If they were going to try to kick her out, couldn't they at least give her a drink first?

It was a few minutes before anyone came to see her. Obviously, they hadn't been hanging out in the back room just waiting for Elliot to fetch them.

Eventually, a woman came out. Reg had seen her around before, but didn't know her well. Mona, a petite, dark-haired woman with a crisp white shirt and little black tie. Usually, there was a man who was in charge. Similar in coloring to Mona, but tall and thin. Maybe her brother.

Did they send a woman out to take care of Reg because they were afraid she might attack a man? She hadn't attacked Elliot.

She hadn't ever attacked anyone in The Crystal Bowl. It was silly to think that she was going to start now.

Mona gave Reg a determined smile. "I'm sorry for the trouble, Miss Rawlins. But you must be able to see the position we are in. We are responsible for the safety of our patrons. And someone like you… who could possibly be a danger… well, we really can't risk it."

"I've never hurt anyone. I've eaten here a hundred times before. I've never caused you any trouble."

Though she did remember a series of glasses breaking. But that hadn't been her fault. It wasn't something she could control. She grimaced and thought it best not to mention that small point.

"I understand that," Mona agreed. "But then, we didn't know about your… nature. And now that it has been revealed, and you have been… hunting in Black Sands…" Mona shook her head. "You can see how it is, can't you?"

"I didn't *hunt* here," Reg indicated the interior of the restaurant. "And I've never hurt anyone. That's ridiculous. I'm not going to hurt anyone here. I'm obviously not here to hunt. Except maybe a fish burger!" Reg laughed, hoping that Mona would join in with an obliging chuckle.

But she didn't.

"Just take my order," Reg urged. "I'm not sitting close to anyone. I'm not having anyone over to join me. I'm just going to sit here by myself and enjoy a meal. I'm not trying to… lure anyone to their death."

Mona shook her head and cleared her throat. "The liability is too high. If something happened to someone here… if it became known that we knowingly let a predatory creature into the restaurant… insurance doesn't cover that kind of risk."

Creature insurance? Was there any kind of rider a person could buy for that? It seemed like they could protect themselves from any kind of risk lately. Though there had been Vivian. She hadn't been able to get any kind of insurance after all the accidents that had happened to her. She had been too high a risk.

"How about a drink and you get me something to go?" Reg suggested, trying to come up with a compromise. She didn't want to go home empty-handed. She didn't want to leave and try to find another restaurant that would accept her patronage. She was hungry and just wanted a meal. Like every other time she had come to The Crystal Bowl.

Mona paused, apparently considering the merits of this suggestion. It would get Reg out of her restaurant. But she would still be getting Reg's trade.

But evidently, Mona decided after due consideration that even just a drink was too big of a risk. She shook her head again. "I'm sorry, but you really are going to have to go."

"I'd like to talk to the owner," Reg blustered, hoping that Mona wasn't the owner of the restaurant and there was still another level to appeal to.

Mona shook her head. "The buck stops here, I'm afraid. Don't make me call the police to have you removed."

"Oh, come on! What are you going to tell the police? That you think I'm a predator who is going to eat your other customers?"

The police in Black Sands were of the non-magical sort. There were a few around, like Detective Marta Jessup, who knew about magic or came from magical families, or even had some minor powers themselves. But those who were "in" on the secrets of Black Sands did not bring it up. If Mona called in the police, she would have to come up with some much more mundane excuse for not wanting Reg there.

"I will tell them that you were making a disruption. Or that you've passed bad checks or counterfeit cash here before. There are lots of reasons I can give."

"But it's a lie. You don't have any evidence that I did any of those things."

"They don't ask for proof. There isn't any big investigation into why I want someone removed from the restaurant. They'll just take me at my word."

That didn't seem particularly fair. But Reg had been kicked out of enough shops and restaurants in the past to know that the police wouldn't be on her side. They would just escort her out. And if she gave them any trouble, they would arrest her and throw her in the tank for the night.

"You won't even give me a drink?" Reg wheedled again. "Does it look like I'm here hunting?"

She remembered when she and Corvin had seen a siren and a mermaid hunting down at the marina. It had been obvious what they had been up to. They had been ensorcelling a sailor. It had been clear. The same as when Norma Jean had been trying to lure Corvin. She got close to him, touched him, smiled, and flirted with him until he was utterly lost, with no way for him to return. Luckily, Norma Jean had not been able to close the deal or something had interrupted her from her plans. Corvin said the bloodlines were weak; a young or inexperienced siren might not have the instincts to take her prey down to the water or otherwise dispose of him. Like an animal raised in captivity that didn't know how to kill. Or if it could kill, didn't know what to do with its prey.

Mona looked pointedly at her watch. "I think we've wasted enough time on this. If you aren't out of here in five minutes, I will be calling the police. We are not serving you, even one drink, so please leave."

Reg stood up abruptly, her anger flaring. There were a couple of pops and the sound of falling glass as a couple of glasses exploded in the bar area. Mona stepped quickly back from Reg, her face pale. She pulled her phone out of her pocket and held it up for Reg to see. One last warning that she would call the cops.

And Reg didn't want any involvement with the police. Nothing that would raise her profile in their eyes or make them want to run background on her. There was too much to be found about what had happened in the past. She had no desire to go back to Tennessee or Maine or any of the other states where she had operated under various names.

She liked Florida, and Black Sands in particular.

Reg sighed in exasperation. "I'm not doing anything to hurt you," she snapped, irritated at Mona acting like she was a violent criminal. She couldn't do anything about the exploding glasses.

Reg headed to the door, struggling to control her breathing to convince herself that there was nothing to be angry about. So they didn't want her there at The Crystal Bowl. There were plenty of other restaurants that would accept her patronage.

As she reached the double front doors of The Crystal Bowl, she felt an unexpected rush of warmth and a magnetic pull toward them.

Reg knew what that meant.

CHAPTER THREE

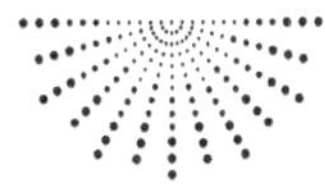

Reg stopped a few feet from the doors, knowing who was on the other side. They parted in front of her and Corvin nearly walked into her.

He stopped abruptly and looked at Reg. A smile played across his face. "Reg. Where are you going in such a hurry?"

"I've got somewhere else I need to be." She stepped forward to push past him. But Corvin anticipated her movement and mirrored it so that she couldn't get out the doors.

"You have… somewhere else you need to be."

"Yes, that's right."

Corvin moved in closer to Reg, drawing in a long breath. His eyes were intent on hers, and she felt a shiver of anticipation that counteracted the warm flush.

"You haven't eaten," Corvin said.

He said it as if he knew it, when clearly, he couldn't have. Was there something different about her smell? Or was he reading her? They had shared psychic powers and experiences in the past, so much so that it seemed impossible to totally close the conduit between them.

Reg gritted her teeth and didn't explain the situation to Corvin.

He looked past her into the restaurant, taking everything in. After a few moments, his eyes returned to Reg.

"Why don't we go somewhere else, then?"

"I don't want to jump from restaurant to restaurant. I'm just going to run into the same thing everywhere. I don't know how word got around, but..."

Corvin nodded slowly. "Your friend Julian Sabat, if I'm not mistaken."

Reg nodded. That would make sense. The investigator from Magical Investigations who had been looking into a death in the Everglades and shared a past with Reg had been very excited with his discovery that she was part siren. She had no doubt that he had spread it far and wide and exaggerated his own involvement with her and the heroic lengths he had gone to in order to close his investigation.

Yes, she had no doubt that Julian had something to do with word getting around Black Sands so quickly. But realizing that didn't help Reg with her dilemma. There was apparently nothing for her to do but to go back home to eat what was in the fridge or to order something in. Or she could stop at the grocery store to get what she needed to make something for herself.

Only Reg didn't cook. And she didn't feel like going back to the grocery store so soon after her last encounter there.

"Julian," Reg muttered.

Corvin nodded his head in agreement. "That being the case... perhaps I could find somewhere suitable."

"Where? Everywhere is going to be the same."

"Don't underestimate my ability to solve a problem," Corvin told her self-importantly. "You haven't even given me a chance."

He waited. Reg didn't want to say anything to him, but he clearly wasn't going to go on until she gave in.

"Fine. What is your solution?"

"You agree to let me try to find a solution for you?"

"Yes. I said fine. So where do you think we should go?" There was, of course, the restaurant they had previously attended at the marina. Reg knew that they allowed sirens and mermaids to get drinks there. But she was also worried that getting so close to the water might affect her ability to control her impulses.

Corvin smiled. He offered Reg his arm. "Shall we?"

Reg rolled her eyes and took his arm. He was wearing a jacket, so there was no electrical shock from skin-to-skin contact. But Reg could still sense the buzzing electricity between them. She had never been so magnetically attracted to someone before. But given Corvin's own nature, that was a huge problem.

"Where are we going?" she asked as Corvin escorted her out to his car. He was in the little white compact, not having anticipated that he would end up out with her. A planned date would have called for the big black luxury car he had taken Reg out in before.

"What about the club?" Corvin suggested.

Reg had been to his private club a couple of times. It was possible they would allow her in as Corvin's guest. Either because they didn't know about her or because of the exorbitant membership fees.

"Well… If you think they would let me eat there… yeah, I guess."

He opened his mouth to answer, but she spoke over him. "In the dining room, not one of those private rooms," she warned.

She wanted to be around other people. When it was just her and Corvin, it would be too easy for him to charm her without anyone noticing. Reg was much better now at resisting him, but couldn't assume that she would be able to fend him off all night. Or however long they were together. In the dining room, she would be able to relax, knowing that there were others around to help if she needed it.

"One of the private rooms would be so much more… intimate," Corvin countered, leaning toward her and breathing into her ear.

"I know that. Why do you think I said I wanted the dining room?"

He gave her one of his knock-'em-dead smiles that nearly took her breath away. Everything about him was designed to charm, from his dark hair and eyes to his perfectly-trimmed goatee and devastating smile. Even the rose-scented pheromones he exuded when he was actively trying to charm her. But Reg had built up a resistance and her powers were much stronger than they had been when she had first met Corvin.

Reg considered telling him that they had to go in separate cars so that she would be able to drive herself home from the club, but she didn't want to argue the point. She was hungry and he was going to take her somewhere there would be a good meal and good drinks available, for as long as she wanted. Hunger and the situation at The Crystal Bowl were making her grumpy, and she wanted the pleasant evening Corvin's smile promised.

So she got into his car when he opened the door for her, and then watched him go around to his own side.

The air inside the car became cloyingly sweet with the smell of roses. Reg buzzed her window down a bit without comment.

Black Sands wasn't the big city, and it wasn't long before they were parking in the underground garage beneath Corvin's club. He went around the car to open Reg's door for her and escorted her to the red door inside the parking structure that would take them into the club. He didn't even have to knock; they must have a motion detector or surveillance camera monitoring the parking garage. The street-side door which Reg had entered through before would be secondary. Most people would drive in and use the provided parking.

The wide red door swung open and a stunning Asian woman stood there to greet them. As with the previous hostesses Reg had met there, the woman's jade green dress had a plunging neckline that left little to the imagination, as well as being backless. Reg would have felt extremely awkward in such a revealing outfit, but the hostesses seemed to take it all in stride, graceful and gracious at every turn.

"Mr. Hunter. So glad to see you tonight."

Corvin nodded a greeting, turning his hungry eyes and charming smile on her and making Reg feel like she had been left behind.

"Melanie. Thank you. Miss Rawlins and I are hoping there is space in the dining room?"

The club had not been busy when Reg had been there before. A few patrons hidden away in private rooms. A handful in the dining room who had bigger parties or who were dining alone. She doubted if the dining room were ever even half full.

"Certainly," Melanie agreed. "Would you like drinks first in the privacy of your own room?"

Corvin turned his eyes toward Reg, but she shook her head. "No. Just the dining room."

"Whatever you wish," Corvin agreed, and nodded to Melanie, who had clearly heard Reg's response.

Melanie wasted no time in escorting them to the dining room. The large room was richly appointed, with a luxuriously deep carpet that Reg couldn't believe had ever suffered a wine stain or other culinary accident, heavy dark furniture, and portraits on the wall that had probably been painted by masters with foreign names that Reg had only heard of.

Melanie led them to a table. "Would this be acceptable?"

Corvin nodded immediately. Reg looked around, making sure that there were people close by and they wouldn't be hidden from view. She didn't want anything happening because they were out of sight. Eventually, she agreed, deciding it would not be necessary for her to sit closer to the kitchen in case she needed help.

Corvin drew out a chair for Reg and she sat down. She always felt awkward when a man held a chair for her. She was never quite sure whether she would land on it properly, if he were going to scoot it in as she sat or if she would need to pull it forward herself once she was situated. And, of course, there was always the possibility of his pulling the chair back and making her fall to the floor, like a schoolboy prank.

She'd never been much good at trust exercises.

Corvin let her pull her own chair in. He chose the chair to her side rather than across the table from her. Closer, more intimate. Less room to work with if she needed to put a protection spell between them. Corvin ordered a bottle of wine from the waitress who floated over to serve them, or what Reg assumed from the French name was wine. When they were seated alone, Corvin smiled at her—the smug, contented smile of a cat with cream.

He figured he had her right where he wanted her.

But if he were going to try to charm her to steal her powers, he would be disappointed. She knew all his tricks.

After perusing their menus and having a sip of the needlessly expensive wine, Corvin initiated the conversation.

"You're having trouble getting service in town?"

"Yes. Apparently, they don't cater to sirens."

He gave an amused smile. "It isn't like you're active."

"Who knows what Julian told people. He probably told people that I attacked him—which I didn't. He wants them to think he was tough to have escaped me. I'm sure he's talked it up plenty."

"I suppose. But it won't last. People will be eager for some scandal, but when it becomes obvious that you're the same old Reg as always, they'll forget about it. Who knows how many people in these parts have some tiny percentage of siren blood in their veins. It doesn't make them dangerous." He chuckled. "Not necessarily."

Corvin had seen Reg triggered twice before, so he knew that her siren instincts weren't quite as dormant as Reg would like people to think.

"If I can get people to believe that," Reg sighed.

He nodded. "I'm sure this silliness will pass. People will realize that there's nothing to it."

"Somebody egged the house last night. And apparently cast a protection spell against sirens."

"They egged your house?" This seemed to take him aback.

"Yeah. That, together with being refused service at The Crystal Bowl… I'm feeling kind of sorry for myself right now. I never thought I'd have to deal with this kind of garbage."

Corvin frowned, shaking his head. "Our community is usually quite tolerant. We are used to being viewed as outsiders. After all that trouble in Salem. Witches are usually—"

"I know. Peaceful. Trying to be at harmony with nature and each other. That's what Sarah said too."

"Yes." Corvin took a thoughtful sip of his wine. "Exclusion is not something that I usually see in Black Sands."

Reg swallowed. It didn't make her feel any better that she was being singled out in a way that others were not. What was she to do when it was the witches who wanted to burn her at the stake?

She looked around, hoping that the waitress might be on her way over with their meals. But it hadn't been long enough. It wasn't a fast-food restaurant. It would probably be half an hour before their dishes were ready. Reg rubbed her forehead, trying to ease the tense muscles that were starting to give her a headache.

"Thanks for this," she said, gesturing at the dining room. "I'm not sure what I would have done if you hadn't come by and suggested it. I guess I probably would have just gone home and… eaten something that Sarah put in the fridge for me."

He gave a dramatic shudder at this suggestion. "Heaven forbid."

Reg laughed. "Her cooking is good. It just isn't my thing. You know, vegetables and things that are good for me. At least her food is better than her tea."

It was Corvin's turn to laugh. "Some witches are very talented in pulling together a remedy that is not only good for you, but pleasant to drink as well."

Reg remembered the tea that Calliopia's mother had prepared as a restorative. It had been surprisingly nice.

"But Sarah does not have that talent," Reg observed.

"No. Unfortunately not."

They both chuckled. Reg took another sip of her wine. She was probably drinking it too fast on an empty stomach. Wanting that pleasantly buzzed feeling to take all the stress away. She shouldn't drink at all with Corvin there. His charms affected her judgment enough without any chemical assistance. She took a couple more swallows anyway. She wasn't feeling it at all yet.

"Why don't we change the subject?" Corvin said considerately. "You probably don't want to talk about this right now."

"No. Not really. I mean, if you had a way to make it all go away… but that's not going to happen."

He didn't even suggest this time that he could take her siren powers away. Reg knew that even if he could, it still wouldn't change what she was and wouldn't satisfy anyone worried about her siren nature.

CHAPTER FOUR

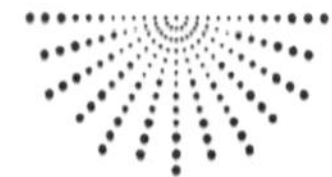

"So," Corvin leaned forward in his seat. "Why don't you tell me about Wilson. With everything going on during the Spring Games, I never heard the details of what happened to him. I talked to Damon, but you know how he is. Got all grumpy with me like I had something to do with it."

"He did miss out on winning half a million dollars. Or a quarter of a million, since he had promised me half. That's enough to make anyone grumpy."

"You weren't grumpy about it."

Reg pursed her lips and looked off into space. "I never really thought we were going to earn it in the first place. It seemed... too easy. If something sounds too easy to be true... chances are, either it is, or you're likely to get arrested for it."

Corvin let out a loud laugh at that. Other diners turned and looked at him dourly, then went back to their own meals and conversations.

"Too true," Corvin agreed. "I'll admit that I didn't expect Damon to be able to find Wilson and get him to sign up for the Spring Games. With you on his side, it was a little more likely to locate him, but it was still a long shot."

"Yeah. Especially if you knew all the details from the beginning. I didn't know that the guy had been missing for fifty years."

Corvin nodded. "It is a little harder to track someone down after that long. You did very well to be able to locate him. But it was obvious from the time that we found him that it would be difficult to get him to the Spring Games. Not remembering who he was, that was a big barrier. If the guy doesn't remember that he is a practitioner of magic, why would he join what is essentially the magical Olympics?"

"I thought we might be able to talk him into it. I hoped so, anyway." Reg sighed and shrugged. "And I thought that if we could help him to remember who he was and how to use his powers, he would be eager to sign up. Show off his stuff. Rejoin the magical world with a splash…"

"So. Tell me about what happened."

Reg gazed up toward the ceiling, recalling the details of what had happened with Wilson. She was embarrassed by her mistakes. It wasn't something she had wanted to talk to Corvin about, and she was sure Damon felt the same way. Even more so because he saw himself as Corvin's rival.

"It was Starlight who gave me the idea to start with."

"Your cat? What did he tell you this time?" Corvin was not a cat lover. Far from it. But he was resigned to the fact that Starlight was Reg's familiar and wasn't going to be going anywhere else. Corvin had even helped when Starlight had been sick. The cat and the warlock put up with each other, though Starlight would still growl and hiss at Corvin if he got too close. Meaning anywhere on the property, since Reg knew better than to allow Corvin into the house. That didn't stop him from coming to her door and trying to wheedle his way in.

"Starlight was getting into my duffel bag. The one from the trip to the Everglades. You know how cats like funky smells like sweaty clothes."

Corvin sniffed. "How pleasant."

"At least they're not as bad as dogs… Anyway, he was crawling inside my bag to smell everything and maybe make a little nest in there. I pulled him out and saw he had been getting into the leaves in my pocket."

"Leaves…?" Corvin frowned.

"Don't you remember? When we went to the Lost Village, the ghost I talked to said that I should take one of the plants with me for when I would need it."

"Ah. Well, I didn't exactly hear the conversation," he pointed out.

"No, I guess not. But she did. So I put them into my pocket and then forgot about them with everything else that happened between then and getting home with Wilson."

Corvin nodded encouragingly. "Which plant was it? Do you know?"

"I took the leaves over to Sarah because I didn't want Starlight getting poisoned by them. And I wondered… whether they were something that we might be able to use to restore Wilson's memory."

"What was it?"

"Sweet bay leaves. Laurel, Sarah said it is called sometimes."

"Ah, yes. I remember picking that. And Sarah told you that it could be used for memory loss? That's not an application I know."

"No, but we thought it might be worth trying. It's one of the plants that the Seminoles use in their medicine, and the ghost said he had something that the Seminoles knew about, called Giant Sickness. So I decided to take the chance that maybe it could be used to treat Wilson."

"And Sarah made tea?"

"Not Sarah. I did."

"You did."

"It wasn't very good. We tried a smudge as well. I did that first. Because the Natives do that sometimes. But it didn't seem to have much effect just waving the smoke at him. The ghost didn't tell me how I should use it. Sarah said they don't have prescribed methods; it is up to the medicine man—or woman—to decide the right approach for each person."

"Of course."

"The smoke didn't seem to make any difference, so we tried the tea. I added some lemon to make it more palatable. But I guess from the way he looked when he tasted it that it wasn't very good. I was going to give him some honey to sweeten it…"

"I don't imagine that would really make any difference to him. Either it would work or it would not. He probably didn't care how it tasted."

"I just crushed it up with my hands, but those leaves are really hard and sharp when they are dry, and I probably should have used one of those things to crush it to a powder..." Reg made the motion of grinding it in a bowl.

"Mortar and pestle," Corvin suggested.

"If that's what it's called, I didn't know what to call it. A grinder?"

"Just a mortar and pestle. So what happened when he drank it? Did it restore his memory?"

Reg blew out her breath. "Did it ever. And I thought... that would be a good thing."

"But it wasn't."

"No."

CHAPTER FIVE

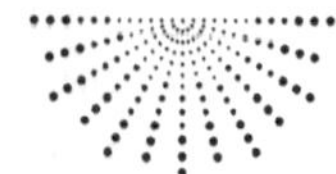

The waitress arrived with their dishes. Reg admired hers, smiling and nodding, but she was too hungry to care about the presentation. "Thanks, this looks great."

For a few minutes, she and Corvin just sampled their dinners. Reg started to relax as her blood sugar got a boost.

"So, what exactly went wrong?" Corvin asked. "Wilson decided he was late for a date? He didn't like the Spring Games? He left the stove on at home?"

Reg frowned at him, remembering that Damon had said something to her about leaving her stove on when they had left for the Everglades. But clearly, Wilson hadn't left his stove on for fifty years. It would have been discovered long before that.

"He was… you know that he was supposed to be a really powerful wizard?"

Corvin nodded. "I remember. He was very well-known. It was a big deal to have him coming to the Games—fifty years ago."

"Yeah. But I guess… he wasn't really satisfied with something like participating in the Games. He wanted to… I don't know. Would it be too dramatic to say that he wanted to take over the world? That he wanted to kill the immortals and be the most powerful person on earth?"

Corvin contemplated this, cutting his rare steak into small bites as he ate. "I guess I can't say you're being overly dramatic if I wasn't there to see. I haven't heard of anyone trying to take over the world and kill the rest of the immortals lately, but that doesn't mean that he's not. I don't imagine you can do something like that in an instant. Your way would be blocked if you moved before you really had a toehold…"

Reg hadn't really thought about what the actual process of taking over the world would be. Corvin was probably right. It would take some time. It wasn't something that Wilson could just do in a day. She had been happy that he had disappeared and she hadn't heard anything else from him. She thought that meant that he had failed in his plan and had kept his oath never to harm her or her friends.

"Yeah… I guess. I never really thought about it. Not one of my life goals."

"I don't imagine so. But power really is… quite addictive. One is never satisfied with just the right amount of power. Every time you consume it… you hunger for more."

Which pretty much described Corvin's existence. Reg didn't want to focus on this point. She felt anxious enough about having dinner with him when she should have just gone home after being turned away from The Crystal Bowl. Corvin was more powerful than Reg, or she thought he was. As he learned to control his new powers, he became more of a danger. Unless she were able to expand her own powers at the same rate, which wasn't as easy for her.

"So… Wilson tried to attack Harrison—"

"Harrison was there?"

Reg nodded. "Well, you remember how he and Weston were talking at the mermaid bar…"

"Yes. So they were both there when you gave Wilson this tea?"

"No. Harrison appeared, but Weston didn't. I don't think… well, we were talking about Harrison, or maybe it was just because he knew what we were planning to do. I don't know. But Harrison was there and Wilson wasn't happy about it. He said that Harrison and Weston had been the ones who had made him forget…"

"And after he remembered, he attacked Harrison because he was one of the people who made him forget for fifty years," Corvin guessed.

"Yeah. Or because Harrison was an immortal. Wilson kind of had a thing about the immortals. He thought… there are so many more humans than immortals, we should just… gang up on them and kill them."

Corvin put down his fork and took another sip of wine. "It wouldn't be the first time a human had the arrogance to challenge the immortals. If you look at the ancient mythology—"

Reg waved her hand, trying to dissuade him from going into lecture mode. "Yeah, yeah, I know. The mortals and the gods were always fighting. I remember that much from school."

"Did Wilson have any chance against Harrison? How powerful is he?"

Reg rubbed the back of her neck. "Harrison said Wilson was one of the most powerful humans he'd ever met. Or maybe *the* most powerful."

Corvin raised his brows. "Really. But Harrison was still able to banish him?"

Reg picked at her meal. Despite being hungry, she had lost her interest in the food. "Well… Wilson attacked Harrison and Starlight. I don't know if he could have done them any harm, but I didn't want to wait to find out, and I didn't want them fighting in my house."

"Of course."

"So I… I put a shield around him so that he couldn't fight Harrison and Starlight."

"Around the most powerful human in the world. Is that… advisable…?"

Reg grimaced. "I wouldn't recommend it. It was sort of an impulse. And… he was too strong for me. I needed Harrison to bleed off some of his power… and then… well, I did like I do with you, when you're targeting me…"

Corvin cocked his head, looking for more information.

"But instead of reflecting his magic back, I kind of… I used the power he was expending fighting me to strengthen the shield. So that the more he fought, the stronger the shield was, and the more energy he expended trying to break it…"

"You have come a long way in using your powers," Corvin said with respect. "And you are very… creative in your solutions."

Reg shrugged. She looked away. "I couldn't hold him forever and I didn't want Harrison to kill him. So I made him promise, to give an oath on his powers, that he wouldn't hurt me or anyone else there."

Corvin wiped his mouth with his cloth napkin and let it fall back to his lap. "And then you let him go."

"Yeah."

"So you…"

Reg forced her breath out in a puff. "Yeah. I restored a powerful evil wizard's memory and then unleashed him on the world. All in a day's work for Reg Rawlins."

Corvin didn't answer immediately.

"Well, he didn't kill you on the spot, so he at least respected his oath that much. But do you think he will keep it? Or will he find a way around it or decide not to keep it?"

"I don't know. Harrison said that maybe it would be enough."

"But Harrison doesn't have to stick around here to take the consequences or see what happens next. You know that he isn't exactly a good judge of human character."

"I couldn't kill Wilson."

"Perhaps you could have found a way to bind him…"

"Even with the way that Francesca bound the Witch Doctor, she admits that it won't hold forever. Eventually, he will be able to gather his strength again. She's a lot more experienced than I am."

"But you are more powerful than she is."

"You said that to bind someone, you needed the strength of the community. You can't do it yourself. I don't know anything about binding. I've never done it."

"No. And I wouldn't expect you to. But you weren't alone with him."

"No…"

"Damon was there. He didn't have any recommendations? Didn't help you?"

"No. He was pretty quiet through the whole thing. I think he was… sort of in shock."

"Harrison should have done something about it. Why didn't he just… obliterate Wilson?"

"I didn't want him to kill him. I thought that if Wilson took an oath… he'd be required to keep it. Isn't that the way it works?"

"For someone with morals, yes. But not everyone intends to keep their promises. With all your experience, you should know that."

Including Reg's experience with Corvin himself. How many times had he made a promise to her and then not kept it? And he was right; growing up in foster care, she'd had plenty of experience with others making promises and then not keeping them. People who were supposed to protect her and provide for her had done anything but. There had been good families, but even they frequently made promises and then didn't follow through. Promising her that if she were good, she could stay with them. That they would send her to some summer camp that she had heard about. That if she tried her hardest, she would be able to succeed at something. Parents were full of promises that never came to fruition.

And Wilson was probably just like they were. He would find an excuse to break the oath that he had made. Maybe he had never intended to keep it. Maybe he had crossed his fingers. He was off building up his power so that he could make a covert attack before anyone knew what was going on. By the time anyone knew that he was planning to overthrow the governments and principalities of the world, he would be there. And no one would be able to stop him.

"Ugh." She rubbed her temples. "This is really not making me feel any better."

"No. I'm sorry." Corvin reached across the table and touched the back of her hand, giving her a pleasant buzz of electricity that sent her heart racing. "Let me remedy that."

Reg inched her hand back away from his touch. She was reluctant. She didn't want to break the contact. But she knew better than to let him ensorcell her.

"You know I can make you feel better," Corvin coaxed.

"For a while, maybe," Reg agreed, "But the way that I felt without my powers…" She shook her head, remembering the bereft emptiness, the silence of the voices, feeling like she was hollowed out and worn thin and would never be happy again. "I never want to feel like that again."

"I wasn't saying I would take your powers. Just that I could help you to feel better. Give you a little boost."

"No. You've done enough."

His mouth twisted into a scowl. "I've done enough? I haven't done anything tonight. Will you never forgive the past?"

"I meant… I didn't mean that. I meant you already took me out, bought me dinner. You've done plenty. You don't need to do anything else for me."

"This?" He indicated everything with a twirl of his hand. "This is nothing. This is dinner with an acquaintance—something I would do with anyone. I want to *do* something for you. Something that will make a difference."

Reg felt a wave of heat. She didn't know whether it was due to his charms or her own emotional reaction to his offer to help without any kind of recompense. She rubbed her burning face with one hand as if she could wipe away the blush.

"How about dessert?" she suggested lightly. "Something chocolate."

Corvin's scowl deepened rather than disappearing.

Reg looked down at her meal and pretended to be concentrating on that instead of on keeping him happy. If he didn't like her suggestion, that was too bad. She wasn't going to let him worm his way inside her psyche and start messing around. If he took away her powers, he would never give them back, and Reg didn't think she could survive without them. The silence inside her head would make her go crazy just as much as a sudden onslaught of voices might for someone else.

CHAPTER SIX

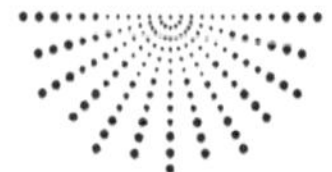

The rest of the meal was spent mostly in silence. Reg couldn't think of what to say to make Corvin feel any better, other than giving in to his desires, and that wasn't going to happen. When the waitress came to clear away their plates, she offered a dessert menu, and Corvin motioned for it. Reg decided to check her email on her phone while he looked it over so that she wasn't staring at him with nothing to distract her.

Corvin didn't say anything to her before ordering a dessert. Reg could only assume that it was something for the two of them to share. Either that, or he was punishing her for expressing a preference for chocolate over allowing him to make her feel "better."

They waited a while longer, ignoring each other, watching other diners, studying the paintings, or checking their phones. Eventually, the waitress returned with some confection as big as her head, piles of ice cream with layers of fudge sauce, whipped cream, and chocolate shavings, topped with bright blue sparklers on top. It was flamboyant enough to capture the attention of everyone else in the dining room. Reg half-expected the kitchen staff to come in and sing *Happy Birthday* to her. It was the type of gauche display that would have seemed more appropriate at a barbecue joint or family restaurant.

"Oh, wow." Reg shook her head, speechless. "I don't know what that is, but… you'd better be planning to help me."

The waitress put it down in the middle of the table, smiling at Corvin. She looked at him expectantly for a minute, then eventually turned away, looking disappointed.

"Who said it was for you?" Corvin challenged. "Maybe I ordered it for myself."

Reg stared. Then she gave an irritated flick of her head. "Fine, then. Eat it."

Corvin picked up a dessert spoon. "It's yours," he conceded. "But I will do my best to help you. As always."

Reg picked up her own spoon, and they dug into it.

* * *

As usual, the end of the date was difficult for Reg. It was tricky getting back to her cottage without acceding to any of Corvin's demands, her powers intact. She usually tried to have someone around to help. Someone like Detective Marta Jessup. She had an unusual hold over Corvin, who she sometimes employed as a consultant on cases that appeared to involve magic that fell within his areas of expertise. Or Damon—but he and Reg were not precisely on the best of terms since the whole *Wilson* scene.

Reg had plenty of friends in Black Sands, but not people who she could call to help her to extricate herself from a situation involving Corvin. He was a force of his own.

She feigned being tired. Not the best ploy, maybe, and one that she had used before, but it was the best she could come up with. Despite her resolution not to have too much to drink, she was feeling a little foggy-headed. It was probably just Corvin's influence over her. Once she was on her own, she would feel a lot better.

"It's a long day and I'm beat," she told Corvin, covering a fake yawn that quickly turned into a real one. "I'm sorry, you probably want to stay out for longer, but I need to get home, take care of Starlight, and hit the sack. Would you take me back to my car?"

"Coffee?" Corvin suggested. "We don't need to hurry off quite so quickly, do we? A little caffeine will keep you going for a couple more hours."

"No, not this time."

"I happen to know that you don't go to bed this early."

"I was up before normal this morning. Because of my house being egged. Sarah woke me up, and I had to help her clean up."

"She made you clean it up?"

"No, she didn't make me, but I couldn't very well let her do it all herself, could I? What kind of a person would I be then?"

"You probably had a nap after that," Corvin suggested. "You're going to be up until at least one or two. There's no reason to end such a pleasant meal so early."

Reg put her hand over her aching stomach. "I couldn't eat or drink anything else. Believe me. If I could, I would." She eyed what was left of the decadent dessert. "But there's no way I can fit one more bit. I'll explode. As it is, I'm sure this didn't do much good for my expanding waistline."

He surveyed her through half-closed eyes. "Your waistline looks just fine to me."

"Ha. You wouldn't say that if you saw me—" Reg cut herself off quickly before he could offer to do a more thorough examination of her figure. "I've put on enough weight. I really do need to watch it. And not eat stuff like this."

"You said you wanted chocolate. This was to ease your stress." He leaned forward, exuding the scent of roses. "Are you feeling more relaxed now?"

Dizzied by the cloying scent, Reg did her best to push back against his charms and reflect the heat she felt coming off of Corvin back at him. He chuckled.

"Are you sure you want to do that?"

"What do you mean?"

"Sending my seducing charms back at me just increases my attraction to you."

Reg hadn't even thought about that. She tried to focus on what to do instead. "I need some fresh air. Let's go to the car."

"Let me get the bill."

"Don't they just charge it to your account?"

"Well, yes. But I would still like a copy for my records."

"So get them to email it to you later. I need to get out of here."

"All right," he conceded finally. "Let's go, then."

He was at her shoulder, taking her arm and helping her to her feet. Reg blinked, but it didn't help to clear her mind. She relied on his guiding hand. Moving and getting out of the dining room where the cloud of pheromones was concentrated helped. Reg took several deep breaths.

If reflecting his charms back to him didn't work, then maybe keeping a protective spell around her would. And slowing her breathing. When she was underwater, she could hold her breath for a long time, but it must be a biological response to the water, because she couldn't seem to do the same thing in the open air.

By the time they got to the car, she was feeling a lot better. But the enclosed space of the vehicle meant that whatever attractants Corvin exuded could build up again. Reg was clumsy getting into the car. Maybe she had consumed just a bit too much of the wine. Though the amount of food she had consumed should have slowed her absorption of the alcohol. She concentrated on building a protective envelope around herself before Corvin got into his own seat. As soon as he had the engine turned on, Reg buzzed the window down.

"It's still a little chilly in the evenings," Corvin objected, using his buttons to roll it back up again. He indicated the vent controls on the front console. "You can turn the air up there."

Reg looked helplessly at the various dials and buttons with their cryptic symbols. Did one of them bring fresh air into the car? Or did it all just recirculate?

Reg felt a sudden surge of energy and inspiration. Her head cleared, and she felt like she was looking down at herself from outside or above the car. She adjusted the various air settings and got the air blowing in her direction, crisp and cool outside air.

Corvin glanced sideways at her as he pulled out of the underground parking, clearly irritated. "That's a bit cold, let me just…" He adjusted a couple of the settings.

The burst of energy Reg felt morphed instantly to fury. "You said I could set it the way I wanted. You are not going to seduce me!"

His eyes widened at her vehement response. "I said it was too cold outside and you're bringing in the air from outside. That's all."

"Take me home and quit the games!"

Despite the protection spell around her, Reg could feel Corvin probing at her mind, trying to figure out why she was suddenly so angry. Reg smashed her hand down on the air conditioner controls. "Get out of my head!"

The car stopped abruptly in the middle of traffic. Corvin stared at her in shock. He was out of her head, at least. Corvin looked at the control panel, where a starburst of cracks radiated out from the display.

"Reg!"

"Take me back to pick up my car."

"I am."

Cars honked their horns behind them. Corvin studied Reg for a few more seconds, then returned his attention to his driving.

Reg stared out the front windshield, on her guard for any other attempts from Corvin to charm her. He apparently decided he didn't need any more damage done to his car and didn't try again.

He pulled into the parking lot at The Crystal Bowl and stopped by Reg's car. "Are you... okay?" he asked tentatively.

"As long as witches like you will leave me alone," Reg snarled.

She'd never called him a witch before. She'd heard it used in a derogatory way to refer to a warlock, but she'd never done it herself. Corvin couldn't look much more shocked than he already did.

Reg pulled the door handle to let herself out. Usually, this would have created another awkward moment, in which Corvin smiled and tried one last time to charm her, making her feel like, if nothing else, she owed him a kiss and pleasantries for taking her out to dinner. Especially when she was pretty sure there wasn't anywhere else in town where they would have served her.

But this time, Reg didn't care about the niceties. She wasn't embarrassed getting out of the car without so much as a thank you. It wasn't like he had just been helping her out of the goodness of his heart. He obviously had ulterior motives and he had done his best to charm her. She'd had enough of his nonsense.

She unlocked her door and climbed into her car, pulling out into the street a bit faster than was strictly necessary so that her tires squealed in protest. In a few minutes, she was home. It was dark and she hadn't thought to leave the cottage's exterior light on, so the pathway was only dimly lit, the shadows under the trees dark and irksome. But there was nothing to worry about; she was home where she was safe.

Reg examined the door before opening it. No sign of the eggs from that morning. No fresh marks. No sign of the magical rune that Julian had left there not so long ago to indicate that she was under investigation by his department. But she still felt like there was something wrong. She didn't get the "coming home" feeling that she usually did when she arrived at the cottage. She hadn't realized how much she had grown to cherish that feeling, after so many years of moving around and not having a permanent home.

She stood there for a moment in thoughtful silence before fitting her key into the lock and entering. She hadn't left any of the inside lights on either. She stepped inside and groped for the light switch but, in doing so, stepped on something that moved, and a yowl of protest assaulted her ears.

Reg got the light on. Starlight glared at her, ears back, standing back from her like she was a stranger.

"Sorry. I didn't mean to step on your tail. You shouldn't be so close to the door, especially when it is dark. You know I can't see in the dark like you can."

He continued to stare at her, lips lifting in a snarl.

"What's wrong with you? Don't growl at me."

She realized that she couldn't feel his aura. She could see his feelings well enough without any psychic connection, but she wasn't emotionally connected with him like she usually was.

"Starlight?"

Maybe there was something wrong with him. He could be sick. When Reg approached him, he backed up, ears still flat and fangs displayed.

Reg looked behind her to see if someone was there, but she was by herself. But there still could be something lurking in the darkness that she couldn't see. She pushed the door shut and looked around, feeling for any shifts in the energy of the room. She didn't want anything unseen entering her home, and Starlight's behavior was making her anxious.

But she couldn't feel anything.

It wasn't just that she couldn't feel an uninvited presence there—she couldn't feel anything at all.

CHAPTER SEVEN

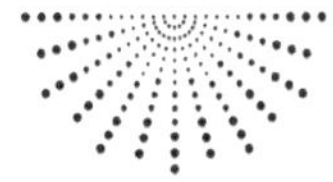

*R*eg's heart pounded in her throat. She stared around her, feeling like she was in a place she had never been before. She couldn't feel any of the presences that were always around her or spoke in her head. She couldn't feel Starlight's warmth or see the auras around the wards and protections Sarah and Reg had placed around the house to keep it safe from intruders or bring other blessings.

Although the house looked exactly the way it always did, it felt sterile.

Her first thought was of Corvin and her hand flew to her phone. She had thought that she had held him off, but was it possible he had somehow managed to steal her powers without her being aware of it?

Could he do that? Did one of his new powers allow him to do what he hadn't been able to before? And to do it so covertly she hadn't even detected him?

She pulled her phone out and looked down at it. Without her even touching the screen or the buttons, the screen flashed on and unlocked. The device launched the phone app and Corvin's name popped up on the screen, with the 'calling...' status at the top of the screen.

Reg stared at it, dumbfounded. She fumbled to end the call, punching at the red button several times before it finally ended. But she had heard Corvin's tiny voice before she managed to hang up the call. Not only had he seen her call, but he'd answered. It was too late to pretend that she hadn't dialed him.

In a second, her phone started ringing again, this time with an incoming call from Corvin. Reg blew out her breath. She might as well take the call and confront him with what he had done. She was going to have to sooner or later anyway.

"Hello?"

"You called me."

Reg nearly chickened out and told him it was a pocket dial. Because it was, really. What else could she call the phone's strange behavior of dialing Corvin all by itself?

"I... uh..." Reg thought fast, trying to come up with an approach. She had no idea what to say to him about the weirdness that had greeted her at the cottage. "Did you... do something?"

"Did I do something?" Corvin's voice was flat. As if he didn't understand what she meant.

"To me. Did you do something to me without me realizing it? I can't... I don't know what's going on here."

"No. What's going on?"

"You didn't? Do you swear you didn't? I don't understand what's going on. You must have."

"You're going to have to give me some information if you want me to help you to figure it out. Do you want me to come to your house?"

"No. No, that's not a good idea." Reg looked around the cottage. Did it really matter? If all magic was gone from the room and Reg herself, what did it matter if Corvin came to the cottage? There wasn't anything more for him to do. "What's happening is... I can't see or hear anything."

"You can clearly hear, or we wouldn't be having this conversation."

"Physically, yes. I can see and hear physically without any problem." Reg shook her head. "But I can't..." She blew her breath out in frustration. "I can't see auras. I can't sense anything. I can't hear... the voices. Not even the usual ones. The ones that are always there."

There was a period of silence from Corvin. She could hear his signal light start to tick.

"I'm coming over there," Corvin told her.

"But… you shouldn't. I can't let you in here."

"I can't sense you reliably from this far away. I'll have a better idea what's going on if I can see you face to face."

"Well…" What further harm could he do? "I don't know. I guess so."

"Try to stay calm. It's probably nothing. Too much to drink. A virus. Something simple."

"Really?"

"Yes."

"Starlight… there's something wrong with him too."

"What?"

"He's… he acts like he doesn't know me. Worse, like I'm someone he doesn't like, someone threatening. And I can't feel him either."

"I'll only be a few minutes. Make yourself some tea and sit down."

Reg tapped the phone screen to end the call. She'd already had way too much to eat and drink to get anything else down, so there was no point in making tea. She wouldn't be able to do anything more than swish it around in her mouth.

She went over and looked at the tea bags and herbs in her cupboard anyway, just to reassure herself that everything was where it was supposed to be.

She was probably just imagining the lack of powers. Or like Corvin had said, she was drunk. If that could affect thoughts and speech and motor skills in a non-practitioner, it must be able to do all kinds of things to her on a higher level. All her senses could be affected, even her psychic powers.

She went into the living room and sat down on one of the wicker chairs. Starlight stayed near the door, watching her. What was wrong with him? She had stepped on him, but she'd done that plenty of times before. Cats were always getting underfoot and Starlight was no exception. Maybe she'd injured him, though, broken a bone in his tail or paw or whatever had been momentarily under her foot. That would explain his reaction to her.

But it wouldn't explain anything else.

"Okay. Just stay calm, Reg. Just stay cool; this is nothing. It will pass. You just have to stay calm and everything will go back to normal."

Saying the words out loud didn't help as she hoped it would.

In a few minutes, she heard footsteps crunching across the cobblestones and a soft rap at her door. Reg got up and went to the door. She swung it open and looked at Corvin for a moment, then looked at her door to make sure that no one had egged it again in the time she had been sitting inside the house. There was not even a fragment of an eggshell.

She stepped back, looking behind her into the house. "You see? It's all gone."

"What's gone?" Corvin asked, peering in.

"All of it. All the magic. The wards, the spirits, all of the protections."

Corvin looked once more into the house and then switched his gaze to Reg's face. "I'm going to have to take your word for that. I can't see most of those things anyway, unless I'm interacting with an object. I can feel, if you'll allow me to come in..."

Reg raised her brows. "There isn't anything to stop you this time."

He raised a wary hand and patted the air in front of him, like a mime feeling an invisible box. Reg shook her head in irritation at his dramatics.

"Corvin!"

Corvin shrugged. "I can't, Reg. I don't know what it is you are or are not seeing, but I still can't enter this doorway without your invitation."

"Yes, you can. There's nothing to stop you."

"Your protections are still in place."

Reg knew that wasn't true. If it were, she would be able to feel the spells. And to see the auras glowing around the wards and charms.

"What about Starlight? Look how he's behaving."

Corvin looked at Starlight. The cat hissed at him. Corvin hissed back. "He's acting the same way as always."

"But he's treating me like that too." Reg took a couple of steps toward Starlight, and he backed away, but then held his ground, letting out a low growl.

"Maybe you smell like me," Corvin suggested. "He often gets grouchy when he knows you've been around me. You said so yourself."

"Yes… he gives me a look. He disapproves. But not like this."

"What was the first thing you noticed?"

"Just when I came into the house. Starlight behaving like that… and then I noticed how… sterile the room seemed. Like someone had just come and swept all the supernatural away."

"It's still here. At least you can be reassured of that."

"Then there's something wrong with me."

"Will you let me into the house? Then you and I can sit down together and discuss this."

Reg stood there, waffling, wavering back and forth on whether to let him in and give him access or not.

But things couldn't get much worse.

Reg took a deep breath and let it out. "Okay," she said finally. "Come in."

CHAPTER EIGHT

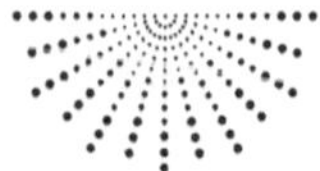

*R*eg saw Corvin out. For once, he wasn't trying to convince her to let him stay over, maybe to watch over her as she slept or to give her the comfort she needed. She didn't know if she would have had the strength or ability to fight him in the condition she was in. He assured her again that everything seemed to be normal and that it was only her perception that was off.

She closed and locked the door and went to her bedroom.

As soon as she opened the bedroom door, Starlight burst out in a frenzy of fur and claws. Reg yelped and jumped back, but didn't manage to avoid a couple of nicks. Starlight flew past her to the front door, where he crouched down and watched her, waiting for her to attack.

Reg instead turned away from him, going into the bathroom. Anything she did was just likely to get him more wound up. She would do what Corvin suggested, and in the morning, everything would be back to normal. She started warm water running and shed her clothes. If they were tainted with some sort of substance that triggered Starlight to turn into a devil cat, she would have to dispose of them. Maybe even burn them. But for the time being, she hoped that just changing out of them and having a hot bath would do that trick.

She added bubble bath and soaked until the water started to turn

"No. I'm not hungover. I feel pretty good. And I was hungry."

"Very strange."

Reg shrugged. "I guess so. A little."

"What are your plans for the day, then? I don't imagine you have any clients lined up for this morning."

"No. I don't know. Maybe I'll go out and sit in the garden. Or go for a walk."

"That doesn't sound like the Reg I know. No danger? No adventure?"

"I don't actually *look* for those things."

"Maybe not, but you seem to find them. I'll be disappointed if all you do is bum around the garden all day."

"I won't stay in the garden *all day.*"

"I should think not—"

There was a crash and Reg shrieked, rocketing out of her seat. She didn't know which way the bowl of rice went. She looked around for the source of the noise, immediately thinking that it must be Starlight, having climbed something and knocked it over. That would have been par for the course for Nico. Ten times a day. But it wasn't normal behavior for Starlight.

CHAPTER NINE

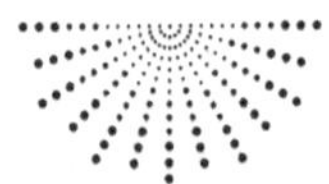

Looking around, Reg first saw the rock on the floor, looking very out of place. So bizarre that she looked around the room, trying to figure out where it had fallen from. But it wasn't a decoration that had fallen off the bookcase. There was a gaping hole in the window behind the couch she had been sitting on. There were slivers of broken glass everywhere.

Reg looked out the window, but whoever had thrown the rock had already made his escape. There was no one to be seen. As Reg was looking out the broken window, she saw the big house's back door open, and Sarah took a few steps out into the yard, frowning and looking around.

She saw the broken window and started walking purposefully toward the cottage. Reg nearly gave in to the impulse to walk over and unlock the door for Sarah, but then, looking down at the glass all around her bare feet, decided that might not be such a good idea.

"Reg, are you up?" Sarah called as she approached the house.

"I'm up."

"Are you okay?"

Reg considered the question, looking down at her body and around the room to compose an answer. She was unhurt, or at least she thought she was. The only thing that had been broken was the glass in the window and Reg herself had not been hit. Whoever had thrown the rock probably had no idea that she was sitting right under that window. Anyone who knew her usual routine would have expected her to still be in bed.

Sarah tried the door and then used her key to unlock it and let herself in. She looked in dismay at the large rock in the middle of the room.

"Oh, my. Who would do a thing like this? Are you all right, Reg? It didn't hit you…?"

"No. Just scared me. I was sitting right there." Reg motioned to the seat under the window. Then she looked around at the shards of glass around her feet. Along with a smattering of chicken and rice, though the bowl had rolled out of sight. "Could you hand me my shoes?"

"Of course. What a horrible thing. I can't understand it. This is just not like Black Sands. The people I have grown to know… they wouldn't do a thing like this."

"Well… they are. I don't know if it's usual or not. Maybe it's just because you've never known a part-siren before. It might happen all the time. But you wouldn't know unless you knew a siren."

"I don't think so. Witches are peace-loving. Accepting."

"Most of them, maybe, but there seem to be a few bad apples."

Reg took her shoes from Sarah and slipped them on one at a time. She was glad to see that she was not shaking and didn't show any other visible signs of having been rattled by the incident.

Just a rock through the window. Nothing serious. Not a gunshot. Not a bomb. Just a rock that someone had picked up on the spur of the moment and thrown through the window.

Sarah next grabbed the broom and dustpan and hurried over to start cleaning up. "I'm so sorry about this, Reg. I don't understand what people are thinking. I'm going to bring it up at the next coven."

"What if they are not in your coven?"

"The members of the coven can help to spread the word." Sarah's expression was set. "If the rumor that you are part siren has gotten around that quickly, then the warning to stop this nonsense can spread just as fast." She flushed a little pink as she swept up the glass, and Reg didn't think that it was the physical exertion.

Reg looked around to see how she could help. The bowl had rolled away somewhere, and as Reg looked for it, she spotted a glowing rectangle under the couch. Her phone.

"Oops. Sorry, Corvin," Reg said. She waited until Sarah had cleared a pathway to the phone, then knelt carefully to retrieve it.

Out of the corner of her eye, she saw Starlight starting to creep closer to investigate the rock and food spilled on the floor.

"No, Starlight! Stay back."

She grasped the phone and started to get up again. Sarah swung the broom toward Starlight to keep him back and he leaped quickly out of the way, hissing and laying his ears back. He'd seen a broom in Sarah's hands before and he clearly remembered how violently she had wielded it.

"It's okay, she's just keeping you safe," Reg told Starlight. She walked closer to him to calm him and put the phone to her ear. "Corvin? Are you still there?"

"I'm here. What's going on? Is everything all right? I was ready to call the bomb squad."

"Sorry. Yes, we're okay. It wasn't a bomb, just a rock through the window. But it scared the heck out of me. I didn't know what was going on."

"I'm glad that you're okay." He paused for a moment. "You think this was... another incident caused by the revelation that you are part siren?"

"Yeah. What else would it be? I don't think anyone else here has reason to hate me. It isn't like I've been giving people bad readings."

"It's not something to joke about."

"I'm really not. I can't think of any other reason anyone would have for doing this."

"I can't either," Corvin admitted.

"Well... I'd better help Sarah. I don't want her doing all the work here. It isn't her fault this is happening."

"Maybe it is time for some protections around the property, instead of just inside."

"Yeah. That makes sense. We'll talk about it."

CHAPTER TEN

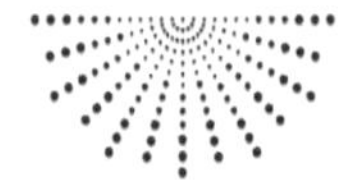

*R*eg had been talking about going out to the garden, so once she and Sarah finished the inside clean-up and Sarah left to call someone about replacing the window, Reg decided to sit for a while in the garden. At least she would be able to see anyone coming.

In place of the lost chicken and rice, she made herself a peanut butter sandwich and took it outside without a plate. She had a travel mug of coffee. Starlight was still stalking around the house, sniffing anything that might be out of place and looking for someone to blame for the disruption. Reg taped a piece of cardboard over the hole in the window just in case he got any ideas about having an outdoor adventure.

She sat on a bench and tried to relax, looking around at the garden's lush growth. Bright and dark greens. Blossoms of a dozen different colors. Forst, the garden gnome, had done a spectacular job of rehabilitating it.

It was peaceful and she liked to spend a few minutes there now and then to reconnect with nature and to let the worries of the world go.

Not that she had ever really been an outdoor, nature-seeking type. She didn't know whether it was because none of the foster families she had lived with had been the woodsy type, or if it was more to do with her stress levels. She had, from the time she was very young, been more concerned with survival than luxuries. For much of her childhood, she had been fighting for her life.

But having the beautiful garden right outside her door had changed that, just a little. Maybe the gnome magic of the place attracted her and drew her into it. She still wouldn't sit there for hours on end. She *couldn't* sit still for that long, even if she were doing something engaging. The only time she was still for long was when she was sleeping, and the way she would wake up wound in her sheets, she knew she didn't stay still even then.

Good morning, Reg Rawlins.

Reg looked out over the garden for a minute before spotting the little man with the red cap a few feet away from her. He always seemed to blend in with the garden, even with his red hat.

Good morning, Forst, Reg returned, speaking to him in her mind, as she usually did. The gnomes were used to talking to each other in their "inside words," not out loud like humans did, and were not very comfortable with spoken English.

Forst pushed a spade into the ground with his foot. *What is it that goes on?*

Reg sipped her coffee. *What do you mean?*

You are not usually here this time. You are worried. Sarah Bishop is upset. The wrinkles in his face deepened as he looked around. *Someone has been here... who is not welcome.*

Well... yes. Someone threw a rock through my window. And yesterday, they threw eggs at the cottage and worked a spell here.

Threw a rock through thy window?

Reg nodded. *Yes. It just has cardboard over it right now, but Sarah will have it replaced soon.*

A rock from my *garden?* he asked possessively.

Reg smiled. *Yes. A rock from your garden. I assume so. I don't expect they brought one with them to do the job.*

Forst shook his head and didn't say anything else for some time while he worked. Reg finished eating her sandwich and sipped the coffee.

Why do they throw eggs? Forst asked.

Just to let me know they don't like me. Reg shrugged, not wanting to have to explain about her being part siren.

This is a spell?

No. It's not part of a spell. Just… a sign. A sign from them to me that they don't want me around here.

'Tis not seemly. He shook his head and continued to work. Reg closed her eyes, resting, feeling the sun on her face. *What spell did they?* Forst asked.

I don't know much about it. There were candles and signs. Sarah said it was a kind of a protection spell.

Protecting you?

No. Protecting them from me.

Forst stopped working for a moment to stare at her in disbelief. *Reg Rawlins is not a monster. Reg Rawlins is kind and helpful to the gnomen.*

Not everyone thinks the same way as you do.

Why is this?

They think I will harm them. That I will… hunt here.

You hunt?

No. I don't. They just think I will.

Why is this?

My parents… my mother… was a dangerous person. People here have heard and are afraid that I will be too.

Forst considered this and continued to dig, overturning the earth as he worked between the brightly blooming plants.

This should not be, he said eventually.

Reg breathed a sigh of relief that he had accepted her explanation and was on her side. But she knew he might not have been if she had told him the details. That her mother was a siren. Reg had seen her on the hunt and did not want to become that herself. If there were anything she could do to keep from turning into her mother, she was willing to do it. Give her any spell or labor to prevent that from happening, and she would do it.

* * *

Reg had almost forgotten that she had set up an appointment with her fire casting mentor, Davyn, a prominent warlock who was the leader of Corvin's coven. Of course, Corvin was currently shunned by his coven, so Reg didn't know if he would actually call it his. But one day, he did hope to be readmitted to its fellowship.

Reg had met Davyn during the course of Corvin's tribunal. She hadn't been too impressed with him at that time, but they had gotten to know each other better after that, and she considered him a friend. Or she had, before he had become friends with Julian Sabat.

Calling Julian her nemesis might be a bit dramatic, but how else could she convey how she felt about him? When she had known him as a child, he had bullied her. As an adult, he had come back into her life, investigating a charge against her relating to the death of a swamp goblin.

That had been resolved, but Reg didn't feel like it was over. She was still irritated with Davyn for having anything to do with Julian when he knew that the investigator was looking to lay charges against her. Even though Julian had since left town, the last Reg had heard, he and Davyn were still carrying on a long-distance relationship. A fact that did not impress Reg or make her particularly happy to see her mentor again.

Without Davyn, she couldn't exercise and develop her firecasting ability, which was too dangerous in the hands of a novice. She didn't know any other firecasters who could teach her, so it had to be Davyn or no one.

Davyn had apparently noticed the cardboard in the window as he approached the cottage. He motioned to it as he entered the house, jabbing a thumb toward it.

"What happened here?"

"There has been… some trouble. Someone threw a rock through it."

Davyn's brows went up. "Really. I'm sorry to hear that."

"Yeah. You're not the only one."

"Maybe you would like to try a little… stress relief?"

If Corvin had said it, his innuendo would have been clear. But Davyn didn't mean that. He meant that it was time for Reg to play with fire. And that was something she had been looking forward to, even if she hadn't really wanted to see Davyn.

"Yes," she agreed emphatically.

"Good. Let's get started." Davyn rubbed his hands together like he was soaping up or trying to warm them. Then, pulling his hands away from each other, he formed a small ball of flame between them. Reg mirrored his actions. Her fire kept flaring, reflecting her emotional disruption. Reg stared into the flame, trying to focus and center herself. A flame was useful for meditation. How many times in her life had she fallen into a trance staring at a candle or campfire? Fire had that power over her.

Her flame stopped jumping and flaring, settling down and behaving more like Davyn's, though it was still larger and somewhat unruly.

"Good," Davyn approved. "That's becoming more natural to you."

"What is? Making the flame?"

"The focus. It's one of the most important parts of your practice. If you can stay focused and in control, your fire will be controlled."

Reg nodded her agreement. She knew for sure that her emotional state affected the activity of her flame and how hard it was to control. When she was angry, she could quickly lose control.

"Did you hear about Julian?" Davyn asked.

Reg's fire expanded so fast it made a popping sound and she had a hard time catching her breath, as if it had burned up all the oxygen in the room.

"Whoa." Davyn held up his hands, calming the wall of flame and trying to gather it together.

Embarrassed, Reg did her best to concentrate and help bring it back under control. Davyn made quieting motions and noises, as if the fire were a living creature. Reg took back control as he pushed a more compact fireball back into her hands.

Reg swallowed, her mouth dry. She licked her lips. "What about Julian?" she asked with difficulty. She didn't know whether he had mentioned Julian's name to elicit a reaction from her, or whether he was just clueless about the way she felt about Sabat.

"Oh, right." Reg's exploding fireball had apparently distracted Davyn from his comment. "He has been promoted."

"Oh?"

"It's still the same job, but his rank has been increased and he was given a special commendation for his work."

At Reg's questioning look, he shrugged. "For the Everglades case."

"You mean for the *Reg Rawlins* case?" Reg let her fire go out, afraid she would end up singeing Davyn's eyebrows if she continued.

"Well, I don't know if he would call it that. I didn't want to…"

"Embarrass me?"

"You didn't do anything wrong," Davyn hastened to say. "I know that you were cleared of wrongdoing in the case. I didn't mean to… bring up something painful."

"Well, you kind of did."

Davyn looked down, clearing his throat. "I'm sorry, Reg. I didn't mean it that way. I was just… Julian is so happy about the advancement, and we were talking about it before I came over here. I just wanted to share some good news."

"It isn't good news to me that he got a promotion. He was already overreaching. He's dangerous."

"You were never in any danger from him," Davyn said soothingly.

"No? You weren't there, were you? You didn't see what happened. You didn't see him pull a wand on me in the middle of the grocery store, did you? Does that sound like exemplary behavior in an investigation? He just got this award because he identified me as a siren, and he didn't even figure that out himself. We had to *tell* him."

"Reg…"

"I know. You think he's great. Best thing since sliced bread. But I don't. I've lived with the guy and I know. Just because you're not willing to believe me—"

"I know all of that is true," Davyn said quietly.

Reg opened her mouth to argue more, then closed it.

"I just see… more in him than that. I see potential. I see what he could be, and what he would be if he hadn't had to deal with all the challenges he did growing up. Like you did. You were lucky. Or strong. You turned out okay. But he still… has a lot of dark places."

Reg gazed at him. "Yeah. He does."

"During the investigation… I know you thought you were on your own and that no one believed you. But that's not true. I did believe you."

"You still went out with him. Acted like…" She couldn't finish. Couldn't put into words how betrayed she had felt by his behavior. She couldn't understand his carrying on a romantic relationship with someone he knew was investigating Reg. And not just investigating her, but a danger to her.

"You don't understand. I was there. I did… keep track of what was going on. Even in the grocery store. If you hadn't been able to handle it like you did, I would have stepped in to help."

Reg stared at him. "What?" She tried to dredge up everything she could of that evening. She hadn't seen Davyn. He hadn't been around. No one had been there to step in between the out-of-control investigator and his quarry.

"You remember that I can cloak myself."

"You can. Oh." Reg considered this. A couple of times while Julian had been in town, Reg had thought someone was there, following her or watching her. But she hadn't been able to see anyone. Had that been Davyn? Watching over her without telling anyone what he was doing? Monitoring his handsome new friend to make sure that he did not endanger Reg? "You were there? Really?"

Davyn nodded. "I couldn't say anything to you at the time. Not without Julian finding out too. But you weren't alone, Reg. And I did believe you."

Reg's anger subsided. Not all the way; she was still irritated that he had thought that bringing up Julian's advancement and commendation to her was a good idea. But her fury cooled. Maybe Davyn wasn't quite as naive or clueless as she had thought.

She raised her hands to rekindle her fire, but nothing appeared and she didn't feel any warmth on her palms.

"I'm sorry, I should not have said anything," Davyn apologized. "I got carried away."

Reg nodded. She stared down at her hands, distracted from the conversation. What had seemed so important a moment before was now forgotten.

Davyn watched her. "What's wrong?"

"I don't know. I can't seem to…"

He cocked his head to the side slightly, analyzing the situation. "You're stressed and upset. It can freeze you up temporarily."

"It never has before."

If he thought about it, Davyn knew that when she got angry or upset, she was more likely to kindle fire, not less. It had happened by accident before she had any idea that she had powers.

"Still," Davyn said, "it can happen at unexpected times. It's one thing to kindle fire accidentally in a moment of emotional instability. But like with anything else, trying to do something when you are upset is a different story."

Reg was disheartened. "Why is it nothing is ever easy?"

Davyn smiled. "It's is the way of the world. We can't control it. There are always new challenges once we have overcome the old."

"That doesn't seem quite fair."

He nodded. He kindled fire between his own palms and reached toward her to hand it over. Reg raised her palms to receive it, but it fizzled out instead of staying in her hands like usual.

"Maybe we should try another exercise," Davyn suggested.

CHAPTER ELEVEN

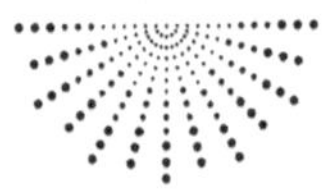

Things did not improve from there. They tried several different exercises, but Reg couldn't seem to get back into the groove. Everything she tried to do with her fire failed, even with Davyn helping her or feeding her his energy.

Davyn shrugged. "Well… I still think it's just because you're a bit upset today. It will go better next time. And I'm sorry. About bringing Julian up. I know you don't want to hear about him."

Reg nodded. She had an uneasy knot in her stomach. First, she had seemed to lose all of her powers on her return from supper with Corvin. Now she seemed to have lost—temporarily—her fire casting powers during the session with Davyn. She had done just fine at the beginning and it had just disappeared. She felt impotent.

What was wrong with her? Since she had started training with Davyn, she had never had a problem kindling fire unless she was too depleted of energy. Once she had recovered or been recharged by Corvin, she had been just fine. This time, there was nothing physically wrong with her. She felt well-rested despite how early she had gotten up that morning and was energetic.

Maybe Davyn was right. Maybe it was just because she had gotten upset about Julian.

But Reg worried it was the beginning of a pattern.

What if she were losing her powers?

* * *

Reg was eating a sandwich at the kitchen island, looking over her schedule even though she already knew that she didn't have any appointments set up for the next few days. Most of her clientele seemed to have suddenly become busy with other things that were more important than going to a fortune teller for a reading or communing with the spirits of their loved ones who had passed. Reg knew that she didn't need them to survive, but she still felt the loss. Worse than the loss of the money was the apparent loss of confidence in her or fear of what she might do.

She hadn't suddenly become a predator and didn't think she deserved to be treated like one.

Okay, there had been a couple of incidents, but she hadn't actually threatened any of the residents of Black Sands.

Except for Corvin, but did he really count? People feared and shunned him, so they should have been happy about it.

She heard the click of heels up the stone path that led to her door, a quick, sharp tapping. Before she could move to the door to see who it was, the knob turned and Sarah stepped into the room. She was still dressed for her coven, wearing a long black dress and robe. And high black heels. Reg raised her brows at that. Usually, Sarah wore sensible shoes. And when she returned from meeting with the witches in her coven, she normally changed right away into her Florida grandmother type clothes. She didn't go around in her cloak.

"Uh, hi."

"You're here. Good. I just wanted to let you know that I have spoken with the coven. Informed them of what has been going on here and made it clear that it *will* stop." Sarah's voice was a little sharp even discussing it with Reg; Reg could only imagine how forceful she might have been in talking to the witches she thought might be responsible for the vandalism.

"Do you think it will help?"

"It will," Sarah said with certainty. "I am not going to allow it to go on."

Reg nodded, not arguing or demanding to know how Sarah was going to prevent it. If Sarah said she was going to put a stop to it, Reg was not about to argue with her.

"Thank you."

Sarah gave a quick nod. "Yes. You're welcome."

Reg picked at a piece of food dried to the surface of the island. She had no idea what else to say to Sarah about it. Or what else Sarah might have to say to her. It was new territory for Reg. In the past, Reg had always run at the first sign of trouble. She would never stay around if she thought someone would target her or that people had decided it was time for her to leave town. By the time people knew what kind of a con she was running, she was usually long gone.

Black Sands had been different. And maybe she should have left months before. But she hadn't been able to bring herself to leave it all behind. Friends and a place she had finally felt like she belonged. She couldn't let that go so easily.

"So…" Sarah let out a breath. "Some friends and I are going out for dinner tonight, and then maybe on a yacht for a nightcap. I was wondering… if you would like to come along?"

Sarah had invited Reg to many kinds of events, so she should not have been surprised by this invitation. There had been community mixers, competitions, plays, all sorts of things. Dinner and a boat trip weren't anything out of the ordinary.

Except for the fact that Reg wasn't sure if she could avoid her siren instincts being triggered if she went to such activities. And after Sarah had just stood up for her in front of her witch friends, Reg didn't think it would be such a great idea for them to see her in that state.

"Uh… I think I have something else going on," Reg said. She looked down at her schedule, which she knew was blank. Sarah was the one who often set up appointments for her and kept her on schedule, so Sarah knew very well that she didn't have anything on.

"Come on, Reg," Sarah coaxed. "Let's go out and do something fun. You don't need to hide around here all day, trying to stay out of sight. That will just encourage people to treat you as an outcast. Be confident and get out there, and people will forget what they're supposed to be afraid of."

It was a lesson that Reg had learned early in her life. Bluster, brag, be confident, never let people know when she felt vulnerable, or they would know she was weak and take advantage of her. If she put on a brave face, they would see she was strong and leave her alone. Hopefully. With Sarah's words behind her, people would soon forget their prejudice about Reg's parentage.

"It's not that," Reg said, although her reluctance to go out at all and be seen around town did have something to do with trying to avoid people's judgment and the possibility of eggs or rocks being thrown at her the next time instead of at her house. "It's, umm… I don't think I should be that close to the water. Until I'm sure I have a good handle on this."

"It won't hurt you just to be close to the water. We'll have dinner in the marina and go out on the yacht. You won't be *in* the water."

"Even just the spray of water was a problem in the Everglades, I had to make sure I sat out of the way… I just don't want to be having to figure out what all the triggers are and avoiding them during an event like that. If it was just a couple of close friends, maybe, but with a group… especially a group that we're trying to convince that I am not a danger…"

"I suppose," Sarah said grudgingly. "But I want you to get out there. I don't want you sulking around here all day, with an empty schedule and nothing to do."

"I won't. I was in the garden for a while earlier… I'll go for a walk. Maybe drive up the coast a bit. I guess it's my opportunity to do all of the sightseeing I never did when I first got here."

Sarah nodded. "There are so many things to see in Florida. And many of the locals never see them."

"Yeah. I looked at some brochures when we were in the Everglades. There are all kinds of attractions. Maybe I'll spend a couple of days in Miami."

"Good. Well…" Sarah looked down at her black dress and cloak.

"Time to get out of this nightmare and into something more comfortable."

Sarah had a houseful of clothes; Reg didn't see why she had to wear something she didn't like to her coven. Even if she were required to wear black, and Reg didn't think she was, there was no reason it had to be a stuffy, uncomfortable dress.

"Okay. I'll see you later."

Sarah nodded and went on her way back to the big house. Reg watched her go, letting out a deep sigh. She really would have liked to go with Sarah. The marina was beautiful at night, and she longed to feel the wind from the ocean and to see the shimmering ripples of the dark water. But she had to be careful. She had to stay in control of herself, and that was getting harder and harder.

* * *

Reg turned on the TV and sat on the couch so that her back would be to the door and window when Sarah left the house. Not that Reg could see out of either one. The window was still blocked by cardboard, as Sarah hadn't been able to get anyone in to install a replacement window so quickly. And Sarah would be leaving by her front door, not visible to Reg from the back of the lot. But Reg didn't want to know when she left, either by the lights going out in the house or by her sense of Sarah's presence in the house, which she couldn't help monitoring.

She flipped through the various options and found a channel streaming classic scary movies. Maybe she would pop some popcorn and enjoy a movie night. The campy black and white horror movies were sure to distract her from everything that was going on in her own life. It was hard to believe that they had once been considered frightening. The melodrama, the cheesy special effects... it was nothing compared to what a computer could generate. Yet those were the classics, the ones that everyone remembered and referenced.

Starlight checked out his bowl to see if anything interesting had materialized there, crunched a few bits of kibble, and joined her on the couch, cuddling up to her so that Reg didn't want to move and disturb his purring meditation even to get popcorn.

* * *

Maybe falling asleep to horror movies was not the best idea. Reg awoke sometime in the night, disoriented and trying to remember where she was and how she had fallen asleep on the uncomfortable couch. She shifted around, waking the black and white cat so that he put back his ears and looked at her with a grumpy expression before stalking away to his food dish. It took her some time to blink away the weird nightmares of monsters and snakes and gangsters with funny hats and guns and to remember where she was, why she was there, and even the tuxedo cat's name.

She used the bathroom and staggered to her bed to go back to sleep where it was more comfortable and, hopefully, she would not have any more dreams.

CHAPTER TWELVE

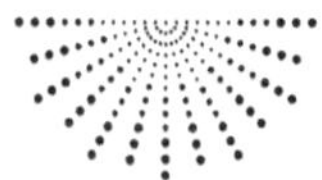

Of course that wasn't the end of the dreams. Reg tried to sweep them away as she woke up in the morning. Just dreams. Nothing she needed to remember. Nothing portentous.

The cat stretched and meowed and jumped over to the bed. Reg scratched his ears, looking at him for a few minutes.

"Star," she said finally. "Starlight." She shook her head. "What is wrong with my head? It isn't even like I was drinking last night. What is going on with me?"

Starlight looked back at her, his eyes steady and expression serious.

"It must be something Corvin did to me. That's when it all started, when I had dinner with him. Did he slip something into my drink? Plant a suggestion in my mind? I don't know what's going on."

Starlight meowed and led the way to the kitchen. Reg laughed. For a cat, everything began with what was in his food dish. How could one expect to solve the world's problems without a proper breakfast?

She followed him out to the kitchen and he indicated his bowl and rubbed against the fridge. Reg checked the fridge and found some fish for him. He supervised while she plopped a couple of spoonfuls into his bowl, and then chowed down.

Reg looked around her cottage. It all seemed familiar and new at the same time. As if she had visited it once or twice before, but it wasn't really hers. Was that because it belonged to the witch in the big house? Or was there something else going on that she didn't understand?

She looked through the other containers in the fridge but didn't see anything that interested her. As if someone else had stocked the fridge with foods that she didn't particularly like. She pushed the button on the coffee machine and put a cup under the spout just in time to avoid it spitting coffee out all over the counter.

There was a phone ringing in the other room. Reg ignored it. She didn't want to talk to anyone. Whoever it was would have to wait.

The cat continued to wolf down his food. Reg watched him thoughtfully as she waited for the coffee machine to finish filling her cup.

It was good that she had a familiar. The cat would help her to focus her energy. The third eye marking on his forehead suggested that he had psychic powers, which would be helpful.

The coffee machine finished dribbling into her cup, and Reg was soon leaning against the counter, sipping the hot, bitter liquid, and wondering where she would go to pick up a newspaper. There didn't seem to be any around the cottage. There was a knock on the door. She decided it wouldn't be polite to ignore it and, since she was up anyway, she might as well answer it.

The blond woman on the steps had gorgeous curls spiraling down to her shoulder and a charming French Creole accent.

"Reg," she trilled. "How ees it? Sarah was telling me about your trouble lately." The woman stopped to look at the door, surveying the whole thing as if she might find a flaw in it. She nodded. "No eggs today."

Reg shook her head at the non-sequitur. She tried to remember what she knew about the woman. They knew each other because of the cats. Reg's black and white tuxedo and the woman's pure black female, who she let wander all over the neighborhood, unlike Reg's cat, who was an indoor cat.

Nicole?

Reg opened her mouth to greet the woman, then closed it again. No. That wasn't right. Nicole was, she thought, the cat's name. She could hear the woman's lilting voice as she pronounced it. *Nee-cole.*

"Francesca," Reg blurted as it finally came to her.

Francesca smiled and raised her brows. "Reg?"

"Sorry. I haven't had my coffee yet," Reg laughed off the blunder. "How are you? And Nicole?"

Francesca was happy to answer and went into some detail about both her recent activities and her and the cat's health. Reg studied her face, trying to remember more about her, but couldn't access much of those memories. Black cats. Singing. *Nee-cole.* She couldn't seem to put it in any order.

"And you?" Francesca was inquiring. "I guess things have been difficult."

"Yes," Reg agreed. She rubbed sweating palms down her robe. She stopped and looked at it. Why was she still wearing a robe in the middle of the morning? She should have been showered and changed by that time. "I really don't want to talk about that right now, though. We should focus on… the positives."

Francesca nodded wisely, as if this were something she often counseled. "Yes. The positive," she agreed. "Not enough people express gratitude for the good things in their lives."

"Exactly," Reg concurred. But she wasn't counting her blessings. She was trying to figure out what the heck was going on without giving away her current deficits to anyone else. In a few minutes, when the caffeine had reached her brain, everything would be back to normal. It was just the previous night's dreams that had not yet left her.

Reg's thoughts flashed back to the dreams. She had tried to push them away and forget them, but all at once, she saw images from several of her dreams almost simultaneously. They were too quick for her to process them one at a time, yet she saw them all clearly.

A man with a claw-like hand. Snakes underfoot, their rattles making her suddenly leap back in alarm. Dark shapes moving in the darkness. She heard words as if they were coming to her from far away.

The venom.

Bring me what I need.

There is no other way.

It was all from watching the movies the night before. She should have known better than to watch horror movies before bed. To fall asleep with them still playing in her ears. Her subconscious brain had picked up on the themes and was bringing the images back to her as if they were her own thoughts instead of echoes of what she had seen on the screen.

"Could I get you something?" Reg offered Francesca, interrupting whatever it was Francesca was going on about. "Coffee or tea?"

"Tea, yes, if you don't mind."

Reg opened and closed cupboards and found a supply of both commercial tea bags and jars of loose-leaf tea and herbs. "What kind do you want?"

Francesca perused the selection over Reg's shoulder. "Just… English Breakfast, I think."

Reg grabbed one of the tea bags and opened another cupboard to find some mugs. She put the bag into the mug and fumbled with the high-tech kettle, trying to figure out if she were supposed to put it on one of the elements on the smooth cooktop or if it worked by itself.

Francesca took it from her and pressed a button. She sloshed it to make sure there was enough water in it, then put it down on the counter to heat. Reg studied it.

"It's new," she remarked.

"It looks the same as the last one," Francesca countered.

"Yes… but there are a few differences."

Neither of them said anything for a few minutes, listening to the ticking of the kettle as it warmed. Reg scratched the back of her neck.

"Where would I go to get a newspaper?" she asked.

Francesca's look became even more bewildered. Reg decided she had better stop asking questions and showing herself to be so unbalanced.

"Are you… okay?" Francesca asked delicately. "I know you were not feeling well; perhaps you need to…"

What Francesca thought Reg needed, she wasn't sure.

"Just a little foggy this morning," she said, trying to wave away Francesca's concern. "I'm sure I'll be fine once the coffee kicks in."

"Is this something to do with... what Sarah said...? About how you are partly..." she trailed off, and Reg was left to wonder. Partly what?

"It's nothing," Reg told her again. "Don't worry about it."

There was a trilling noise from the direction of the bedroom. Francesca looked around. "Is that your phone?"

"It can wait."

Francesca's eyes grew wider and rounder at this suggestion. There was a lag in the conversation as they both listened to the phone ringing in the other room. Whoever it was, they were very persistent. Reg didn't like phones. It was reprehensible the way that young people were always glued to their phones, ignoring everything going on around them. They needed to just put them down and get out there in the real world. Quit hiding from everything outside their own doors.

"Why don't you look up the news on your phone?" Francesca asked. "Isn't that what you usually do?"

Reg considered this. But she wasn't sure what it was she usually did. Just that there were not any newspapers around the cottage. Not even in the garbage bins of varying colors under the kitchen sink.

"Yes, of course," she agreed. "I just felt like... I'd like to be able to see everything spread out in front of me, instead of crammed onto that tiny screen."

"Oh." Francesca nodded politely. "Of course."

"Not everyone likes reading on their phones."

"No. That's true. I just always thought you were... a phone person. You've always got yours with you, and you haven't seemed interested in... books and newspapers."

"I made a resolution. For the Spring equinox. I want my life to be more balanced, so I decided to quit relying on the phone for every-thing. To have a better, more well-rounded life."

The kettle whistled. Francesca turned it off and poured water over her teabag. She looked around the kitchen and found sugar in the cupboard and a small carton of milk in the fridge. Then she nodded her head toward the wicker furniture in the living room.

"We should sit. Enjoy the tea like civilized people."

Reg nodded her approval at this. She carried her coffee cup over and sat down in one of the chairs. Francesca sat down with her tea. Reg appreciated the calm, unhurried atmosphere. Much better than gulping the hot drinks down and rushing off to something that seemed so much more important but was really just an excuse for not visiting properly.

"So, how long since you moved to Florida?" Reg asked.

Francesca looked at her, frown lines appearing between her eyebrows. "Just when I moved here to Black Sands. Right before we met."

"Oh. Right. I was thinking you had lived in Orlando first. I'm not sure why I thought that."

"No. When I left Haiti, I came here. I had only lived here a couple of weeks before… that business."

That business?

Reg smiled and nodded her confirmation. Of course.

The tuxedo cat—Starlight—wandered into the living room and went to Francesca for attention. Then rather than going to Reg, he hunkered down a few feet away from her and just stared at her. Reg snapped her fingers beside her chair.

"Come here, Starlight. Come on over and say hi."

Starlight didn't budge. He just sat there in the shape of a bread loaf, unmoving, and looked at Reg.

"He is sleepy this morning too?" Francesca suggested in a light tone.

Anger flared up inside of Reg. She didn't like Francesca's tone or the suggestion that Reg's explanation hadn't made sense. Francesca thought that there was something wrong. Wrong with Reg and wrong with the cat.

Why did the stupid woman come forcing her way into someone else's house with all kinds of expectations? She wasn't in charge of Reg. They weren't best friends. They had spent some time together, and now the little witch thought that she had the right to pass judgments over Reg's life. And her cat. What kind of person did that?

Francesca's eyes narrowed. She drank another sip of her tea. She looked toward the door as if measuring her chances of a quick escape.

"You can leave whenever you like," Reg snapped. "Don't feel like you have to stay."

Francesca looked as if she would argue, putting a determined smile on her face and making demands, but then she apparently thought better of it.

"I don't want to take up any more of your time," she said graciously. "I'm sorry, I should have called first."

Her words hung in the air, and Reg wondered if she had, in fact, called first, and that had been one of the calls that Reg had ignored, leaving the phone in the bedroom where she didn't have to deal with it all the time.

"It was nice to see you," Reg offered up a platitude.

"Yes, always a pleasure," Francesca returned woodenly. There was no warmth between them. Reg simmered at Francesca thinking she could just show up out of the blue and would be welcomed with open arms.

Reg escorted her to the door, still smiling in a way that stretched her face unnaturally. Francesca cast a couple of quick glances in her direction.

"Let me know if you need anything," she said in a low, urgent way, as if someone might overhear them. "Just give me a call; I would be happy to help."

Did she think that Reg was being held hostage? Or did she have some other scenario in mind?

Reg just shook her head. "Of course. I'm fine, but if I need anyone, I know who to call."

Francesca gave her one more perplexed look, and then walked out of the cottage.

CHAPTER THIRTEEN

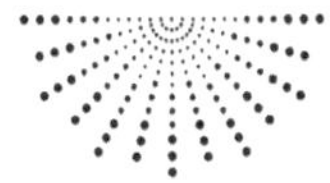

Reg watched Francesca walk away. She shut the door and locked the two locks.

"I wonder what that was all about." She spoke to Starlight, though the words weren't really meant for anyone but herself. "Why did she come over here? Just to gossip? To see if Sarah was right and I am… whatever Sarah said?"

Reg looked toward the big house. That was, she knew, where Sarah lived. She searched her memory for any fragments. Sarah Bishop. A witch so old she might have lived in Salem during the great witch furors. Reg didn't think Sarah had ever told her whether she was part of that situation, but it wasn't out of the realm of possibility.

What had Sarah told Francesca about Reg? Reg didn't like being out of the loop. But Francesca had been too cagey, not wanting to declare out loud what they were talking about. That Reg was part… what? Part of a group Francesca or Sarah had a low opinion of? Or the opposite, of a group they admired? And what had that comment about eggs been about? Reg didn't know if she had been hinting at a desire for eggs for breakfast? Or was it something else?

No eggs. No eggs today.

Maybe she meant that she only wanted toast and not any eggs. It was impossible to guess.

"People should say what they mean," Reg told Starlight. "They shouldn't come over here hinting and acting like they know what they're talking about. Or like I know what they're talking about."

The first thing to do was to go out and get a newspaper. Reg could read up on what was going on in the community and around the world. It would trigger memories, and from that, she would be able to reconstruct her life. No one would have to know that there was anything wrong. Francesca might have some lingering doubts for a few days, but when everything went back to normal with Reg, she would soon forget that she'd ever had anything to worry about. In Reg's experience, people were very quick to forget things that didn't fit properly. They would rather believe that everything was just the way it had always been, ignoring any minor differences that might have given it away.

That was what allowed people like Reg to hide in plain sight.

* * *

She should have guessed that it wouldn't be long before that busybody Sarah Bishop got involved. She had always been a thorn in Reg's side. Instead of reassuring Francesca that everything was fine with Reg, she had apparently bought into Francesca's concerns. Now there were two of them Reg would have to convince that everything was fine. And just the way it always had been.

Almost as soon as Reg stepped onto the pathway outside the cottage, Sarah popped out of the back door of the big house. "Oh, Reg!" she greeted, as if she were surprised to see her there and it was only coincidence that they both went out at the same time. "How are you doing this morning? Going out already?"

"Yes, lovely," Reg agreed. "Just thought I'd pop out and pick up a newspaper."

Sarah frowned and cocked her head to the side. "A newspaper. Well, why don't you come in? I get it delivered every day."

Reg hadn't been expecting the offer. She could still go out to find her own, but then it would probably look even more suspicious. If Reg weren't the type of person who usually read the paper, then going out to get her own when there was already one available would be strange. Unless she needed a copy of her own because she wanted to save a clipping. But of what? She wasn't quick enough on her feet to come up with something, so she nodded acquiescence and followed Sarah into her large, comfortable kitchen.

"I'll just get today's, why don't I?" Sarah offered. She disappeared down the hall for a moment and returned with the local rag.

Reg spread it out on the table, glancing through headlines, trying to get up to speed on what had been happening in Black Sands lately and if she'd had anything to do with it. There were a few articles on the Spring Games and saying goodbye to the many visitors who had brought tourist dollars into the town. It had been a good boost to the economy.

There were some local happenings around spring equinox. Nothing specifically about Reg or about psychics. Whatever the gossip was about Reg around town, it apparently hadn't made its way to the news.

"Are you looking for something in particular?" Sarah asked. "I thought you would find it on your phone…"

Her phone again. Reg ran her fingers through her red box braids. "It's not working right now. I'm not looking for anything in particular… just seeing what's going on."

"Oh. Well, it's all been pretty quiet since the end of the Spring Games. You know how it is; unusual things always happen during Ostara, and when you throw the Games and all of the visitors in, it does cause a certain amount of… disruption in the magical balance."

"Yes." Obviously, Reg would be familiar with that. "Yes, it looks like things have quieted down. Gone… back to normal."

"No unwanted intruders last night," Sarah said. "It looks like the wards are holding. Or what I said at coven had some impact."

Intruders? Reg's ears perked up at that. What kind of intruders?

"You slept well?" Sarah asked, when Reg didn't contribute anything of interest.

"Yes. I slept just fine." Reg thought about that after she said it. "Well… other than dreams, I mean. But I felt reasonably well-rested this morning."

Sarah scratched her ear. "That's good to hear. You are up early, that's why I wondered. I thought maybe you weren't able to sleep and were still up from last night."

"No. I slept. I guess I was just ready to get up earlier today."

"Can I get you a coffee? Tea?"

Reg shook her head and looked around the kitchen. Reg might be friendly with this witch, but that didn't mean eating and drinking with her. Not when Sarah could slip something into her coffee that could affect her. A truth serum or something to calm her nerves.

She looked back down at the newspaper, paging through it more slowly. She even paused to skim classified ads, looking for any unusual patterns or coded messages. But everything seemed normal. Boring, even.

"Thank you for the use of your paper," she said finally, closing it. "That was very nice of you."

"Did you find what you were looking for?"

"I'm not looking for anything particular," Reg told her. "Just seeing what's going on."

* * *

Walking back through the yard, Reg had an uneasy feeling that someone else was there, watching her covertly. She looked around a few times, trying to catch them at it, but she couldn't see anyone. Shifting shadows under the trees, but no person.

She looked down just in time to avoid stepping on a snake. She halted abruptly, foot still in the air. The snake's head bobbed up and down, watching her with wary eyes,

"Well, hello," Reg greeted in a low, even voice.

She put her foot down carefully. The snake's head weaved back and forth. She half expected it to strike, but it did not. She bent closer to it, staring into its black, empty eyes.

"Reg Rawlins!"

She startled, just a small muscle twitch, nothing big enough to trigger the snake. A little old man hurried toward her. He held a spade, and when he got close, he moved it cautiously toward the snake, trying to move it off the pathway. The snake struck once and, finding its way blocked by the man with the shovel, it eventually uncoiled and slithered off into the grass, disappearing into the bushes.

The little man looked up at Reg expectantly.

"Thank you," Reg acknowledged, but she really hadn't been worried about the snake, so she wasn't sure why he had acted the way he had.

He stood there for a minute looking at her and not saying anything, then eventually, he said tersely: "Poison."

Reg nodded. "I know. But it wasn't going to strike."

His eyes rounded. He cocked his head to the side as if expecting her to say more, but she didn't have anything else to say. She had thanked him for his perceived good deed. What else did he want?

"You can't hear Forst?" he asked finally.

Forst was, she assumed his name.

"I can hear you just fine."

He looked doubtful. "But inside words?"

Reg blinked at him, uncertain what this meant. She shrugged. "I need to get back into the house. I think I might have left the stove on when I went to see Sarah."

His forehead wrinkled in consternation. Clearly, he expected her to stay outside chatting with him for longer. They were friends, and he was used to more attention.

"Sorry. We'll talk later."

He nodded his head, pointed red cap bobbing, and he turned to go back the way he had come. Reg looked into the bushes to see if she could find the snake again, but it was gone.

CHAPTER FOURTEEN

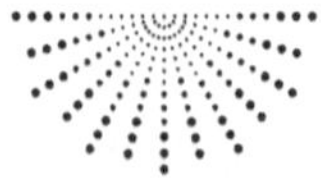

Maybe because Reg had gotten up so early, she hit a wall shortly after noon, finding herself exhausted and hardly able to keep her eyes open. After resisting for a little while, she finally decided she wasn't going to get through the day without a nap. Though she had felt good when she had woken up in the morning, she had not had enough sleep to make it through the day.

Starlight was curled up sleeping on her bed. He raised his head to look at her, making an inquiring purr-meowing noise. Reg scratched his head and crawled onto the bed, curling up in the middle to close her eyes. Starlight got up and stretched, his whole body trembling with the effort. Then he made his way over to her, curling up against her leg and purring contentedly. It was nice to have the warm, soft form fitted against her.

While she had only intended to lie down for twenty minutes or so, just long enough to get her engine going again, but she knew when she woke up that several hours had passed. She sat up and rubbed her eyes. They were sticky and her vision blurry. She blinked and petted Starlight, who rubbed against her and head-butted her.

"Yes, I had a good nap. How about you? Did you have a nice one?" She asked.

Starlight seemed to be happy; she assumed his nap had gone well.

He jumped off the bed and made a noise for her to follow him. Reg grabbed her phone from the bedside table and followed.

She rubbed the back of her head and neck. She turned her neck, cracking it several times and trying to work out the kinks and the stiffness. That was one of the problems with sleeping in the afternoon. Headaches, grogginess, and a stiff neck were common side effects. She wandered out to the kitchen and put some food in Starlight's bowl without really paying much attention. She tried to remember what she had done during the morning, but wasn't sure what she had done that had made her so tired. It had just been a regular day. Other than the fact that she had gotten up too early.

There were still no appointments on her calendar. Sarah hadn't been by, or if she had, she hadn't added any more appointments for that week. Reg didn't look any farther ahead than that.

"What should we do for the rest of the day?" Reg inquired. "I should probably go for a walk, stretch my legs. Sitting around at home all day isn't good, and I haven't exactly been keeping up my activity level. If I'm going to eat more, like I have been, then I'd better step things up a bit."

She could even start exercise classes at the community center or a nearby gym. She knew they did yoga classes. Maybe spin and some kind of aerobics, though she knew they called it by a different name now. She'd never been a member of a gym before, but then, she'd never had any leisure time either. Now that she had the one, she might need to balance it out.

Reg decided she should just take the bull by the horns instead of debating it with herself. She didn't want to talk herself out of going for a walk and end up just spending the rest of the day in front of the TV and phone screen. She put on what she hoped were good walking shoes and a hat, and set out. She walked around the path to the front of the big house and saw Forst watering the garden. He looked just like one of the ceramic gnomes people posed in their gardens as decorations. She smiled at his studious look and reached out to him in her mind.

How's the garden coming along?

He looked around, startled. He frowned for a moment. *Is Reg Rawlins feeling better?*

Reg stopped. She had intended to just call out to him as she passed, but his question gave her pause. *Better? I suppose. I had a nap this afternoon, and I'm feeling pretty good. A little groggy, but I figured a walk and the fresh air would do me good.*

Forst stroked his long white beard. *That is good. I was worried this morning…*

Reg tried to remember what he would have had to be concerned about. Had she even seen him in the morning? She was getting her days mixed up. *Umm… this morning? Why?*

Forst pulled the curvy pipe out of his pocket and fiddled for a few minutes, preparing the tobacco and lighting it, then puffing rings of smoke.

The snake, he reminded her eventually. *You did not heed my warnings… When I chased it away, you seemed… disappointed.*

Reg's mouth fell open. She looked for words but couldn't find them, even though she only needed to form them in her head and not have to explain herself to Forst out loud. She shook her head slightly, trying to understand what he was talking about.

The snake?

Forst raised his bushy gray eyebrows and nodded, puffing on the pipe. *Very dangerous. Most humans would panic. But not Reg Rawlins.*

I don't like snakes.

He didn't seem to believe this. *And also, you did not… hear me. When I spoke the inside words, you did not answer. Only outside words.*

Knowing how difficult it was for Forst to express himself out loud, Reg would never have demanded he speak to her audibly. It was baffling.

I don't… I don't even remember what you're talking about. There was a snake? And I couldn't hear your telepathy? Are you sure… this wasn't a dream? It sounds like one of my dreams. I've been having a lot of nightmares about snakes lately.

She remembered before when she had been dreaming about

spiders. There had been a reason for that. She considered whether there was a psychic explanation as to why she had been dreaming about snakes. And why Reg could not remember it.

Not a dream, Forst insisted, shaking his head. *This morning, on the pathway.* He pointed back the way Reg had come. *A diamondback.*

Reg didn't know a lot about venomous snakes, having grown up in the north where they were rarer, and usually in the city where snakes did not venture, at least not in the areas where she had lived. But she knew that a diamondback rattler was one of the most deadly snakes in Florida.

In the yard here? She gestured at Sarah's back yard. *There can't be one here, in the yard!*

Forst nodded seriously. *Snakes come and go. In the garden, there are places to hide. They do not usually bother humans, so noisy and clumsy are they.*

And did I see it? I must not have seen it.

You saw, he insisted. *You were looking at it. Talking to it. But you heard not my words. I had to run over,* he made a gesture, *chase it away. Could have been hurt if I didn't have my shovel. Reg Rawlins could have been hurt.*

Yes… well, thank you so much for doing that. I'm so sorry that I don't… Reg shook her head. *That I don't even remember it. It's very strange.*

Forst nodded, smoking and considering the strange occurrence. *Things have been bad lately for Reg Rawlins?* he asked. *First, the eggs and the broken window? And now…*

But this isn't something that the witches did. This is… just a coincidence, right? They couldn't have had anything to do with this.

He took the pipe stem out of his mouth, tapped the bowl, and put it back in his mouth. *Talk to Sarah Bishop about the spell they cast. What kind of spell?* He shook his head grimly.

Well… I don't know. It was just supposed to protect them from harm. That's what Sarah said.

Forst shook his head doubtfully. *Other magic going on here. Strange happenings.*

Reg swallowed. *I'm going for a walk now,* she told him. *But I will ask Sarah about it later. She said she was going to put wards outside to keep us safe… so there shouldn't have been anything dangerous in the garden, should there? That diamondback… I just don't understand it.*

Wards against witches are not wards against snakes.

No. I guess not.

He nodded meditatively, and Reg left him there smoking his funny-looking pipe.

CHAPTER FIFTEEN

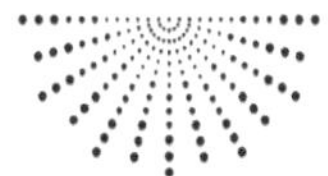

Reg had never been big on walking. When she was a kid, she had walked or ridden her bike a lot, because as a kid, it was the only way to get around. But as an adult, she'd avoided extra physical exertion. She was often counting her pennies to be able to eat, so less activity was better if she were to be able to afford enough food to keep her healthy.

All of which was to say that she didn't enjoy her walk around her Black Sands neighborhood nearly as much as she had imagined she would. She tired quickly and the walking shoes were rubbing where they shouldn't, making her worry she would get blisters. There were a lot of elegant houses like Sarah's with beautifully tended grounds. No gardens quite as nice as Sarah's had been since she had hired the garden gnome, but that was to be expected. Reg had thought she would enjoy looking at the architecture and at the bright greens that abounded in Florida, but she had quickly become more concerned about her feet than anything around her.

So she was back before she had traveled as far or as long as she had planned to.

Reg looked at the house and tried to decide whether to talk to Sarah about what was going on. There were too many strange things happening for her to figure it out, but she wasn't sure she wanted to tell Sarah everything. Some things a person just wanted to keep to herself.

But a diamondback rattler in the yard? Wasn't it more important for Reg to protect her health and safety than it was to guard her privacy and what someone else might think about her? Sarah had always been friendly and supportive. Or mostly, anyway. It had been a little different when she was sick, but a person couldn't be expected to expend all her energy on her friends when she is sick.

Reg went to the back door even though she had been standing outside the front while trying to decide. She knocked and then opened the door, as Sarah had repeatedly encouraged her to just "come right in."

"Sarah? Are you home?"

She could feel Sarah's presence there. And someone else's too. Reg closed her eyes for an instant to clarify the feeling. Detective Marta Jessup. That was who was there visiting with Sarah.

"Come in, Reg," Sarah called back.

Reg considered. She was hesitant about talking to Sarah about what had been going on. But she was even more reluctant to talk about it in front of Jessup.

"Reg?" Sarah called again.

Reg sighed and followed their voices into the sitting room. "Hi," she greeted, poking her head in. "I didn't realize you had company. We can talk later." A clue to Sarah that she had something they needed to discuss in confidence.

"No, no," Sarah said. "Come in. This affects you too. You weren't home when Marta got here, so I said we would just go ahead, but I would much rather you were part of this."

Reg hovered in the doorway. "I don't know, I just wanted to talk to you about..."

"Come on, Reg," Jessup encouraged, smiling at her. But she was in her full cop uniform, which not only triggered Reg's desire to flee, but also meant that it was official police business, and Reg didn't want anything to do with a police investigation.

Beside Jessup sat another cop. A man, balding, barely taller than Detective Jessup, with a round face and a belly that extended past his duty belt. Senior to Jessup; a babysitter. A partner who was supposed to keep her in line, since she'd gone over a few too many lines in previous months. Reg hadn't seen Jessup with a partner since they had first met, when Jessup had been warning Reg off and poking around to see if she was really a psychic or just trying to bilk people out of their money.

The cop's name bar said Devaughn. His presence made Reg doubly anxious.

"Come in," Sarah encouraged again, patting the seat of the easy chair next to her. "I want you to be a part of this."

Reg eventually caved. She tried not to slink like a cowardly dog as she approached the chair next to Sarah's and sat down, hoping that if she stayed quiet, she would be invisible to the two cops.

"We were just talking about some of the things that have been going on around here," Sarah explained. "The vandalism and such. The police ought to know about it, be on the lookout in case they see anyone around who doesn't belong here."

But they weren't going to know who belonged and who didn't, which meant that there were likely to be random stops of suspicious-looking characters, which might just include Reg herself. Jessup wouldn't arrest her just for hanging out around her own home, but she could still be targeted by other cops who didn't know her. And so could Forst and anyone else who came over to visit Reg or consult with her. Forst's twin, Fir, had previously been arrested by cops for vandalism of some industrial equipment.

"I think we can take care of it ourselves," she told Sarah and Jessup. "I don't think we need to involve the police."

"After a rock through the window?" Jessup demanded. "What if that had hit you in the head instead of just sailing over it? What if they decide to start throwing rocks at you when they see you out on the street? You were out there walking just now... you're lucky that no one bothered you. How would you protect yourself if you were attacked?"

"I can take care of myself," Reg insisted. "I have... skills." She looked at Jessup's partner, not knowing whether he was someone who knew about the magical practitioners in Black Sands or not. Some of the police knew or were practitioners themselves. Others just turned a blind eye to anything they could not explain and continued to operate as if the magical world did not exist.

"I know you do," Jessup acknowledged. "There aren't many people around here who are… more skilled. But that doesn't mean you would be able to withstand any number of attackers. What if there are more than one or two? What if it's a whole group of people intent on hurting you?"

"We've already put… systems in place to deal with that," Reg said carefully. Let Devaughn think that they were talking about burglar alarms or a night guard.

"I'd like to read this to you," Jessup said, pulling up the statement that she or Sarah had written out in longhand on a clipboard holding carbonless triplicate forms. Reg was glad that Jessup offered to read it, rather than forcing Reg to read the cursive writing. Bad enough when it was regular cursive writing. Reg would have trouble reading more than a few short words. But even worse was the archaic flavor of writing that witches in the area seemed to all use. Spiky, with longer tails and stems than Reg was used to, often written with a fountain pen or a quill.

Jessup proceeded to read the statement. It was short, but accurately described the eggs and the rock through the window. It didn't say anything about the candles and symbols of the protection spell. Reg supposed that was too inflammatory for the official report. They didn't want anything in writing about witches practicing magic there.

Reg nodded when Jessup was done. "Yeah, that all sounds right."

"And you haven't seen anyone hanging around? Don't have any idea who might have done this? If you do, I should bring them in for questioning. And make sure that they understand they will be prosecuted if they come back."

"No. I don't know who it is." Reg glanced over at Sarah. Had she figured out who was behind the attacks when she spoke to her coven?

Sarah's pleasant smile didn't waver. She gave nothing away. Reg admired her poker face.

"Okay." Jessup closed a cover over the clipboard to keep everything neat and tidy. "Thank you for reporting this. It's important for us to stay on top of social disorder, so that we can curb it before it turns into something dangerous. It may seem like a minor thing, but we know from experience that they can escalate. I want people in our community to feel safe." Jessup smiled encouragingly.

Sarah and Reg nodded.

Devaughn took his cue from Jessup that it was time to go and hefted himself to his feet with a grunt. "You take care, folks," he said with a nod.

They saw themselves out. Reg didn't know whether that new cop might have psychic abilities and be waiting to see what they had to say after he left the house. Or whether they might turn around and pop back in to see if they overheard anything interesting. So she waited until they were some distance from the house before turning to Sarah.

"I thought that you figured it was going to be okay after talking to your coven."

"It will be fine," Sarah agreed, giving a nod. "I'm just covering all of my bases."

"You don't think that they'll 'escalate'?"

"I don't imagine so. After having spoken to them, word should get around that we're not going to just sit here and take it. And that you're not going anywhere. Eventually, things will settle down and go back to normal."

"You don't think that they would do something like… a spell that would call poisonous snakes, do you?"

"No, certainly not." Sarah's smile disappeared, and she stared at Reg. "Poisonous snakes?"

Reg shrugged. "I know there are a lot of poisonous snakes in Florida."

"Certainly. But not a lot in town. And they won't go after a person; they will flee in the other direction."

"Yeah. That's what I thought."

Neither of them said anything for a while. Sarah's gaze remained steady on Reg. "What kind of snake?"

Reg chewed on her thumbnail, a habit she had broken years ago which still reappeared every now and then in times of stress. "Diamondback."

"A diamondback rattler. In my yard. Are you quite sure?"

"I, um… to tell the truth, I don't remember anything clearly. But Forst was there, and he says it was a diamondback. I think… he probably knows his snakes."

"Yes. I would trust his identification. When did this happen?"

"Today. Earlier."

"Where did it come from? What did it do?"

"I don't know. Forst chased it away. With a shovel. But I don't have any idea where it came from or whether it was related to this other business. Forst suggested that it might have something to do with whatever spell they cast the other night. He said I should ask you. You looked at the symbols and everything that they left behind after their ritual."

"So untidy," Sarah said with a grim shake of her head.

Reg giggled about Sarah being concerned about the witches not cleaning up after themselves properly. "But it's good for us because you can read what they left behind, right? You can tell me what it was all about?"

Sarah tapped her fingers on the arms of her chair. "I don't know. There was a siren image. There were some other lines and symbols that I couldn't be sure of. Crude drawings. A couple of squiggly lines could be the waves of the ocean or they could be snakes. It would make more sense if they were waves of the ocean, because of your nature, but I can't be sure."

"If they were clumsy about their drawings, maybe they were trying to draw waves and accidentally summoned snakes."

"Uh, no, dear. That's not how it works. It is the intention of the practitioner, not his artistic ability, that guides the spell. Despite what you may have seen on TV or the silver screen, mispronouncing a word in a spell or chant will not cause something completely unexpected to happen. The practitioner's will guides it."

"But you don't think they were calling snakes."

"No. I don't. But I would like to hear more about this. I will have to talk to Forst." Sarah sighed. "But you know that he doesn't speak to me like he does to you. Would you mind… relaying for him?"

Reg nodded slowly. "Sure." She pondered what Forst was going to tell Sarah. Unlike if she were translating for someone who spoke a different language, Forst would know if she misrepresented his answers to Sarah. And he would want Sarah to know everything that was going on that was weird. Not just the unexpected appearance of the snake. "There are… other things I should probably tell you before you talk to Forst."

"Okay. What should you probably tell me?"

"I have… there are some… blanks in my memory."

"Blanks. How big are these blanks?"

"Uh… I don't remember much of what happened from the time I got up this morning until I got up from a nap in the afternoon. So… pretty big."

"Have you been hit on the head?"

Reg couldn't repress a laugh at Sarah's matter-of-fact question. "No. Uh… not that I remember."

"Have you been sick? Maybe… something to do with your recent… changes?"

"No. I've been feeling okay. Other than the other night, after I got back from a… date. I sort of… didn't seem to be able to use any of my powers."

Sarah noted her hesitance. "What happened on this date? Could he have put something in your drink? Did he give you a gift or do something else to ensorcell you?"

"No. Nothing like that. I just… I maybe indulged a little too much. I felt pretty wrecked going to bed. But I was fine when I got up in the morning. Not a sign of a hangover, physical or magical. Everything was back to normal."

"But that wasn't last night. Or this morning. It doesn't explain your memory blanks."

"No. It doesn't."

"So we have had these attacks or warnings, a spell was cast, and you have had a loss of your powers and memory blanks. And the appearance of a diamondback rattler where there really shouldn't have been one. Is that everything?"

"Forst said… that he tried to talk to me. To warn me about the rattler and to talk to me about it afterward, and when he did, I couldn't hear him. Telepathically. He had to speak out loud for me to understand him."

Sarah nodded slowly. "That is strange. Another loss of your powers. Something is going on here, but I don't think this is just the protection spell. Why would that stop you from being able to communicate telepathically or to use other powers?"

"And I can now… it was just then, before my nap. Now… it seems to be okay again. I talked to him a few minutes ago and everything was normal again."

She should probably tell Sarah about not being able to kindle fire with Davyn either.

"Have you tried… meditating? Or using your powers to find out what has been going on? If you're able to use them right now, you could ask the spirits about yourself and what has been happening with your gifts. Or you could look in your crystal ball and see what you can see."

"I didn't think of that. I guess I can try. It's just been so strange the last few days. Switching between normal and these… hiccups."

"You should try it. See if you can determine the source of these changes in your energy field. If we know what it is being caused by, we have a better chance of being able to do something about it."

Reg pushed herself to her feet, thinking about it. "And you don't think…"

Sarah waited for her to finish, and when she didn't, prompted her. "I don't think what, Reg?"

"You don't think this is… because of being part siren? That my siren part is somehow… taking over and erasing everything else?"

"I don't know. It is not something I have any experience with. Sirens are very rare in this world, and interactions between sirens and humans are practically nonexistent. We know of each other, but we generally try to have nothing to do with each other."

"*Positive* interactions," Reg amended.

"Hmm?"

"There aren't very many *positive* interactions between sirens and humans. But sirens still hunt. And so do humans, for that matter."

Reg knew that sirens had been hunted in the past when they had gotten too close to human civilization. Maybe that was one of the reasons they were so rare. Other than the fact that they tended to kill each other over territorial rights. Even their own children.

"Well, yes. I meant that… we don't talk. We're not friendly with each other."

"Yeah. And you don't think I have some siren disease? When she was here, Norma Jean seemed like she had periods when she was unaware of what she was doing. I thought it was the drugs. How much of her brain she had killed with her addiction? But what if…"

"We really don't know what is normal and what is not for a siren. I wish I could help you more. Maybe Corvin knows something about it. He's always been interested in deep studies of other magical species."

"And he has particular reasons to be interested in sirens now," Reg agreed.

Sarah raised her brows.

"Because of Norma Jean," Reg clarified quickly. "Not because of me. She could have killed him. He was lucky."

It was just one example of Norma Jean's odd, un-siren-like lapses. They had speculated that it might be because her siren blood was too thin and she didn't have more than the initial instincts to seduce but not to drown. Reg thought that it might be something more.

"I'll think about it all," Reg said. "Maybe, like you say, I can see something in my crystal. There must be a reason that all of this is happening."

Sarah nodded. "I hope you will be able to sort it out. Let me know if you think of any other clues. I'll try to help you out if I can."

CHAPTER SIXTEEN

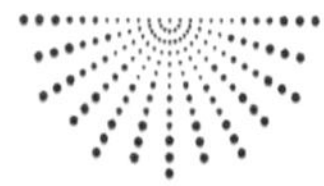

Reg went back to the cottage, dissatisfied with the way things had gone. She'd wanted answers but had gotten nowhere. Sarah didn't know anything else about the protection spell the other witches had worked in the garden and what effects it might have had. Could they have called the snake? And if they had, then why? How did it help them? Did they mean to kill Reg off to get her out of the neighborhood? That seemed quite a bit more extreme than the vandalism. She would have thought it would take more steps to get from throwing eggs at a building to trying to kill someone.

And Sarah had insisted that witches tried to stay in harmony with nature, each other, and the community. That was in direct opposition to something like calling venomous snakes to attack someone. They were many kinds of magic, and Sarah assured her that there was no bad magic or black magic, just magic that could be used myriad different ways, depending on the practitioner.

But Reg didn't believe the line that there were no bad witches. She had met practitioners who used their powers to harm others, no matter what the old witch had said.

She discovered she had left the cottage door unlocked. She needed to be more careful about that. She didn't want someone breaking in and lying in wait for her.

Starlight was lying in the middle of the floor waiting for her. Reg grinned at the juxtaposition of her thought and Starlight's behavior.

"I don't mind *you* lying in wait for me," she told Starlight. "Just everyone else." She picked him up and cuddled him to her face for a few minutes, until he started squirming to get away. She let him jump back to the floor.

"I'm going to try looking in the crystal," she told him. "Do you want to help?"

He sat watching Reg as she moved the crystal ball off her shelf onto the coffee table where she usually put it during a client session. Starlight looked at the door as if checking to see if anyone else were coming in to join them.

"Just you and me, Star."

When Reg sat down with the crystal, Starlight jumped up into her lap and started kneading her legs.

"Not too much there. Watch the claws," Reg warned.

After a few minutes, he settled. Reg stroked him a few times, feeling his comforting aura and the focusing of her powers.

She stared into the crystal, searching for anything that might hint at the cause of her troubles. Why was she experiencing such swings in her powers? Where did the disconcerting memory blanks come from? Was it just her siren nature? Was that normal for sirens? Or for a human fighting siren instincts?

She saw her own face reflected in the surface of the glass and let her eyes focus there instead of in the darker depths of the crystal. Her image was distorted, but she ignored that fact, looking for anything else out of place. Had something changed in her? If so, what? And why?

As she watched, she saw herself pouring hot water into a teacup. That wasn't much of a help. How many times had she poured tea for one of her clients? Unless the message was that she needed to drink some kind of tea in order to recover her powers, just as Wilson had to recover his memory after fifty years in the Everglades.

But Sarah hadn't suggested any herb or remedy that she thought might work in Reg's current circumstances. And Sarah was always quick to jump in with a remedy if she knew of one. Maybe the same remedy as had worked to recover Wilson's memory could help Reg with her memory lapses? Would a tea of sweet bay leaves put things to rights again for her?

Reg wasn't sure it was the right thing to do, but she thought she might as well at least give it a try. Sweet bay leaf was, she knew, an herb with many beneficial properties, and she couldn't see it doing her any harm, even if it didn't do her any good. She scratched Starlight's ears and chin for a few minutes, just feeling safe and cozy sitting with him, then eventually nudged him off her lap.

"I'll just make some tea," Reg said. "If it works, it works. If not…" she shrugged. "Then we'll try something else, right?"

Starlight sat there blinking at her, but he didn't seem to object to her plan. Reg nodded, resolved. She went to her kitchen cupboards and looked through them. She was pretty sure that she hadn't used all the leaves that she had brought from the Everglades. She had learned through her lean years never to waste anything that might be useful in the future. She had judged the herb to be of some use to her still.

It was, appropriately enough, in the cupboard with the teabags and jars of tea leaves and herbs. Neatly labeled laurel in Sarah's printing. Reg vaguely remembered Sarah taking care of it after Wilson was gone.

Reg pulled out the leaves and looked for something to crush them with. When she had prepared the tea for Wilson, she had just broken the leaves up with her fingers, but she had found the leaves to be very tough and sharp, pricking the pads of her fingers and thumb painfully. She still didn't have a mortar and pestle like Sarah did, but she was bound to have something she could use.

Reg eventually settled on an extra-heavy freezer bag and a hammer, and pounded away at the leaves inside the bag until they were a fine powder. Well, a coarse powder. Maybe not exactly powder, but certainly small enough to be used in the tea. Reg started the kettle heating and poured the crushed leaves from the plastic bag into a teacup. She knew that the lemon hadn't exactly made it palatable for Wilson. Sarah was always rolling her eyes at how much sugar or honey Reg put in her teas. But Sarah's teas always needed the extra love.

When the kettle whistled, Reg poured the boiling water into her teacup and watched the leaves steep. How long should she wait? She didn't want it to get too cool or bitter. It would be easier to get down while it was hot. But the leaves might need time to release their essential oils and special little molecules and magic into the water. She stirred it, watched a couple of short videos about cats on her phone, and then stirred in a bit of lemon juice and a couple of tablespoons of honey. She sniffed the steam coming out of the cup.

It didn't smell too bad. Not as bad as some of the stuff that Sarah tried to make her drink. Reg sipped the tea and added another tablespoon of honey into it. She watched more videos to distract herself from the taste while she sipped the rest of the oversweetened tea.

"It's not *that* bad," she told Starlight.

Starlight paid her little attention, sitting like a sphinx sculpture, unblinking, staring off into space.

But then he gave a jump as if startled by a noise, and he looked back at the coffee table where Reg's crystal ball still rested. He walked over to the table and stood up on his hind legs, sniffing the ball and looking down into it.

"What's going on?" Reg inquired. She joined him beside the coffee table and sat down, looking at the crystal ball and trying to figure out what had suddenly interested Starlight so much. "What is it?"

Shapes were moving in the core of the crystal. Reg stared down at it, letting her eyes focus on the depths of the crystal ball rather than focusing on the surface. If something in the ball had enough power to call to Starlight from across the room, she thought it must be very important and powerful magic.

Large shapes. Vaguely human. She couldn't see well enough to recognize who it was in the ball, not even to discern the species. Was it Calliopia again? Hurt or in need of some other kind of assistance? Reg hadn't heard from either her or Ruan, her mate, recently. Not that she had expected to. She had known that they were leaving town, and that, both having been shunned by their communities, they would be trying to remain inconspicuous during their travels.

She didn't think that the main figure in the ball was a fairy, though. It seemed too bulky overall to be one of the slim fairies, even with a puffy winter coat. It was spring and, while they would probably still be wearing winter jackets in the northern states, most people in Florida had no need for such things. Reg thought that with the strength of the revelation in the glass that it was something close, not halfway across the country.

"Who is it?" she asked softly. "Who is in my crystal today?"

She put her hand on Starlight, trying to strengthen the vision. The picture became clearer. She thought, was almost sure, that it was a large man in a cloak. There was nothing to compare his scale too, but Reg got the impression of size and strength. The man's build was largely hidden by his coat or cloak, which was hooded so that she could not see his face.

As if he had heard Reg's thoughts, the man turned toward her, looking for someone who was not actually visible to him. With his movement, light fell across his features, and Reg knew who it was.

CHAPTER SEVENTEEN

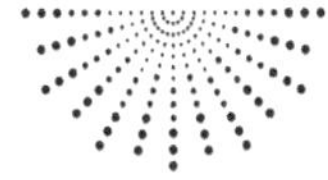

*E*tienne.

Reg sat back in her seat, smiling.

She hadn't expected to see or hear anything from the creature for several months. She knew that Bruce, a skinwalker, received Etienne's postal mail from him once a month and, at the same time, passed on any mail he had received for Etienne. And Etienne had made it known to Reg that he was very deliberate in his letter writing and might take the whole month writing something to his girlfriend who lived in… where was it? Russia?

So the chances that he would take the time to write a letter to Reg and that it would reach her less than a month since she had left the Everglades seemed very low. More likely, it would take a year for him to decide that he should write to Reg, a month or two to compose a letter, and then another month for it to get to Reg. That seemed more like his pace.

Watching him in the crystal ball, Reg frowned, trying to figure out where he was.

He wasn't out in the wilderness where his cabin was, all by himself. He seemed to be moving among crowds of people, as if he were walking past them on the street. But what would possess him to go into town? He kept the cloak wrapped tightly around him so that he wouldn't attract the attention of those around him, but there wasn't much he could do to disguise his great height and bulk. He was at least a head taller than any of the other human shapes he passed by. As if he were the only adult among a crowd of children.

"Where are you, Etienne? Where are you going? And why was it important for me to see you?"

Unsurprisingly, Etienne did not answer her. Nor did he magically appear in front of her.

Reg looked at Starlight. "He is a friend from the Everglades. He's… well, there they call him a skunk man, but he doesn't smell bad. He's very clean, just like a cat. He's… very large and hairy. A Bigfoot."

It occurred to Reg that she hadn't asked Etienne what he preferred his species be called. One would think that after her experience with Tybalt, who had complained about how the humans called the various magical species by whatever name they liked instead of by the way they self-identified, she would have learned. And of course, many of the names that the humans used historically had derogatory meanings and were used as slurs. Reg didn't like to give other races offense by calling them something other than they wanted to be called.

"I don't know if that's the right word. Forget I said that. Until I find out what the right word is."

Starlight blinked at her, unfazed.

But she still didn't know why she saw Etienne in her crystal. Had the bay leaf tea triggered a memory, and that was what she was looking at? She didn't think so. She had never seen Etienne out among people. At least, not that she remembered. Reg swore under her breath at the circular thinking. She knew it wasn't a memory because she didn't remember it?

"He can't be coming here. That wouldn't make any sense. Do you think maybe I'm supposed to go see him in the Everglades? It doesn't even look like that's where he is. And why would he want to see me again so soon?"

She had sent him a box of Hershey's bars, apparently Etienne's one indulgence. Maybe he just wanted to tell her thank you, so he had sent her a message in the vision. But then wouldn't it have been something more straightforward? Etienne mouthing "thank you," or showing her the Hershey's bars in his special cupboard? Or toasting her with an opened Hershey's bar?

Walking through a crowd didn't feel like a message.

So if it wasn't a memory and it wasn't a message, then what was it?

Thinking about Hershey's bars made Reg hungry, so eventually, she let the vision go and got up to see if she had any ice cream or other treats.

CHAPTER EIGHTEEN

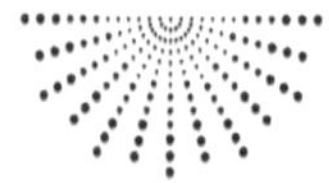

eg tried to keep to what was her normal schedule, staying up until the small hours of the morning before going to bed, hoping that the regular sleep schedule would reset things and everything could go back to normal. Sleep deprivation could do a lot of weird things to the body and the brain. If she had accidentally deprived herself of sleep, perhaps her memory lapses and problems accessing her powers could be attributed just to that. She needed to get the right amount of sleep, and then everything would turn out right.

Going to sleep at the right time of day should have minimized nightmares. She would be tired enough that she could just go to sleep within minutes and rest comfortably until her usual wake-up time. But it didn't turn out that way.

Reg tossed and turned, falling asleep and then waking up again repeatedly. She saw Etienne in her dreams again. And Sarah, with the candles and markings of the spell that had been cast. And snakes. Slithering in the darkness. Rearing up before her, rattles shaking and buzzing noisily.

Other shapes in the darkness. A watcher she couldn't identify. Was it Davyn, cloaked? Was it Etienne or someone else who simply did not wish to be seen for his own personal reasons? Or was it something more sinister? Someone watching Reg and trying to force her out of the neighborhood? Someone who didn't appreciate being hoodwinked by a siren.

Reg shook off the thoughts. They wouldn't think that way if they knew her. If they knew her, they would see that she was not going to hurt anyone. She wasn't going to hunt on the land or the waters. She wasn't that kind of person, no matter what the fractional amount of siren DNA in her blood.

She tossed and turned some more and found herself in another dream. The quality was different. She was immersed in it, as if it were real life, instead of being aware that it was full of symbolism and meanings. She didn't feel like herself and she didn't know what she was doing, there in the graveyard, moving from one row of tombstones to another. She had no idea why she was there or what she was looking for.

But she knew something. She wasn't going to like what she found there.

* * *

Reg jolted awake. Going from the darkness of the dream to the brightness of the room was disconcerting. She took several deep breaths, trying to calm the pounding of her heart. She had not known that it was a dream and it took her a while to convince herself that it was. There was no graveyard. She hadn't been there. The grittiness that she could still feel on her skin was only an illusion and would fade within seconds.

What had she been looking for?

She tried to shake the dream off without asking the question, but it kept coming back into her mind, forcing itself into her consciousness. What had she been looking for?

She was glad to be awake. She was not interested in trying to find sleep again. She would just keep falling into nightmares and she would rather be tired during the day than have to go through another dream.

Starlight meowed loudly from the floor beside the bed. Reg

looked over the edge at him. He stared up at her, imperious, commanding her to get up and fill his bowl with good fish. She had lazed around in bed too much already.

"A cat is telling me I sleep too much?" Reg demanded. "You're the one who sleeps the day away in the sunshine."

He just glared and didn't explain himself.

"All right," Reg grumbled. "I was getting up anyway, though. It's not because of you."

He waited until her feet were on the floor and then led the way to the doorway. He waited for Reg to lead the way through the door, then ran ahead of her to his dish, to sniff at it and remind her that her first priority needed to be his welfare.

"Bathroom first."

He stood by his dish, watching her disappear into the bathroom and shut the door. But she didn't linger for too long and, in a few minutes, was back out and looking through the fridge for the tuna she remembered being there. She looked through all the bowls, with Starlight winding around her legs and encouraging her loudly the whole time, before finally giving up and deciding that she must have finished it off the last time she had fed him, even if she didn't remember.

"Okay, okay. I'm opening a new can. But you could eat your kibble, you know; you're not starving."

But kibble was not for breakfast. Starlight would eat it throughout the day because, unlike the tuna or canned cat food, it would stay good, but he liked something better for his first meal of a new day.

Reg managed to get the food from the can to his dish and put the rest away in a bowl in the fridge, carefully sealed so that it wouldn't make everything else in the fridge smell like fish.

"Okay." Reg started her coffee brewing and went over to the couch to sit down and look at her phone while waiting for it. She had not put her crystal ball away after the previous viewing and it still sat on the table in front of her. Reg did not look into it; she just gazed toward it, her eyes focused somewhere beyond the crystal, letting her brain wake up at its own speed.

She was aware of shapes in the crystal, but didn't want to exert herself by seeing what they were. Not before having her coffee. She suspected that it was still the same vision as the day before, Etienne moving through the crowds of people. But even without looking at it, she sensed that he was closer now. Was he coming to her? Why would he? He would never leave the Everglades. And if he did, why would he go to her?

There was a heavy knock on the door.

Reg hadn't even pulled on her robe. The day was advanced and it was warm inside, the A/C already running. She was in shorts and a t-shirt. Not exactly dressed for company. She rubbed her eyes with her fingertips and tried to figure out whether to answer the door or just to ignore it.

What if it were someone who didn't want her there? Someone come to bully her into leaving Black Sands? It wasn't Sarah, or she would have just let herself in. If it were Corvin, Reg would have felt his pull. Jessup usually announced herself, and Reg didn't think she would have let her new partner show up there by himself. The heavy knock did not sound like a client, though, of course, it could be.

Reg sighed and boosted herself up off the couch.

The wards inside the house would protect her from intruders and those with malice in their hearts. And Sarah had now set wards in the yard, so no one should even be able to get to her door if they had evil intentions toward her.

She opened the door a crack with the chain still on. "Who's there?"

A red-brown, furry face appeared immediately in front of her face, making her jump.

"It is I," Etienne announced.

Reg slid the chain and threw open the door. "Etienne! What are you doing here? I saw you in the crystal, but I didn't know you were coming here."

He nodded, smiling shyly at her. He straightened to his full height, so her eyes were somewhere around his chest level. "It has been a strange journey," he admitted. "It was unexpected." She loved his faint French accent and old-world way of talking.

"So why are you here?" Reg realized herself and motioned for him to enter the cottage. "Come in, come in. Tell me all about it."

Etienne entered. He looked at the wicker furniture and hesitated. He was not a small man and the furniture looked too fragile to hold his weight. He grabbed one of the sturdier wooden kitchen chairs and put it into the conversational grouping of wicker furniture. He sat down with a sigh and pulled off the dark cloak, which he certainly did not need in the warmth of the room. He ran his hands over his furry arms and legs and settled himself in.

"Do you remember I told you about Ilka?"

"Ilka. Your girlfriend. Yes, I do. I remember she is from Russia and that her coat turns white in the winter."

Etienne's whiskers bristled and pointed upward as he smiled. Reg suspected that if she could see his skin through his hairy face, he would be blushing. He was both shy and proud of his girlfriend.

"Yes, that is right," he agreed, nodding. "And I told you that… our courtship is not so quick, as with *Homo sapiens*. We have traditions… we take time to get to know each other, discuss families and arrangements, and get the proper blessings of our family and community. It is not a quick process."

"Yes, I remember." Just like with letter writing, and the fact that he still considered himself to be just settling in at his cabin in the woods, when he had lived there for ninety years. Reg couldn't imagine taking so much time for anything. But they were clearly a much longer-lived race that had the benefit of time.

"Well…" Etienne rubbed his whiskered chin thoughtfully. "I got a letter from Ilka. You remember my friend Bruce who took you to the settlement. He brings me my mail…"

"Yes. The last Tuesday of the month."

"It is so. And this month, there was a letter from my Ilka."

"Is she okay? Is everything all right?"

"She is well…" He nodded. But Reg could sense his hesitance to say everything was all right.

CHAPTER NINETEEN

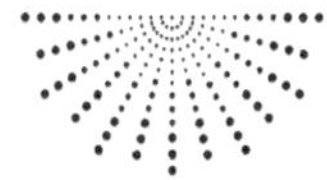

Starlight finished eating his food and wandered over to greet the new guest. He stopped a few feet away from Etienne and began to wash, watching him. Etienne began to preen, not licking his fur, but smoothing it with his fingertips, laying down the hair of his arms and legs and fussing over his grooming. Starlight watched him. Reg wondered how much the two could communicate with each other just by their body language and movements. She remembered that Etienne had communicated with the panther in the Everglades without any spoken words.

After a couple of minutes, Starlight finished his grooming and jumped up into Etienne's lap. Reg moved to take him away if Etienne were uncomfortable with him taking such liberties.

"Starlight, you should wait to be asked," she chided. "Is it okay, do you mind? I try to keep him from jumping on company…"

"It is fine," Etienne informed her. "I did invite him."

He stroked Starlight's back, thinking about what he wanted to say. Starlight began a low, rumbling purr.

"Ilka is coming here," Etienne said finally.

"Here? To the United States?"

"To Florida. She is coming on a boat that is supposed to dock tomorrow!"

"Oh!" Now Reg knew what had pulled Etienne away from his cabin in the Everglades in such a hurry. There was probably nothing else that would have convinced him to leave, especially so quickly. But a letter from Ilka that she was on her way to see him, that was a different story. "Well, you must be very excited!"

"Yes, of course." He nodded. His bushy brow pulled down. "But… I don't know what to think. We hardly know each other. And what does she expect? I am supposed to go meet her, and then what? I cannot take her home with me. I do not have family near here, and neither does she. So where is she going to go?"

"She must have some plan. She didn't say in her letter?"

"No. Only that she would be on her way to see me when I got her letter, and when it landed."

"Then I guess… you discuss it when you see her. Find out what her expectations are, and see how the two of you get along. You don't have to do anything you're not comfortable with."

"But there is no agreement between our families. Even to see her alone is… that is not the way our people court."

"What do they usually do?"

"After they have gotten to know each other, there is discussion between the families, and the families arrange for a meeting. Supervised. Chaperoned. And if the couple is willing, after they have met, then the family begins to make arrangements for them to marry and to raise a family together."

"Do you have any family? I know they are not in Florida, but is there someone who would help you to negotiate?"

Etienne thought about it. He nodded slowly. "I have brothers and an uncle. I do not know of the younger generation. We do not exchange many letters."

"Do you know where they live? How to get ahold of them?"

"I have their addresses."

"Yes, but what about phone numbers? Email addresses? If you needed to talk to them right away, how would you do it?"

"I would not. We write letters."

"What if it was an emergency? If there was a death? Or someone was sick and needed a kidney transplant? How would you contact your family members?"

He scratched his jaw meditatively. "I suppose… I could try to reach the general store or post office where they live. Perhaps they could send a messenger." Etienne shook his head. "Once upon a time, we could send a telegram."

"A telegram. I don't even know what that is. It's like an email?"

Etienne just stared at her.

"Okay. So I don't know. Where did your brothers move to? Somewhere there are more people? Less? You said that some of your people get laser hair removal and try to blend in with human beings."

"*Homo sapiens*," Etienne corrected. "We *are* human beings."

"Oh, okay. With the *Homo sapiens*. Did any of your brothers do that? Do they live where there would be more people, an easier way to contact them?"

"James. He was very interested in that." Etienne waggled his fingers toward Reg's phone. "Computers, phones, technology."

"Okay. Let's see if we can find him. Tell me his name and where he lives."

* * *

James Legrande of Minnesota was not too difficult for Reg to find on social media. Although Etienne had not seen him since his transformation, it was evident from his photos that he was a big man, and he still had a bushy beard and hair that, although not as thick as Etienne's, looked quite Sasquatch-like. Etienne agreed that the man looked like his brother, but was hesitant to say for sure that it was him. She sent James Legrande a couple of messages through her profiles and hoped that he would get back to her.

"When does Ilka get here?"

"Tomorrow afternoon. Two o'clock."

"Okay. Well, hopefully, James will get back to us before then. What about Ilka? Does she have a family? Someone who will negotiate for her?"

"She has a father. But I do not know…" Etienne shook his head. "She has run away. I don't know if she will allow him to speak for her. This is not the way things are done with our people. She is very headstrong."

"And… do you like that?"

Etienne considered it. "Well… I don't know about that."

"You said that the women of your people are very…" Reg tried to remember the word he had used.

Etienne smiled and smoothed his mustache and beard, perhaps remembering their conversation. "Formidable?" he suggested.

"Yeah. So do you like her taking control and coming here to see you, or not?"

"It is very… flattering. That she would take it upon herself to come all the way here to see me. That she would be so sure we are compatible."

Reg nodded. "Well, then, what do you need to do before you see her?"

"What do you mean?"

"First impressions. How do you want her to see you? Do you need… a suit? Flowers? A haircut? A dowry? Do you need to talk to her dad before she gets here to ask for her hand?"

Etienne's big hands were very gentle as he petted and scratched Starlight. His eyes widened a little as he considered the question, recognizing that he was going to see his sweetheart the next day, and he had very little time to prepare for it.

"That is an excellent question."

* * *

It had been good for Reg to get out of the house and to be focused on someone else's problems instead of obsessing about her own situation. Everything seemed to be just fine, and she wondered if she had been blowing things out of proportion. Maybe she had just been short on sleep and had exaggerated the issues she was having. Everyone had problems when they got overtired; why would she be any different?

Etienne needed a number of things in short order. A couple of gifts for Ilka. Inquiries into hotel availability. He tried to reach Ilka's father, eight time zones ahead of them but, like Etienne, Ilka's father did not have a phone in his house, and it was nearly impossible to find someone to act as an intermediary to track him down and pass a message along. Etienne stopped in at the barber, not for a haircut, but to have special oils rubbed into his facial fur and to have it combed out until it shone.

The whole process was fascinating for Reg, who had never been involved in so much as arranging a bridal shower or bachelorette party. She didn't know what would happen once Etienne and Ilka met face to face, but she could only assume that Ilka believed they were compatible and would find a way to be married shortly after her arrival.

Was she arriving on a passenger ship or some other kind of boat? Did she fit in or was she hiding on board? Did she need a visa to visit the US? Some other special type of permit or travel papers? It couldn't have been easy for her to make all the arrangements that would be required. It had been a big step to separate herself from her family and just head out on this adventure on her own.

Back at the cottage, they were both resting and relaxing after clearing out most of the contents of the fridge. Etienne had his feet up on the coffee table and was snoring gently. Reg's phone rang. She looked at the screen and saw it was a video call. She knew the face on the display from that morning.

"Etienne!" She nudged him to wake him up.

Etienne snorted and his feet fell from the chair to the floor with a bang. His eyes flew open and he looked at Reg. "What? What's wrong?"

"Nothing is wrong. Look, it's James."

Etienne stared at the screen. Reg tried to hand it to him, but he didn't know what to do with it. Reg swiped the call to answer it. She held it up to her face.

"James? Thanks for calling. Here is Etienne." She turned the phone around for Etienne to talk.

Etienne stared at his brother on the screen. "James?"

"Little brother! I never expected to see you on video. Unless some paparazzi caught a glimpse of you running through the trees." He laughed a deep-throated chuckle.

"James." Etienne leaned close to the phone and spoke louder than necessary. "I have a serious problem."

CHAPTER TWENTY

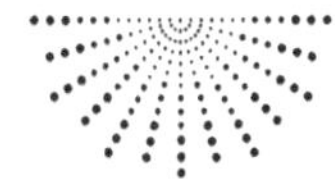

James and Etienne talked for a long time. Apparently, making decisions was another thing that Bigfoots did not do quickly. Reg became bored with the minutiae and turned on the TV, keeping it quiet so it wouldn't interfere with the conversation. Though with how loudly Etienne was speaking into the phone, she probably could have had it much louder without them even noticing it was on. Starlight curled up on the couch with Reg, purring away contentedly.

Since she had reacted so strongly to watching the old horror movies on TV, Reg was much more careful about the entertainment she selected. She flipped back and forth through several different options, including a kids' movie that had something to do with time-traveling wizards, a nature show, and some light mystery fare. It all seemed innocuous, not likely to cause her any nightmares. She would just sleep soundly and wake up feeling refreshed in the morning.

Starlight lifted his head to stare at Reg for a few minutes. He curled back up again, needling her leg gently with his claws. Not enough that it bothered her. It just reminded her that he was there, trying to keep watch over her. Provided she didn't do anything stupid.

After a while, the time-traveling wizards became too inane; Reg couldn't stand watching them anymore. She flipped back over to the nature channel, which had been showing a program on bird-watching in the area. Reg had been keeping an eye on it, figuring she might pick up some ideas on setting up a bird feeder or birdbath for Sarah, since she liked birds so much. They would keep Starlight entertained at the window too. But the birding program had apparently ended, and Reg watched it for a few minutes before she figured out that the men in khakis and sun hats were hunting snakes in a Florida swamp. She stared at the screen, eyes wide, unable to bring herself to change the channel before seeing what they found. If she didn't see where the snakes were hiding, then she would be sure to have dreams of snakes hiding in her house or in the garden outside. She didn't need another disrupted night.

Starlight apparently didn't like the new show. He jumped down from the couch with a huffing sound and stalked away. Reg didn't try to call him back. He could do something else if he didn't feel like sitting with her. Reg could still hear Etienne and James talking in the background, but their voices seemed faint and far away. She watched the snake hunters on the screen, exchanging jokes and colorful stories as they poked through foliage and set traps. They speculated whether they would find the creatures they were looking for sunning them-selves on rocks out in the open, or hiding in a cool, dark cave or corner.

Starlight returned, dropping something long and black at her feet.

Reg jumped back instinctively, sure that it was a snake.

But of course it wasn't. There weren't any snakes in the house and Starlight wasn't allowed outside. Even if he were, she didn't imagine that he would have brought her snakes. Mice, maybe, but snakes?

It was just a shoelace. Reg had bought shoelaces for her favorite pair of shoes, but as soon as she had bought them, one of the pair had disappeared before she had a chance to use them. She didn't know whether Starlight had the lost shoelace, which he had hidden away from her somewhere, or whether he had the one that she hadn't lost, which she had thought she'd put out of his reach so he couldn't steal that one too. Sooner or later, she would either find the lost shoelace, or would remember to buy another pair when she was at the store. Then she'd have three shoelaces, one for a backup.

Reg bent down and picked up the shoelace. She stretched it out in a long line for Starlight, then slowly tugged it around corners and behind the furniture. Starlight's pupils were big and black. A few times, he attacked it, but mostly he just seemed to like making it slink around. Reg waved and twitched the shoelace, making it undulate down its length like a slithering snake. Starlight watched it, the green and blue of his eyes just barely visible around the huge pools of black pupils.

He pounced, bit and clawed at it, and then leaped back away so that it couldn't retaliate. Reg's heart was pounding hard and fast as she watched the cat attacking the snake. Attack and retreat, attack and retreat.

She watched the undulations that she herself was causing, almost hypnotized by the movement. It wasn't real, but she could feel it. The strong muscles that stretched down the length of the snake. Its cool, dry scales. The writhing movement she would feel if she picked it up.

"Reg?"

She didn't look up from the picture of the snake she held in her head. It was so clear. She could reach out and touch it. Reg reached out her hand, but couldn't quite reach it. It was an illusion of some sort. It looked and felt so real to her. It was there. In another plane. In another reality. She knew that snake was real.

"Reg Rawlins, is everything all right?"

She blinked her eyes, trying to reset her brain. She needed to stay in the physical world around her. It wouldn't do to disappear into a trance while she had company. Though she couldn't think of a reason Etienne couldn't take care of himself.

"Etienne...?" The shape of the word was strange in her mouth, like she'd never said it aloud before. Reg shook her head and tried again. It didn't sound right. Not crisp enough. Like her tongue was too slow. That was what she got for being mesmerized by a shoelace. She made a fool of herself in front of her guest. She'd never had a real guest in her cottage before. Not an out-of-town guest. Well, except for Norma Jean, but there was no way Reg would have even considered letting Norma Jean stay there any longer than it took to ask. She saw her on her way. But she really didn't have a place for Etienne.

There was a spare room, but it was set up as an office; there was no bed. There was no pull-out, and Reg could see that the wicker couch would be a big fat "no" for the Sasquatch.

Etienne's hand was on her arm. Big, warm fingers. Gentle. But he was also asking questions, and Reg couldn't answer any questions.

"No. It's fine. Finish your call."

"My call with James is done. Do you need to do something now? You are very white."

"I'm a redhead. I'm always white unless I'm burned, and then I'm red."

"You are white."

Reg closed her eyes, concentrating again on the picture of the snake. She needed to catch it. To make a full examination.

CHAPTER TWENTY-ONE

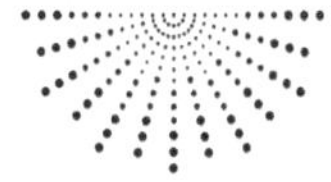

"Do you need to lie down?"

Reg shook off the questions. "Everything is fine."

"Should I get you some tea? Coffee?"

She wasn't looking at the man, but could feel him moving around, figuring out what to do.

"I don't want tea or coffee," Reg snapped, her voice an explosion. "I want the snake!"

The room fell utterly silent. The tuxedo cat had been stalking and chasing the shoelace, but he froze and looked at her. The TV program had been playing, but it shut off. She hoped she hadn't damaged it beyond repair. She didn't like having to get rid of broken things.

The large, hairy man stared at Reg, looking concerned. He didn't offer tea again, but he was probably trying to think of something else he could do for her. But the truth was, Reg wanted to be left alone to figure things out. What was she going to do? How was she going to get that snake? She would have to stay and make the guest feel comfortable, but all she wanted to do was fulfill her quest.

"What snake?"

Reg ground her teeth in frustration. Couldn't she get anyone around her who was competent? Did they all have to be such dunces?

"I need the snake I saw," she told him through gritted teeth. "It's like that," she pointed to the shoelace. "I could see it just now…"

"You are not feeling well," the man suggested.

"I'm feeling fine. Stop saying there is anything wrong with me. I just need some space. I need to figure this out. I saw the snake…" She struggled to finish the sentence. "Before. In my dream. I was looking for it in my dream. And I found it, but it was in…" She grasped for it, trying to remember where she had seen the image before.

The man sat down on the chair he had been using earlier. Reg stared at him, then stared at the place that the snake had been. She wished he hadn't been quite so quick to notice her behavior and to address her. If she had been able to grasp the image of the snake, then she wouldn't be in this state. She would have known exactly what to do.

Reg pressed her thumbs into her temples.

"Why do you want a snake?" the hairy man prompted. "You don't want it for… dinner?" he looked displeased by this image.

Reg rolled her eyes. "No, I don't want to eat it. I want…" The reason hovered on the tip of her tongue, but try as she might, Reg couldn't access it. "I need that snake."

The man looked down at the shoelace. The cat pawed at it for a moment before looking up at Reg and at the large hairy man. He put his ears back and sneezed.

"Get away," Reg snapped, sweeping her arm at him threateningly so that he jumped up and ran several feet away before looking back at her in consternation. Reg picked up the shoelace. She wiggled it on the floor. Not for the tuxedo cat to chase, but to imitate the movement she had seen earlier, in the hopes that she could bring the memory to the surface.

"This is not like you," the man reproved.

"I didn't ask you."

"What has changed? What happened?"

"Let me think. Just *let me think!*"

He was quiet, watching her warily. His nostrils flared, and she knew that he was scenting her, trying to detect the reason for the change in her mood. But he wasn't going to find anything out, because nothing had actually changed.

Reg watched the movement of the shoelace, willing herself to slide back into the trance.

She didn't see the snake in front of her again, but suddenly flashed to the dream.

She had been searching for something. She had seen the snake and had been hunting for it. And she knew where she had been.

"Why don't you stay here and relax a while?" she suggested to the man. "I'm going out to get some things."

"Oh, I will come with you. I can help to pick out victuals and help you to cook."

"Cook? I'm not going to cook."

His whiskers bristled. He was looking as unhappy as the cat was.

But they would go back to normal when she had what she wanted. They would see that she was happy and normal, and they would relax and forget all about it. Everyone went through moody periods. She was sleep deprived or tired out from the Spring Games. There was an easy explanation, and once she was back to normal, they would shrug it off.

"You stay here," Reg told him firmly. "You can look through the cupboards and fridge if you want to make something. Or go up to the main house. The witch back there, she would be happy to help."

"You won't be long?"

"No. Just a few minutes."

Just as long as it took to find the snake.

* * *

It took much longer than it should have to extricate herself from the cottage and get to her vehicle. Why couldn't she just go out and run a few errands? They made it sound like she was trying to get away with something. She hadn't done anything.

Yet.

She slid into her car and started the engine. It was starting to get dark outside. Twilight. The darkness fell quickly in Florida. She should probably have brought a flashlight with her. But she hoped to still be able to achieve her goal without one.

In a few minutes, she was at the cemetery. She remembered being there once before, not inside the graveyard itself, but outside the walls, detoured because of what the Witch Doctor had been doing. Only they hadn't known yet that it had to do with the Witch Doctor. They had stopped and talked to the police, but the cops had been tight-lipped and hadn't told Reg what was going on. Reg looked around for them. There didn't seem to be any activity within the walls of the cemetery. She didn't see any police cars or security vehicles. It was probably a pretty quiet place at night. They wouldn't have much call for a big security presence.

Reg drove up to the entrance and found her way blocked by a tall gate, like something out of a Gothic horror movie. Big black bars stretching upward, the graying sky behind them as the sun went down.

There was a sign on the gate that was not so Gothic, clearly setting out the hours that the cemetery was open. A cemetery had hours? Who knew? She could try driving around to the other entrances, but suspected that they would be similarly barred. There might be another way in, an unobtrusive caretaker's entrance that only someone who worked there would know about. But Reg didn't have the patience to go looking for one. She turned off the car, got out, and scaled the fence without another moment's consideration. She had things to do; she wasn't going to let one little gate get in the way of her goals. Well, one big, tall gate. She imagined the hairy man would have been able to just toss her over. But she did reasonably well on her own, considering out how of shape she was. She resolved again to start a more vigorous diet and exercise program.

She dropped down on the other side of the gate, landing lightly on her feet like a cat.

Reg looked around the rows of graves and markers, trying to orient herself and figure out what course to take. She just needed to remember her dream. What had she seen in the dream? Where had she gone? If she followed the template of what she had seen in the dream, then she would find what she was looking for.

She walked up one of the rows, pausing at each aisle to reach out with all her senses. She waited for an instant to see if she felt a little tug and, when she didn't, went on to the next one.

Reg felt compelled to go down an aisle with a cherub marker on the first row. Was this it? She kept walking, kept trying to feel whether she were in the right place. It was getting too dark to see. If there were still any snakes around, she wasn't even going to be able to see them. She pulled out her phone and turned on the flashlight mode. She was going to run down her battery, but chances were, she was not going to be there long anyway. She would either find what she was looking for, or would go back home. She couldn't leave a strange man in her cottage for that long.

CHAPTER TWENTY-TWO

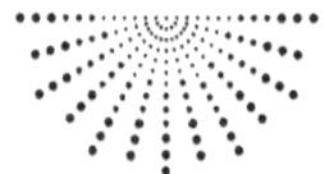

$\mathcal{R}$eg heard a rustling in the grass.

Was there someone else there with her in the cemetery after closing? Or was it the snake she was looking for? She knew it couldn't be far away. She could feel it.

There was a presence, but it slipped away quickly. Just a small night creature. Nothing for her to worry about. More of a worry for the small night creature. The dark was full of predators.

She could see a shape in the grass ahead of her. Maybe a grave that had recently been dug, so it didn't yet have sod laid over the top to match the carpeting over the rest of the graveyard. Reg crept closer, keeping her light low in case someone walking by the cemetery looked in through the bars of one of the gates and saw her. She had no idea how visible or hidden she was.

There was definitely something there on top of the grass. Not a freshly dug grave.

The shape looked vaguely human. But they wouldn't have placed a body on top of the grass like that. It would be in a casket or an urn. People didn't just throw bodies anywhere in a cemetery. There was an order to things. Reg leaned down as she got closer, so she was hunched low to the ground. Like it wouldn't be a surprise to her when she finally saw what it was, if she was just close enough.

There was more rustling. More night creatures? Reg looked back and forth, and even took one quick glance behind her to show that she wasn't afraid. Nothing was going to scare her there. She wasn't afraid of the dark. The Witch Doctor wasn't there reanimating corpses. There wasn't anything for her to worry about in a cemetery closed after dark. It wasn't some kids' thriller movie.

Reg's light fell on the corpse. It was a man. Little blood or violence. But there could be no doubt that he was dead and not just sleeping. Reg's flash of light and quick look at the face and body of the man told her that much.

"Freeze! Police!"

Reg stopped where she was, looking down at the body.

"Get your hands up," the voice told her. Reg slowly raised both hands to shoulder level. "No, I want them way up. Get them up, up!"

Reg obeyed, raising her hands as far as they would go. She kept her cellphone in her hand, making it as visible as possible so no rookie would think that she was carrying a weapon. It was just a phone, obvious from that little rectangle of light in the rapidly-falling darkness. Clouds scudded across the moon, deepening the twilight even more quickly.

One of the police officers came around in front of Reg. A woman. Asian. Pretty features. Reg couldn't see her name bar in the darkness.

"Reg?" the cop asked incredulously.

Squinting, Reg tried to access her memory banks to come up with a woman's name and background. She obviously knew Reg and was surprised to find her there, which meant she didn't think that Reg was someone who would normally wander around cemeteries stumbling across dead bodies.

Reg tried to smile in a friendly way. "Oh, hi…"

"What are you doing here?" the woman cop asked in a way that was not friendly at all.

And then her eyes dropped to the corpse in front of Reg.

And that was not good. Not good at all.

CHAPTER TWENTY-THREE

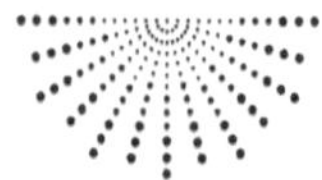

*R*eg cleared her throat and tried to come up with some line that would make the woman cop laugh. Or something that would make it plain that Reg hadn't had anything to do with the killing of the man. She searched her brain for something that would work. Something light, and yet calm and composed. An excuse for being there. After dark. After closing.

With a fresh corpse.

She had nothing.

"We've got a body," the woman yelled to her male counterpart, shining a powerful flashlight at the corpse.

"A what?" the man asked, stunned. But of course he had heard her correctly, and there wasn't much that the cop could do that would clarify matters for him. Or that Reg could say that would make them both feel better disposed toward her.

"I just found him," Reg said finally. Not her most brilliant response. "He was just lying there."

"We got a grave robber?" the male cop asked, grasping for an explanation.

"No. Not a grave robber. This guy is fresh. Hasn't been buried. Hasn't even been embalmed."

"I didn't do it," Reg told her. Another brilliant conversational gem. They would definitely be convinced by an explanation like that.

"Don't move," the woman cop commanded, as Reg started to lower her hands a little. Holding her arms up so high without moving hurt. Reg did her best to hold them steady. The three of them looked down at the corpse.

"What the heck happened here?" the male cop mused.

"I don't know. I just… was going for a walk…"

In a graveyard. At night. After climbing over the fence.

"I'm going to pat you down," the woman cop told Reg, handing her flashlight to the man. "Just hold still."

Reg did what she was told, keeping her hands high above her head as the cop did a quick pat-down and turned Reg's pockets inside out.

"No weapons," she told her partner. "No drugs."

"I didn't do anything to him. He was dead when I got here."

Neither of them responded to Reg's protest.

"I'm putting you in handcuffs. That's to keep us safe while we call for backup and get this sorted out. You're not under arrest at this time, but we will want you to answer some questions."

Reg felt numb as the cop took each of her arms and closed the bracelets around them, restraining her hands behind her back. The cop clicked her shoulder mike and started making reports and requests.

"What do you think happened to him?" Reg asked, looking down at the body.

With the bright flashlight on him, she could see that it was an older man, his scalp shiny and mottled with liver spots, his skin white or gray. His hands were strangely twisted. Not like he had arthritis, and they didn't look like they had been recently broken. But maybe the result of some accident when he was a child, and they had never healed straight. He had a few tattoos, old and fading. It didn't look like he had fallen and hit his head or been attacked. It looked like…

Reg resisted the thought, not letting her brain go down that path.

She didn't know what had killed the man. It was probably natural causes. A heart attack. He had simply dropped while he had been there visiting a departed loved one. And now they were together again. It was a good thing. A happy thing for him.

Or not.

"I'm not going to speculate on cause of death," the woman said. "We'll leave that up to the medical examiner. Why don't you tell me exactly why you're here? You saw the signs saying that the cemetery is closed. What are you doing here?"

"It must have closed after I got here," Reg offered. "I didn't hear them closing the gates. And I guess they didn't see me. Maybe it was while I was crouched down. Uh, kneeling. Praying. I guess that's why they didn't see me, and I didn't see them."

She hoped the lie was believable . She wasn't sure what she was going to come up with if it didn't.

"Your car is parked outside the gate," the cop told her flatly. "You got here after it was closed."

"Oh."

"Why are you here? And how did you know what you were going to find?"

"I didn't. I thought it would be… I didn't know that there was a body here. I was looking for something else." Reg looked for a reasonable explanation. What would she be looking for in a cemetery? A lost cat? Her eyes caught on one of the headstones. "An inscription," she offered. "I wanted to see the verse on one of these headstones."

"And you had to do that at night?"

"No… the client wanted me to hurry on it. And I didn't realize that it would be closed already. I guess I should have waited until tomorrow, but I didn't want it to be a wasted trip."

"Yeah." the cop shook her head. "That just doesn't wash."

Reg would have to come up with something better by the time they got around to asking her for an official statement. She looked at some of the headstones around the body to come up with something that sounded logical.

Before long, Reg could see flashing red and blue lights around the cemetery, even though the police cars were parked outside the walls and locked gates. Someone would have to wake up the caretaker to get him to open the gates and let the medical examiner's and crime scene investigators' vehicles in, but in the meantime, the cops were all getting in the same way as Reg had, by scaling the gates.

The female cop took Reg outside the perimeter they were setting up. She looked sideways at Reg a few times, as if expecting her to explain herself. Reg got the idea that they must be friends, and the woman was waiting to hear the inside scoop now that their conversation was more private. But Reg didn't have her story fully-formed yet. It wouldn't hurt her case to wait, and might prove beneficial as she gathered more information.

* * *

"Finally," the cop grumbled, seeing the first van roll up to the crime scene. "That means the gates are open and I can take you in."

Reg appreciated that they hadn't made her try to climb over the gate with her hands cuffed. She didn't need a broken ankle on top of everything else.

"Can I drive my car home?" she asked. "You said that I'm not under arrest, right?"

"You'll have to pick your car up after they are done with the crime scene. Until then, it is staying right where it is."

"I don't want to get ticketed or towed."

"I can't promise anything. But they're not going to let it go until they're sure it isn't evidence in a crime."

"He didn't look like I ran over him with my car," Reg pointed out.

"Let's walk." The cop nudged Reg ahead of her, indicating that she should head for the open gate. "Nobody said that you ran over him with your car. But you could have had him in the trunk."

"And I carried a dead body over the locked gate? So I could put him on the ground in the cemetery? I don't think that one is going to fly."

"You could have something else in your car that was used in the commission of a crime. I don't know. A crowbar. Poison. Duct tape. Until we have the cause of death, I don't know what we're looking for."

"I didn't have anything to do with his death. I just happened to find him."

"And why didn't you call the police?"

"I didn't have a chance. You showed up right after I tripped over him."

"But you would have."

"Of course." It didn't hurt Reg to say what she would have done. It was all speculation, since she hadn't had the chance. Her reaction probably would have been to get as far away from the dead body as possible. But there was no way for anyone to know that now.

"Do you know the victim?"

Reg didn't answer, thinking about it. She didn't recognize the man, but should she? Was it someone she had been seen with? Had she had dealings with him in the past that others would know about?

"I didn't get a good enough look at him," she fudged. "I'm not sure. It was kind of a shock."

"I'm sure it was," the policewoman agreed dryly.

Reg wasn't sure how to respond to that. They continued in silence, until they reached the gate and could see all the emergency vehicles gathered outside the cemetery fence.

"Here we go," the cop offered, and opened the back seat for Reg.

"You said that I'm not under arrest."

"That's right."

"Then I don't want to sit in the back. I'll sit in the front. And you can take the handcuffs off."

The cop rolled her eyes. "Not a chance, Miss Rawlins. Totally against department policies. No one in the front. And no one transported without handcuffs."

"Come on. If it was a ride-along, you wouldn't make me wear handcuffs."

"This isn't a ride-along."

"How is it any different? If I'm not under arrest, then I can leave anytime I want to. And I want to now. Take off the handcuffs and I'll go home."

"We still need to take your statement."

"I can drive myself to the police station."

"You can't have your car. That is needed for evidence until it has been processed."

"Then I'll walk," Reg said stubbornly. "Take off the handcuffs."

The woman eyed her warily, as if she might throw a tantrum or suddenly break free of the restraints. But Reg didn't. She wished she could, but she couldn't. Her powers were strangely restricted, and she wasn't sure what she could and couldn't do. She wasn't about to start experimenting in front of an audience.

"Just… stay here for now. I'll try to get things worked out. But we really can't release you without a statement."

"I'm a witness. That's all. And I didn't even witness anything except that there was a body on the grass. If you are going to treat me like a suspect, then I'm going to have to call a lawyer, and I'm not going to tell you anything."

"Why are you being so difficult?"

"Why are you treating me like a suspect?"

"Reg," the cop's tone changed to a wheedling note. "Reg, you know I can't show my friends any favoritism. And I'm already in enough trouble from letting things slide on other investigations. I have to act professionally and go above and beyond the rules or they're going to think that I've intentionally messed something up. So please, just cooperate, come to the police station and make your statement. Then you can go home."

Reg wondered what kinds of things the cop had let slide before. Her partner would be watching her closely and making sure she couldn't get away with anything. And he might just decide that Reg was a criminal trying to get police favors rather than an innocent citizen.

She looked into the back of the police car. "How long am I going to have to stay here?"

"I'll officially hand off the scene as soon as the homicide detectives drag their butts over here, and then we'll go. No longer than I can help. All right?"

Reg sighed. "Fine. But you'd better not be jerking me around." She obediently slid into the seat.

CHAPTER TWENTY-FOUR

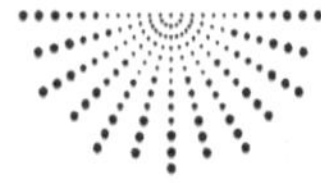

Reg awoke abruptly. She straightened up and hit her head on something solid. She blinked, looking around. She was in a car. In the back seat of a car, and it looked suspiciously like a police cruiser.

What was she doing in the back of a police car?

Had she been sleepwalking? She couldn't even remember leaving the house. Maybe she had been kidnapped. Maybe the witches who had been vandalizing the house and conjuring spells had gotten so bold as to try to remove her from Black Sands by force. Reg didn't know how. She supposed they could have put something in her coffee or tea to make her sleep and then stepped in once she was unconscious. Though how they would do that with the wards set in the house and in the yard, she had no idea. They shouldn't have been able to get past them without permission, especially if they had evil intentions.

Unless Sarah was also involved. She could get past the wards, most of which were her own, without any problem. Reg had allowed her free access at all hours of the night and day, whether she were home or not. There was nothing to keep Sarah from getting into the cottage.

But Reg didn't think that anyone had kidnapped her, with or

without Sarah's help. She wouldn't be sitting in a police car if she had been abducted.

So what did they have on her?

Reg peered out the window, trying to make sense of the scene. She saw her own car parked outside of the tall iron gates, and lots of other vehicles around, most of them with flashing lights. It was enough to make her dizzy.

Something big, then, or there wouldn't be so many emergency vehicles. And Reg hadn't been sleepwalking if her car was there. Sleep driving, maybe, but not sleepwalking.

She had seen the bars of the iron gate before. At first, she couldn't think of anything but old horror movies, ghostly mansions surrounded by premonitory fences. Fences that would keep the visitors in as well as keeping intruders—or rescuers—out.

It took a few minutes to realize that she was at the cemetery. Which was not any better than her first thought. She would rather be at a haunted mansion than the cemetery.

Why had she gone there? Was it because of her dream? She knew she had dreamt about being there, but she hadn't thought it to be second sight. She had been to the cemetery before, so she assumed that it was a memory. Or a mishmash of memories and dream imagery, all the things that had been stressing her over the past few days.

"Reg."

Reg turned her head toward the voice and saw Jessup through the grille that divided the back seat from the front. She sounded impatient. She was probably the reason Reg had just awakened. Reg tried to rub her head where she had bumped it, to indicate to Jessup that she had been hurt and to give her a bit of a break. At least time to wake up and answer. But she couldn't raise her hand to her head. Her hands were restrained behind her back and she had lost all feeling in her fingers.

"What?"

"I'm sorry for being so long. We can go to the police station now."

"Uh… okay."

"Are you okay? I didn't think you could sleep back there."

"No, you wouldn't think so, would you?" Reg rubbed her bump against the plastic surrounding the door, where she had clearly bumped her head. She touched the sore part to the window, which was cool and helped to soothe the bruise. "What happened?"

"Nothing happened. I just had to wait for the homicide detectives. They are here now, so I can take you in and get your statement."

"My statement?"

"About why you were at the cemetery and what you saw."

"Oh. Right." Reg considered. "But I didn't really see anything. Do you think I could get out of it?"

"No. They're not going to give me any latitude on this. I have to do everything by the book. And that means getting statements from everybody at the scene. And that is you."

"I'm not feeling very well. Do you think we could do this tomorrow?" By that time, maybe she would be able to remember something of what had happened. Or she would have had some time to think up a pretty good story based on what she could glean from gossip and media.

"Reg, please. I know you don't want to do this, but let's just get it over with. We need to put it to bed."

Reg leaned against the side of the door, closing her eyes. "Fine. But I don't have anything to tell you."

"You're going to have to answer some questions anyway, even if you don't think you know anything of value."

"It isn't what I *think*. I know I don't know anything."

Jessup turned around so that she was facing the front again and turned her key in the ignition. Her partner, Devaughn, got into the shotgun seat. He looked over his shoulder at Reg briefly, but said nothing to her.

Jessup took a direct route to the police station. Reg wouldn't have minded more of a scenic tour in order to get her story straight. But since she didn't have anything to work with, it didn't really matter.

"Okay," Jessup shut off the engine and forced cheer into her voice. "Here we are. It will be quick and painless, I promise."

Reg knew it wasn't going to be quick or painless.

Not one bit.

She waited until Jessup made her way around to the door and opened it, then struggled out of the seat, putting her feet on the pavement and standing up. Jessup put her hand on Reg's handcuffs and guided her into the building. Reg was relieved that they did not immediately book her. That was a good sign, anyway. Once Reg was in the interview room, Jessup removed the handcuffs. Reg sat back in an uncomfortable plastic seat and looked around. Not much to see. Walls that had been painted over many times due to the number of people who had spit, vomited, or peed on them. Cheap, difficult-to-damage furniture, anchored to metal loops cemented into the floor. There would be a camera somewhere in the ceiling, along with a microphone to record everything that happened there.

Not the kind of place that you took someone who was just a witness. Not unless all the other conference rooms were booked.

But at least Jessup had removed her handcuffs without any prompting.

"I don't know anything," Reg warned again.

"We just need to know your movements tonight. Can you tell me what you were doing this evening?"

Reg thought back to what she could remember. "I had a guest. We talked, did some errands, went home, and talked to his brother on the phone. That's it. I went out to… look for something."

"Look for what?" Jessup asked, her pen hovering over her notebook.

"Uh… I don't know. That wasn't important; I just wanted to get out for a while. You know, get my own space."

"Because you had a guest."

"Yeah."

"Who is your guest?"

Reg eyed her. "No one you know."

"Not a certain warlock?"

Corvin. Sheesh. "No. I said it was someone you don't know."

"First and last name, please. We'll need to cross check."

"Uh… no."

"Reg. You promised you were going to cooperate."

Reg knew she had promised no such thing. She would never promise to help with a police investigation. She would find out what the least she had to say was, and go with that.

"I don't think it's relevant to your investigation."

"I'll be the judge of that. Just give me the information, and we'll decide what is relevant or not."

Reg shook her head. "No one you know. He's not from around here. He didn't have anything to do with... what you're investigating."

Reg hoped for a little more guidance in precisely what they were looking for. It was difficult trying to guess. There had been many police vehicles and what looked like an ambulance, so she had to assume that someone had been hurt or even killed. But what did that have to do with her?

"We'll come back to this," Jessup said slowly. She made a note in her notepad. "So you went out to get some space. Where did you go?"

"I don't know. Here and there. I wasn't really going anywhere in particular, just wasting some time."

"How long were you out?"

"I'm not sure. Not long."

"Why did you go to the cemetery?"

"They just... such interesting places. I thought it would keep me occupied for a while, walking around, looking at the tombstones, maybe talking with some ghosts."

Jessup's eyes flickered over to her partner, and she gave a bit of a laugh. "Sure, of course."

Her laugh warned Reg not to say anything else about her psychic abilities. Her partner wasn't part of the paranormal community in Black Sands. That was going to make it a lot harder to provide any kind of statement.

But Reg advertised services as a psychic. So it would still be in keeping with her role in the community, even if Devaughn didn't believe in psychic phenomena himself.

"I do that, you know," Reg said, emphasizing the point Jessup had just warned her away from. "I'm a medium. I talk to the ghosts of those who have passed on."

"Right. As part of your psychic services business. Your *entertainment* business," Jessup emphasized.

Reg shrugged like it didn't matter. "Some people believe in it."

"I'm sure they do. I'm not sure I believe that you just wanted to walk around in a cemetery to blow off some steam. That doesn't make any sense to me."

"You're not a medium."

"Why did you go in when you knew the cemetery was closed?"

"I didn't know it was closed."

"We've already been through this, Reg. You parked outside the locked gate. You knew very well that it was closed and locked. You chose to climb over the gate. Why?"

"I told you. I just wanted to walk around."

"Maybe you could walk around a park that was still open. Or you could leave your communing with the dead for another day. Why the closed cemetery?"

"Best place to go if you're looking for ghosts. And the best time to reach them is when they are strongest. At night."

Jessup tried to stare Reg down, but didn't succeed. She looked away, consulting her notes again. "What did you see when you got there?"

"Not a lot. It was getting dark. There was no one else around. I thought I was alone."

"You *thought* you were alone?" Jessup repeated.

"Yes." Reg tried to think of what might have happened at the cemetery and what she could tell Jessup that she would believe.

"I heard something when I was there. Like… footsteps. But I could have been wrong." She gave a shrug. "You know how I have such an active imagination. Sometimes, the dark plays tricks with you, especially in a place like that. So full of potential."

"I'm sure we've all had the experience where our imagination got away from us. Describe the footsteps."

"Uh… footsteps. What else can I tell you?"

"Fast or slow? How close? Was it someone big or small? Carrying or dragging something? You must have had some kind of impression."

"Uh… no. It just all happened so fast. I didn't know what to think. It was very… fleeting. Just a sense that someone else was there. Maybe it was the wind or an animal."

"Did you call out? Call 'hello' to see if there was someone else there?"

Reg raised her brows. "Would you? No. No way. I wouldn't call out in a creepy cemetery. I don't want to run into someone else there in the dark."

"I guess not. And then what did you see and hear?"

"Nothing else, really. It was just like… when you… well, you know how it was…"

"It was just like it was when we found you?"

Reg shrugged.

"Did you know the victim?" Jessup demanded.

"The victim…?" Reg thought about it. She couldn't remember anything Jessup was talking about, so she had to be very careful. "It was dark… and I was confused."

"You said you didn't get a good look at him in the dark."

"No. Sorry."

Jessup nodded to her partner. Devaughn pulled out a small tablet and rested it on the table. Without looking at Reg, he tapped the unlock code into it and pecked at the screen with fat, clumsy fingers. Eventually, he turned it around and showed Reg a picture.

Then Reg understood what the questioning was all about. A dead man in the cemetery. Not one of the ranks of the buried dead, but lying out in the open under the moon, waiting for someone to find him. And Reg had been that lucky someone. Had the sight been so traumatic that her brain had refused to process anything else, leaving a memory blank? Or was it just coincidental?

It didn't seem like wandering into a cemetery on a whim and finding a body was a coincidence. Something had drawn Reg there. Something had called to her, pulled her into the cemetery to find the body. Was it the man's ghost? A spell? Had someone told her to go there and meet them? She couldn't imagine that she would have just left Etienne at the cottage and gone off to meet someone in a cemetery. Even if it were someone she knew well, that was just... a bit too spooky for her liking.

Where was Etienne? Reg assumed that he had not gone with her. That it wasn't anything to do with him, and she hadn't asked him to accompany her.

He wouldn't have been a bad guard, if she had asked him to go with her to ensure her safety. But if she had done that, then where had he gone when the police showed up? Would he just run?

"I don't recognize him," Reg said, after examining the picture closely, trying to glean all the clues from it that she could. She swiped the tablet to look at the next and previous pictures, and Devaughn pulled it back before she could get too far. Only far enough to see the body from a few different angles. But even that was helpful. "I'm sorry. I don't know him, and I can't tell you anything else about what happened. It wasn't anything I was involved in. I just happened to be... the wrong place at the wrong time."

"You've never seen this man before."

Reg shook her head. She reviewed the man's features mentally. Bald crown, aging, twisted fingers, old tattoos. Someone that she would expect to have known if she had seen him before. But then, she wouldn't have expected half her night to be missing from her memory, either.

"I'm sorry. I don't know him. If I've ever met him before, I don't remember it."

"He's pretty distinctive."

"I know. And I don't remember him. I didn't know him. We just happened to cross paths..."

"At the end of his life."

"Yeah. I can't help that. It wasn't planned."

"Did someone call you and tell you there was a body in the cemetery? Were you looking for him?"

"No."

"Or looking for a client that had asked you to meet them there?"

"No."

"Come on, Reg, help me out. I know there was a reason you went to the cemetery. That isn't somewhere you just go to on a casual car ride. You don't go there without a reason."

"Well, this time, I did. I just wanted some time and space to myself. It seemed like a good place to get some peace and quiet. I didn't think anyone would bother me there."

"I'm sure you didn't. What would you have done if we hadn't shown up?"

"What do you mean?"

"You find a body on your little walk in the park. What would you have done?"

"I don't know… I would have called you, I guess. Called 9-1-1."

"Would you?"

"Why wouldn't I?"

"Maybe because you didn't want to end up here, being questioned."

Reg shrugged. "Maybe. But I didn't have to call anyone. You were already there." She thought about that fact. "Did someone call you and tell you to check things out? Or tell you that I was there?"

"We're obviously not going to tell you about our internal workings. This is an investigation, not a free exchange of information."

Reg stretched. "That's everything I know. Can I go?"

"I have a few more questions."

"And I have a houseguest." Reg stood up. Having remembered Etienne's attendance at her cottage, she knew she'd better get back to him. He would be wondering what had happened to her. Maybe getting worried. Maybe snooping through her things to see if he could figure out where she had gone and if she needed help.

"We'd like to get your statement typed up and signed."

There was no way Reg was going to stick around that long. "Go ahead and get it typed up. I'll come back in to sign it tomorrow."

"If you could just stay around for a few more minutes…"

"This is not a 'few minutes' job. And I've already been here and cooperated with you long enough. I'm going to head home. Take care of my guest and… have a drink and relax."

Jessup looked at Devaughn for any other ideas of ways to keep

Reg there. But Reg wasn't going to stick around to hear his views. She headed for the door. "I'll just find my own way out."

She knew that Jessup wouldn't let her do that. They would have to escort her to ensure that she didn't get into any secure areas or see anything that she shouldn't. Jessup was right behind her.

"Slow down, Reg, let me just take you out. You might not remember the way."

Reg remembered the way very well. She always took note of escape routes. She didn't want to be stuck in a maze of corridors, not knowing the quickest way out.

"I'll drop you at home," Jessup offered, and Reg remembered suddenly that she didn't have a car.

"Where is my car?"

"I'll find out whether it has been released yet. Just come on out to my unit."

Reg scowled at the thought of having to sit in the back of the police cruiser again. "I'll just get an Uber."

"You don't need to do that. I told you I would drive you home."

"No, thanks."

"I have my own car in the parking lot."

Reg turned to face her. "Your own car, not the police car?"

"Yes."

"So I don't have to be handcuffed in the backseat?"

Jessup looked embarrassed, flushing despite her complexion. "I'm sorry about that. I had to follow protocols."

"Yeah. I'll remember that next time you want to do another girls' night out."

"Reg! That's not fair. I'm just doing my job."

"And I think that you should probably not be consorting with someone like me. We should just go our separate directions."

"You don't mean that."

"I do tonight."

Jessup nodded understandingly. "You're still upset. Once you've had a chance to relax and get a good sleep… things will look better in the morning. You're just emotional right now. You don't want to make any decisions based on emotion."

Reg rolled her eyes. She didn't know whether she'd be able to forgive Jessup for the way she had been treated. She didn't know if she wanted to forgive her. But it wasn't going to be for a while.

Jessup led the way to her civilian vehicle and let Reg in. They got settled and Jessup pulled out of the parking lot.

"So, you want to tell me now what exactly was going on at the cemetery? Why did you go there?"

"I can't tell you."

"I won't put it into any reports. But I'd like to know what's going on."

Reg shrugged.

"Come on, Reg. Don't you think I should have some idea of what's going on in my own town? Even if I can't do anything about it officially, it's still good to know whether I'm going to have more grave robbing or murders or if there's something else coming down the pipe."

"I don't know what's going to happen. Can't help you there."

"Do you know how this guy died? Was it something super-natural?"

"I only walked up on him when you showed up. You know more than I do about it."

"He didn't have any identification on him. Do you know who he is?"

"No. Never seen him before that I can remember."

Jessup shook her head in frustration. "So you're just sticking with the story that you went out for a walk and happened to stumble across him."

"Yeah. That's what I'm sticking to."

"You won't tell me anything else, off the record, one friend to another."

"Nope."

"You didn't go there just for some fresh air."

Reg shrugged. Jessup could ask it in as many ways as she wanted to; Reg wasn't going to give her any more information.

Because she didn't have any more information. She had no idea what had happened that night.

CHAPTER TWENTY-FIVE

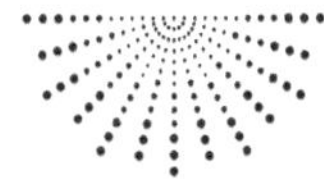

$\mathcal{R}$eg was glad to be home. She couldn't wait to be in her own space again and away from the cops and even Jessup's probing questions. She needed to figure out what was going on. Or she needed to get to bed. Something. As long as it was in her own cottage and she didn't have to worry about anyone looking over her shoulder.

Except there was still Etienne. Reg didn't really think about him until Jessup was a block away from the house and asked, "Who is your house guest?"

"Oh." Reg's face warmed as she remembered who was waiting for her. She wasn't even sure what she had told Etienne before she left. He would certainly be thinking that her behavior was strange. But then, he was used to *Homo sapiens* acting impulsively rather than sitting and thinking things over for a few weeks or months before deciding. Or years. Maybe it wouldn't seem any stranger to him than the typical *Homo sapiens* behavior. "Right. I forgot about him."

"Him?"

"Yeah."

"And it isn't Hunter."

"No, it isn't Corvin. I already said that."

"But I still don't know if you're telling me the truth."

"Then why ask again?"

"I guess I shouldn't expect to get a different answer. So who is it? I thought you and Damon were sort of on the outs."

"Why would Damon be staying at my house? He has his own place. I'm not inviting anyone over romantically. That's not what this is. A friend of mine who isn't from here is… may be getting married. I'm just putting him up and helping him for a few days."

Though she still didn't know where she was going to put him. It would be better if Etienne found a hotel, since Reg didn't even have a pull-out bed for him to use.

"And what did he have to do with this business at the cemetery?"

"Nothing."

"A mysterious out-of-town visitor and it's just coincidence that you stumbled over a body? I don't believe that."

"Believe what you like. Et—he doesn't have anything to do with a mysterious body showing up in the cemetery."

"What are we going to find out about his cause of death?"

"I don't know."

"Maybe you could use some of your psychic ability to find out."

"Why should I? Leave it to your medical examiner."

"Did you see his ghost?"

"No."

"Hear it?"

"No. I didn't communicate with him in any way. I keep telling you, there wasn't time for anything. You just showed up when I came across him. Like you were waiting to ambush me."

"Nobody ambushed you."

Reg looked at her, eyebrow raised.

"We saw your car parked at the gates where it didn't belong and stopped to see what was going on. We could see that you had climbed the fence and followed you in. That's all. It was just a simple trespass investigation."

"Seems a bit convenient."

"Well, unless you told someone else you were going to be there, I don't know how we would have found out to plan anything ahead of time. Did you tell people that's where you were going?"

"No."

"Then we couldn't exactly have ambushed you. How do you think I would know you were going there?"

Reg had to admit that it made some sense. But she wasn't about to tell Jessup that. She wasn't feeling particularly charitable toward Detective Jessup.

Jessup pulled the car over at the curb in front of Sarah's house. Jessup clearly intended to talk some more, but Reg didn't have to stay and listen. She yanked the door handle and slid out. "Thanks for the ride and a lovely evening," she said in a sweet tone, and left, ignoring Jessup trying to call her back. She stomped around the big house to the cottage in the back, hoping that no one would cross her path. Not because she was afraid for herself, but because she might just fear for them. Nothing was getting in between Reg and her safe haven.

When she got to the door, she found she had left it unlocked, which had been a stupid thing to do. She let herself in and looked around. Etienne was cooking something on the stovetop. Whatever it was, it smelled good. Etienne turned and looked at her. With his bushy whiskers, it was hard to discern his expression. But she'd could feel his concern.

"You are back."

"Yeah. Sorry about all that. I shouldn't have left you alone here."

"I am fine alone. But I was concerned about you. You seemed… very strange."

Reg folded herself into the couch. "Why? What did I do?"

"You do not know?"

Reg didn't answer that. She waited for him to tell her more.

"You were very white, very pale. I thought maybe you were sick. But you said you were not, that you didn't need anything… except a snake. Then you had to go out… for a few minutes, you say." He looked at the window. "It was several hours ago."

"I feel bad about leaving you here to fend for yourself. I should have known that you would need to eat," she nodded to the stove, "and I don't know what other help you might need to get ready for Ilka, or how your talk with James went. Did you get everything worked out with him?"

"He is going to call Ilka's family. Try to get it smoothed over." Etienne nodded at this. "He is a good brother. I should do more to keep in touch with him."

"Does he write letters?"

"Not much. A Christmas card, sometimes. But he likes to send those emails. Through the clouds. I do not do that. He says I should at least get a phone like you have."

"We can look at some while you are here. Maybe you'll find something you like."

He waved away this conversation with a gesture of his hand, then stirred what was cooking on the stove. "Did you find a snake?"

"No." Reg tried to remember what she had been thinking before she left. Why she would have given Etienne the impression that she wanted a snake. But she couldn't come up with anything. "Is that all I said? That I wanted a snake?"

"I think you said *the* snake. Like it was a certain one. I do not know."

"I guess I owe you an explanation. But I don't have one. I have these... memory issues."

Etienne cocked his head slightly, without looking at her. "More than memory issues."

"Well, I suppose. But I don't know what it is being caused by." She sighed. "Everyone says get more sleep. Maybe I'm fighting a virus."

"I do not think so. You acted like... you were someone else."

"What does that mean?"

"I do not know. You talked differently. Looked at me differently. You were very... irritable and angry."

Starlight was crouching nearby, watching Reg. She made a noise to call him and patted the couch beside her. He didn't jump up. "Oh, come on, Starlight. Don't act that way."

"Perhaps he wants to make sure you are yourself again."

Reg looked back at Starlight. With the way that Starlight and Etienne seemed to communicate without words, she couldn't very well argue that he didn't know what he was talking about.

"It's me, Star. Really. I'm back to normal again."

"What was it that changed you?" Etienne asked. He pulled a couple of bowls out of the cupboard and started ladling the pot's contents into them.

"I don't know."

"You were playing with Starlight. With a string."

Reg looked around and saw the shoelace. She vaguely remembered Starlight bringing it to her.

"I guess… I don't know, it must have just hit me suddenly. I don't remember."

"You said the snake looked like that." Etienne pointed to the shoelace. He shrugged his wide shoulders. "I have not ever seen a snake that looked like that." He carried the bowls over to the table and put them down. Reg got a couple of spoons from the utensil drawer. A bigger one for Etienne. She sat down at the table, where she actually never ate. The steam rising from the stew was hearty and fragrant with spices.

"Mmm. I didn't think I was hungry, but this smells delicious. Thank you. I didn't even know I had the ingredients to make this."

Etienne made a snuffling, laughing sound. "You did not have very many provisions here. And I could not rely on what you might be bringing back. Some is from your fridge, some from the witch you said to ask, and some from plants growing in the garden."

"Really? Wow. You're really good at this stuff. I can't make anything without a recipe. Actually, I can't make anything *with* a recipe. The best I can do is warm something up."

Etienne took his first bite of the meal, closed his eyes, and nodded slowly. "It is very good. My grandmother was an excellent cook."

"Is that who you learned from?"

"I taught myself, living alone in the swamp. But I suppose I must have remembered something from her in my early years. I must have watched her cook dozens of times, and perhaps I absorbed some of it from her."

"Yeah."

Reg took a couple of bites of the stew. It was delicious and satisfying, and she knew she was going to want more than just the one bowl he had dished up. And she generally ate a steady diet of fast food, which she had been told would destroy her taste buds for anything else. "It's awesome. Thank you so much. I'm exhausted tonight."

"How about your grandmother? You did not learn to cook from her?"

"No. I don't even know who she was. I was taken away from my mother when I was four."

"So young!" Etienne *tsked.* "I feel sorry for the child Reg Rawlins. Why did they take you from her?"

"She wasn't a good person. She couldn't take care of me. She was a drug addict. I didn't get much to eat or much care." Reg hesitated, wondering whether to tell Etienne that her mother had been part siren. It explained her inability to parent. Sirens were very competitive and often killed off their own children. If Reg had not been taken away from Norma Jean when she was so young, she probably would not have lived to adulthood. She had been upset to be taken away from her mother, but it had been a good thing.

But Etienne might react the same way as the others did when finding out she was part siren. She didn't want to have to face his disappointment and fear or anger. It was nice to just have a friend, even if he was only there for a day or two.

"Are you going to stay here tonight or find a hotel? I don't have a second bed; I don't really have anything to offer you."

"I don't need anything special. A couple of blankets. Nothing much."

"What are you going to do, sleep on the floor? That's not going to be comfortable." She'd been to his house. It had been furnished just like a *Homo sapiens'* house, with chairs and a table, and beds in the bedroom. He wouldn't want to go from sleeping in a soft bed to sleeping on her floor.

"I could pay for a hotel for you. I don't like to think of you laying on the floor."

"I would prefer sleeping on my friend's floor to sleeping alone in a hotel," Etienne said. "I sleep alone at home. This is... like a vacation. It's my one chance to be around people. A person. It's been nice."

Reg felt even more guilty for having neglected him while she went off gallivanting to the cemetery and police station. She sighed, looking for a half-way point, some kind of compromise, but she couldn't find one. He was happy to sleep on the floor. She didn't need to provide any amenities. She just had to accept his presence there.

She could go to the store and buy a blow-up mattress or cot. But she really didn't have the energy to go out again.

"You're welcome to stay here," she told him, not wanting him to think that she was trying to get rid of him. "I'm just afraid you won't be able to sleep."

Etienne ate a few more bites of the stew before speaking, chewing it slowly. "I do not know if I will sleep tonight," he confessed. "Thinking about Ilka being here tomorrow. My whole life could change."

"Yeah. That's big news, isn't it? I'd have a hard time sleeping too. I'm excited just thinking about the two of you meeting, and it isn't anything to do with me. After all the time you spent writing to each other, are you ready to see her in person? I mean, it doesn't matter if you are ready or not, since she is going to be here. But how do you feel about it?"

His hair bristled. Etienne patted it down, trying to look calm and collected. "I am very excited," he confessed. "I did not think something like this would ever happen to me. If I met my mate, it would only be after a long courtship and negotiation. Not like this, all at once." He dropped his eyes to his bowl for a few minutes before looking up again, shyly. "She is magnificent."

CHAPTER TWENTY-SIX

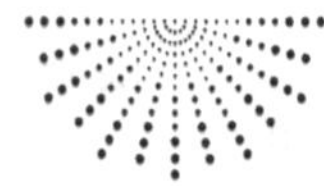

Since Etienne didn't think he would be able to get to sleep, and Reg didn't usually sleep until several hours after midnight, neither of them made any attempt to go to sleep until very late. Or early, depending on who was calling it. They stayed up watching streaming movies, which Etienne viewed with some level of shock and alarm, frequently looking over at Reg to see how she would react to an intense scene on the screen.

"The last time I watched TV, it did not look like this," Etienne said, staring at the picture.

"What did it look like?" Reg laughed.

"Well, it was smaller. This is very large, like a movie theater. And it was not colored like these. Sometimes a movie was in color at the theater, but it wasn't like that on a person's TV. It was just grays."

"You haven't seen color TV?"

"I have seen TV. And I have seen color," Etienne clarified. "And I have seen colorized movies at the theater." He drew his chin up when he said that, obviously proud of the fact.

"But you haven't seen color TV."

He hesitated for a minute before shaking his head. "No."

"Wow. I've seen some of those old movies. I was watching some old thrillers just a couple of days ago. You know, *The Blob* and stuff like that. Really old, cheesy special effects. It was amazing, cutting edge when it came out, but now we look at it and just shake our heads." Reg looked at the image on the screen of an army descending on a contingent of aliens. Little did they know that there was a whole other army of aliens in the next valley. They thought they were powerful enough to beat the aliens, but it wasn't even going to be close.

Etienne turned his eyes back to the screen as well. He put one furry hand over his eyes to shut out the images, but still didn't want to take his eyes off of it and peeked out through the cracks.

"Do you want me to find something that isn't so scary?" Reg asked.

"No, no. It's your house. You watch what you would like to."

"You're my guest. That means we watch what you want to watch. And I have a feeling this is a bit much for you."

Etienne peeked through his fingers and winced, squinting at the screen for one more look. "Well…"

"I have the nature channel, you know. You can watch animals."

"The nature channel?"

"Sure. Shall we try that?" Without waiting, Reg switched away from the movie. There was a picture of a bear walking in the woods with a calm, peaceful narrator describing the scene for anyone who couldn't figure it out for themselves.

"Oh." Etienne stared at the screen intently, sitting forward. "This is very nice."

Reg broke out the ice cream and they both ate while watching the action slowly unfold.

* * *

They both fell asleep in their seats, which is where they were when Sarah came strolling in the next day. Reg had fully intended to sleep in her bed, but it didn't happen. So much for her sleeping on the bed and Etienne sleeping on the floor. She didn't have to worry about that inequality.

"Well, this is cozy!" Sarah observed, waking them both.

Reg straightened up, looking around and trying to get her bearings. "Oh… I guess we fell asleep. We were just watching movies. Sarah, this is Etienne, he is here—"

"Yes, we met last night," Sarah agreed. "Though you might have told me who was staying with you before I had one of the forest people show up on my doorstep."

"Uh… yeah, sorry about that. I didn't really think… I wasn't planning to go out, but when I had to, I told Etienne he could ask you for anything he needed…"

"And of course I'm delighted to help out. But it is nice to have a bit of a warning. Especially since… they are so very large."

"But he couldn't have gotten through the wards if he had intended to do either of us harm."

Sarah studied Reg for a moment. "No," she said finally. "Not unless his magic was much stronger than mine."

"Good morning, Sarah Bishop," Etienne greeted formally.

Sarah gave a nod in his direction. "Good morrow, Etienne."

"I am sorry," Reg said with a shrug. "Things ended up going… a little off the rails yesterday."

"Not to worry. As it turns out, Etienne and I have met before. When he was just a cub."

"Really?" Reg looked at Etienne, remembering how he had referred to ninety years being a short time. She supposed it proved Sarah Bishop was centuries old, as she had claimed. "That's cool. You remembered each other?"

"Etienne has always had a fondness for chocolate," Sarah said with a mischievous smile. "I'm afraid I might have had something to do with that."

Etienne gave his soft, snuffling laugh. "It was good to meet you again."

Sarah nodded her agreement. She looked at Reg. "Maybe you and I could walk in the garden for a few minutes. I have something to show you."

"Etienne could—"

Sarah shook her head. "He'll stay here and see what he can whip up for breakfast. He always was good with a skillet. Come with me."

Reg followed her outside and into the garden. "You have something to show me?"

"Well, if I had brought it out with me, I would show you the newspaper. What were you doing out last night? What is all this nonsense about you being somehow involved in an investigation regarding a dead body found in the cemetery? An *unauthorized* dead body, of course," she said quickly, "I do note that there are many other dead bodies that you didn't have anything at all to do with."

"That's in the paper today?"

"Yes."

"With my name?"

"With your picture as you are escorted out of the cemetery in handcuffs. No mention of your name, and the police have not yet given an official statement or acknowledged your involvement in the case, but I can read between the lines. What happened? What were you doing there?"

"I wish I could tell you, but I can't. I don't know why I went there, and I can't tell you anything about the dead guy, other than the fact that he was dead. I didn't have anything to do with it."

"You don't know how he died?"

Reg had a strange tremor run through her body.

She looked for a way to deny it. Of course she didn't know anything about how the man had died. She'd only caught a very quick glimpse of the body in the dark, under the glow of her phone and then Jessup's flashlight. She didn't *know* anything about it.

But her body wouldn't let it go. When she tried to explain how she didn't know anything, her body reacted like a lie detector, throwing a huge wrench into the works. How was Reg supposed to lie convincingly when her body told the tale to anyone looking at her?

"I didn't have anything to do with it," she said instead, shaking her head. "Why don't you call Jessup or wait for the official statement from the police force? This isn't anything to do with me."

"You just happened to be where there was a dead body."

"Yes. Exactly."

"I don't imagine that's what Marta had to say about it."

"Jessup wasn't happy," Reg agreed. "Especially when I wouldn't tell her anything. She said she could have kept it a secret, but you know that's just a ploy to get me talking."

"Are you going to tell me anything about it?"

"How can I? I don't know anything."

"Why did you go to the cemetery?"

"I don't know. I had… another blackout. A memory blank. I went into the cemetery looking for something… and I found that man. I don't know his name or anything about him. The police were right behind me. That's it, that's the whole story."

"Another memory hole."

"Yes."

"From when to when?"

"From… I guess the time that I left the house, until Jessup put me in the police car."

Reg wondered what the photo of her had looked like. What was her expression? Stunned? Confused? Tired? Or just blank like a zombie?

"And you don't know why you went to the cemetery? You said it was to look for something."

"Etienne said that I was talking about a snake. Looking for a snake. But I don't want to see a snake. I hate them. I think that I must just have been thinking about snakes because of the one we saw in the yard. That's all."

"Why would you be looking in a cemetery for a snake?"

"I don't know," Reg repeated, for what seemed like the millionth time. "I'm sure there are probably some around there, but I wouldn't expect it to be… snake Mecca. Just a few random snakes living in the trees or some mausoleum."

Reg turned around to go back into the cottage. She should be helping Etienne to make breakfast. Or at least pretending that she could do something to help. Or feeding Starlight.

Coming the other way down the path was a familiar figure. Reg groaned.

CHAPTER TWENTY-SEVEN

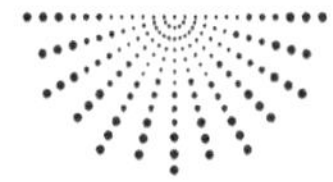

"Jessup? Don't you sleep?"

"Not last night," Detective Jessup acknowledged, smothering a yawn. "When you discover a body, there is a lot that needs to be done. Interviewing witnesses, logging evidence… it's the homicide detectives' job, of course, but I want to keep my hand in this. I don't want someone else screwing it up, and then me getting into trouble as if it were my fault."

"I already told you everything I could yesterday. Which is nothing. Because I didn't know anything."

"I have a few details that might help us to sort it out."

Reg didn't know what to say to that. She wanted to continue to be oppositional and challenge everything Jessup said, but it didn't work if Jessup was going to be nice and to come bearing gifts.

"Maybe we should go sit down," Sarah said. "Do you want to sit in the garden, or go back into the house?" She gestured toward her house, not Reg's.

Jessup looked at her, frowning. "This is a police matter. I really can't involve you in it. Reg, why don't we go into the cottage, and we can discuss it privately there."

"Uh… no. Let's just stay out here."

Jessup looked at Sarah to leave.

Sarah stayed where she was. "I'm already discussing this with Reg. We're trying to figure it all out. So you can either include me in the conversation or be on your way." When Jessup opened her mouth to argue, Sarah beat her to the punch line. "And it is my property, so I have every right to tell you that you cannot be here."

Jessup thought about that for a minute. She looked at Reg. "You want me to share this with both of you?"

Reg nodded. Sarah was already involved, like it or not.

Jessup sighed. "Do you know how he was killed?"

Sarah was expecting Reg to shake her head and say no. Reg was expecting herself to shake her head and say no. But that wasn't what came out.

"He had a mark on his neck," she told Jessup. "Did you see that?"

"I didn't. Not at the scene. There was too much else; I guess I missed it."

Sarah cocked her head. "Bruises?" She suggested. "Strangled?"

"No." Reg looked up into one of the trees. There could be a snake up there now. Snakes climbed trees, didn't they? "It wasn't left by fingers or a rope. It was a bite."

Sarah blinked rapidly, looking from one to the other. "A bite? What kind of a bite? A vampire? A wild animal?"

Reg looked at Jessup for her answer. Reg had wondered that too. What had bitten him? She didn't know anything about real-life vampires, though some of the things she knew about vampires made her wonder about Corvin... But would a vampire have just left the body there like that? It would have been drained of blood, wouldn't it? Reg had a pretty good idea that the man had not been completely drained.

But Reg didn't know anything about real vampires and how they worked in the real world. Many of the magical species Reg had met were different from the way they were described in fairy tales and movies. So she couldn't assume anything.

Jessup looked steadily back at Reg as if expecting her to answer the question. She had just claimed to have seen the bite. So how clearly had she seen it?

Reg broke the eye contact. "I think... maybe a snake."

Jessup nodded. Reg looked at Sarah, who raised her eyes thoughtfully. They had just been talking about snakes. Reg had said that she had gone to the cemetery looking for a snake. Then she had found the body of a man who had been bitten by a snake. Not just bitten, but bitten and killed. How did Reg explain that coincidence?

But she didn't. She couldn't remember looking for a snake. Etienne had told her that part. It was another mystery shrouded by her memory blackouts.

"You think this man was killed by a snake?" Sarah asked Jessup. "Then it was natural causes. It isn't as if he was murdered in the cemetery. With all the stuff in the paper this morning, one would swear that the police thought this was a suspicious death. You said that you're investigating. But investigating what? A snake bite?"

"We're investigating a suspicious death. Until the medical examiner declares cause and manner of death."

"And then you'll let it go. If she says it was accidental or natural death."

Jessup nodded. "Of course. We're not going to investigate it any further if the ME declares that it was natural causes."

"Then you don't have to keep treating me as a suspect," Reg said.

"I'm not. Would I be here talking to you now if you were a suspect?"

"Cops can be tricky."

"And so can cons."

"So you don't suspect me."

Reg waited to see if Jessup would actually agree and put it in so many words.

"Someone could still have planted the snake," Jessup said slowly.

"What? *Planted* the snake?"

"The man who was killed… he was very big in the snake-handling community."

"Snake handling—?" Reg pressed her lips together, determined not to be an echo chamber. Jessup would have to take the time to explain it to her instead of just dropping tantalizing little clues and expecting Reg to understand the whole picture. *Snake handling community?*

"Some people believe that handling venomous snakes shows that they are faithful," Jessup informed her.

"You mean, like, a religious thing?"

"Yes. I don't know all the details, but they believe that if they can safely handle snakes, it shows that they are true believers. God is protecting them."

"And this guy who was killed, he was one of them?"

"He was part of that group… but I'm not sure whether he did it because of religious beliefs or if he just liked snakes. Some people get off on taking risks. I think that's a big part of why religious folks do it. It gives them an adrenaline boost. A euphoria when they manage to do it without getting bitten."

"But what if they do get bitten?"

"Most snakebites won't kill you immediately. With most types of snakes, it would take more than one bite before your life was in danger. And most snakes don't bite multiple times, if what I've been told is correct. They use up their venom on the first bite, and all the bites after that, if there are any, are dry bites. So it would take multiple bites from multiple snakes."

"But that guy, he only had one bite that I saw. Were there more?"

"Just the one that I know of. Unless the ME uncovered more. We didn't strip the guy. And apparently those hands—you saw how his hands were misshapen?"

Reg had seen it in the pictures Jessup had shown her. She nodded. "Yeah."

"Apparently, that's from being bitten before. It kills tissue, causes deep damage like you saw on his hands. So he's been bitten before and should have some immunity to the venom. If he handles venomous snakes regularly, then he might have been injecting himself with venom to build up his resistance."

"But you still think that he died from a poisonous snake bite."

"Until I'm told differently, that's the working hypothesis."

"Then it must have been… a really poisonous snake. Super poisonous."

"There are a few in Florida that can kill you with one bite."

"What about a diamondback?" Reg asked, remembering the one she had seen in the garden. The one that Forst told her she had seen.

"Yes," Jessup frowned. "Why specifically a diamondback?"

"I don't know. It was just on my mind." Reg shrugged. "Maybe a psychic insight. Maybe it's something that you needed to know." She was still good at bluffing about paranormal phenomena in the cases she didn't actually experience a psychic connection.

Jessup considered for a moment, then wrote it down. She studied Reg and Sarah, eyes moving back and forth between them to discern whether they were telling the truth or whether there was something they were trying to hide from her.

"So you think he was killed by the bite of a diamondback rattler."

"It's as good a guess as any. I guess you'll know for sure when your medical examiner calls you."

"And you say you don't know the man who was killed."

"No. Never seen him before, as far as I can remember." She left the remembering part in there just in case it came up that she had seen him in another time and place that was lost in the memory blanks.

"We have an ID on him now."

Reg waited. If Jessup were going to tell her about him, she would.

"His name was Nagendra."

Reg waited for more, but that appeared to be all Jessup was going to say. "Well… that's a new one. I don't remember ever hearing that before."

"It's not a common name."

"Is that his first name or his last name?"

"His only name, apparently."

"But you have to have a first and last name."

"Humans do," Jessup agreed.

"Oh. So what was he?"

"Troll."

"He was a troll?" Reg thought back to Tybalt. "Wait, are goblins and trolls the same thing?"

Sarah giggled.

"No," Jessup answered. She smiled in Sarah's direction. "They are both humanoid in form, but they are very different creatures."

"Trolls are the ones who hide under bridges, right?"

"They historically prefer a hovel by the water. Some kind of dugout or shack under a bridge is not uncommon. But most of the trolls that I am familiar with have left that traditional lifestyle and blend in with human society."

"So the ME isn't going to find out that he has a tail or something?"

"That would be awkward! Physiologically, they are quite similar enough to humans that a basic autopsy will only find minor variations. As long as they don't do a DNA test."

"What is she going to think when she finds these minor variations?"

"People live with quite a range of mutations and differences in development. Sometimes they don't even know that they had a misplaced organ or something that works differently than we would expect and it isn't discovered until after they die. She'll just put it down to abnormal development that had nothing to do with his death."

"And can trolls be killed by poisonous snakes? They're not immune?"

"I've never heard anything to that effect. You'd have to talk to someone like Hunter, who has made a study of other species."

"So…" Reg tried to tie it all together and see the bigger picture. "A troll who is known to be a snake handler, someone who has been bitten by snakes before, is found in a graveyard, dead with a snakebite on his neck."

Jessup nodded. "By a psychic who claims to have just stumbled over the body."

Reg sighed. "It's true, though. I didn't have any idea who he was."

"And why were you there? In the cemetery. It's important, Reg. If I can't get your full story, I'm going to be in trouble and so are you. If we need to… finesse it, then we can talk about that. But I have to have something to start with."

Reg looked at Sarah to see what she thought. Sarah gave a one-shouldered shrug. "Do whatever you think is best."

CHAPTER TWENTY-EIGHT

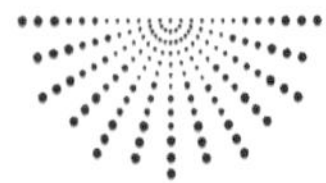

Jessup looked at Reg, waiting for the explanation.

"I've been having… some issues."

"Psychic stuff? Voices? What?"

"I have… missing memory. I can't tell you what I witnessed or what I was thinking. Because I can't remember any of it."

"You remember something."

"No."

"You knew about the snakebite. How did you know about that if you don't remember what happened in the cemetery?"

"You showed me a picture."

"It didn't show up in the picture."

"Yes, it did. I don't remember anything that happened from the time I left my house until you took me back to the police station. Everything that happened in between is gone."

"You can't remember it."

"No."

"Why wouldn't you be able to remember it? You seemed perfectly fine at the time." Jessup stopped and reconsidered this statement. "Well, pretty normal. You did seem a little… distant."

Reg nodded.

"How long has this been going on?"

"Just for a few days."

"Have you seen a doctor or something? I think I would want to know what was going on if it was me."

"I've been trying to figure it out. I talked to… Sarah."

"That's it? That's the sum total of your research?"

"That's not any of your business. Now I've answered your question. You know why I can't tell you anything."

"But there has to be a reason. And if we can figure out what that is, maybe we can unwind what happened here."

"I don't know why I went there. I was looking for something, maybe. But what or why… I don't know. I was just… driven there. That's all I know."

"What about your houseguest?"

"What about him?"

"Did you start having these memory blanks after he started staying with you?"

"No. I was having trouble before he showed up."

"Does he have psychic abilities?"

"I don't know." Reg thought about Etienne's interactions with Starlight. "Maybe some. Like, with animals. I don't think he communicates with humans telepathically. I don't see how he could have had any influence on me."

"Does he have anything to do with snakes? If he can communicate with them telepathically, then maybe he sent the snake to bite Nagendra."

"He's not that kind of person. He wouldn't do something like that. He's peaceful."

"What is he?"

"He's human." Reg didn't look at Sarah. She didn't want Sarah to give it away. Etienne had said that he was human, that the Bigfoots considered themselves to fall into that category. So even if he weren't *Homo sapiens*, Reg at least wasn't lying about him being human. "A friend."

"Can I meet him?"

"No. He's kind of a hermit. He doesn't like being around other people. But he had to come here for some family business. So he's staying with me until he goes back home."

"What's his name?"

"Etienne," Reg said after a moment of consideration. "And I don't know what last name he uses." He could use Legrande like James did, but Reg suspected that he didn't use a last name at all. He lived by himself in the woods. He didn't associate with other people, other than the skinwalker who did the mail runs for him. What use would he have for a last name? He must have put something on his letters to Ilka, and must have introduced himself to her and her family some-how. But it might have been through a complex genealogy rather than a last name.

"He doesn't live around here?"

"No."

"Does he have a criminal background?"

Reg laughed. "I don't think so. I never asked him."

"This isn't some con that you've worked for before? Are you shel-tering him from the police?"

"No. He just doesn't want to have to deal with other people."

"What is it he's here for?"

"What does that matter?"

"I want to know how it connects up. If it does."

"It doesn't."

"What is his business here?"

"Meeting his bride."

"Oh." Jessup looked taken aback. "Okay. Yeah, I'm not sure how that would have anything to do with this business unless she's the daughter of the troll."

"No, she's not. I told you, he's human. Not troll. He's not connected. This all started before he showed up."

Jessup stared off into the distance, probably trying to go through everything she already knew to see if there were anything else she should be asking Reg.

"You're not aware of anyone in town that has anything to do with snakes?"

Forst had chased away the snake in the back yard. He hadn't had anything to do with it being there in the first place. Not that Reg could figure out, anyway. Etienne hadn't had anything to do with the shoelace Reg had said looked like a snake.

"I don't know anyone who handles snakes or even has a pet snake."

CHAPTER TWENTY-NINE

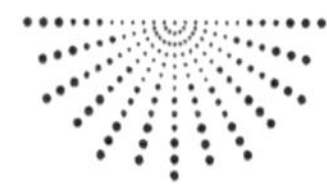

*E*ventually, Jessup went on her way. Reg looked at Sarah, rolling her eyes. "Well… that was interesting."

"You didn't tell her anything about having seen a snake here."

"No, I didn't see how that could help her. There are snakes all over the place. It isn't like they're going to go hunting them down and bringing in every snake in the area to see if it is the one that bit this… Nagendra. I don't see any connection between seeing a snake here and a troll being bitten by one somewhere else."

"Don't you?"

"Coincidences do happen."

"Yes, but when magic or other paranormal forces are involved… coincidences may flag spells and sorcery."

"Why would anyone put a spell on a snake? If you wanted to kill someone, there have to be more efficient ways."

"Maybe Nagendra was trying to perform a spell in the cemetery. Maybe his snake turned on him. He was known to be a snake handler, so it's not surprising that a snake was near him before he died. It was more likely to be his own snake than one that just happened to wander by."

A picture flashed through Reg's mind of a snake wandering along in the cemetery, swaying from side to side, just casually on a slither through the grass. She snickered at the picture.

The door to the cottage opened a crack. Reg looked toward it. "Etienne?"

"Is she gone?"

Reg nodded. "Just me and Sarah here."

He opened the door a few inches. "Breakfast is ready. If you talk for much longer, it will get cold."

"Sorry. I'll come eat. Sarah, would you like to stay and have a bite?"

"I've already had my breakfast today. I'd better not start doubling up." Sarah patted her slightly thick middle. "Got to keep in shape for the young men, you know."

Reg laughed and went back into her cottage to join Etienne. They sat down at the table as they had for stew the night before, taking the same chairs as if it were already an established routine. Reg watched Etienne spoon vegetables from the skillet onto his large plate, then took it from him and put a few on her plate. Mostly the potatoes and carrots. She wasn't really a vegetable person, but Etienne's meals had always been delicious, so she was willing to try a little. If she didn't want it, she could just tell him that she wasn't used to eating breakfast, which was true. She rarely had anything but coffee before noon.

She speared a potato and put it into her mouth. It was salty and savory, with the sweetness of caramelized onions. Reg chewed slowly, enjoying it. She wasn't sure how he had gotten it crisp on the outside and soft in the middle. She remembered a number of failed dishes from when she was younger, trying to take her turn cooking for the family at a foster home or attempting to be domestic once she had moved out and had her own apartment from time to time. Her potatoes had ended up either burned on the outside and raw in the middle, or mushy all the way through.

"Very good," she told Etienne. "Thank you. I normally don't even eat breakfast, but this is really good." She kept eating.

Etienne nodded his thanks and worked on his large mound of vegetables. "It is nice to be lazy and not have to go out and forage my own food."

"Yeah, I guess I never thought about that. It's nice to always be able to have freshly-picked stuff, straight from the garden… or the wilds. But you do have to go to the work of collecting it before you even start cooking."

A person would have to know what he was making before beginning to cook—no rummaging through the fridge to find what you had bought at the grocery store. Reg would probably have starved if she had to live on her own in the wilderness like Etienne did. She wasn't exactly made of the right stuff.

"If you had been raised to survive in the swamp, you would be able to," Etienne commented.

"I guess so. But I didn't learn everything I was trained to do, so there's no guarantee. I might have been the first one in the family to have a terrible accident."

Etienne looked at her for a moment, then nodded his head very slightly. "Accidents are not uncommon," he admitted. "Unfortunately, not everyone survives to a ripe old age."

Reg hadn't thought about that. She didn't mean to make him feel sad about family members he had lost in unfortunate accidents. "Oh… I'm sorry. I didn't even think about that. I was just joking."

"What were you talking about with your friend outside?" he asked, changing the subject.

"With Sarah?"

"Your other friend who came by."

"Oh… I'm not sure I would call her my friend. I mean, we have been, but she's more of a cop than a friend."

Etienne was looking at her questioningly.

"She's a policeman," Reg explained. "She was coming to talk to me about… something that happened last night. I didn't actually have anything to do with it, but they think I am somehow involved. I have to keep telling them that I'm not…"

"Ah."

"Can you communicate telepathically with snakes?"

He stopped eating, fork raised partway to his mouth. Reg realized that the question had been a little abrupt. She should have done a better job building up to it. She ate a few bites of her own meal to try to cover up for the awkwardness.

"I can… have some communication with most animals," Etienne said slowly. "It isn't exactly like talking to them."

"Yeah. I couldn't hear you when you talked to Starlight or to the panther in the swamp. So I didn't think that it was… actual words."

Etienne nodded his agreement.

"So you can communicate some things with them. Feelings. Impressions. But what else? Do you understand them? And if so, how clearly?"

Etienne made a muffled noise and didn't try to answer the stampede of questions for a while. "Why do you want to know this, Reg Rawlins?"

"There was a snake in my yard. I don't know if it is still there. I don't know why it was there. Or if it has anything to do with… what happened last night. It wouldn't slither all the way from here to the cemetery, would it?"

She realized belatedly that Etienne probably had no idea where the cemetery was. She scratched the back of her head, trying to figure out how to ask for what she needed a little more clearly.

"I am not a snake charmer," Etienne said slowly. "And I cannot call them. I would have to see it gaze-to-gaze to communicate with it."

"I'm sure it's nothing to do with the cemetery anyway. That was just… something stupid. Something that my friend wondered about."

"Snakes do not usually travel far from their birthplace," Etienne confirmed. "The ones around here do not migrate."

"Yeah, that makes sense. So it had to be another snake at the cemetery."

Etienne looked across the table at her. Reg thought that he was going to discuss it further, but then decided not to complicate things any more than they already were.

"Are you looking forward to seeing Ilka this afternoon? Is there anything you need to do before then?"

"Oh, so many things," Etienne groaned, shaking his head and

pulling his whiskers anxiously. "Why did she have to come without any warning? I cannot have anything prepared for her."

"Maybe that's why. She didn't want you to go to the trouble. She wanted to see you and talk with you face-to-face without all the artificial stuff. Just you and her, in your natural states."

Etienne scratched his ear vigorously, turning away from her. She wondered if he were embarrassed by what she had said. She hadn't meant to insinuate anything.

"Anyway… if you need to run any errands or need me to pick something up for you, we should talk about it now. Even though it is early now, the time will go quickly."

"I would like to bathe. I want to be very well-groomed when I meet her."

"Sure, no problem. I don't need the bathroom for any length of time today. You can shower or bath, whichever you like. And there is plenty of soap and… hair care products in there."

"Thank you, that is very kind. I got everything else I needed yesterday, though I may need some time today to make sure that everything is prepared."

"Do you know where she is going to stay? I can't really offer her any space here. Not that you don't already know that."

"If she has not made arrangements for lodging, we will help her with that. James said that he could… e-transfer me money if we needed to do anything for her." He looked at Reg, eyes wide and helpless. "I don't know how."

"If you don't have a bank account, he can send it to mine and then we can take out cash or pay with a debit card."

His eyes were still wide. He had no clue about all the modern conveniences. He was still stuck back in the old days using cash and gold. He had no idea how the rest worked.

"Don't worry about it. We'll work it out. Your brother said he would help you with the negotiations too?"

"Yes. Though he is not experienced in matrimonial negotiation. I think… he never thought that he would need it. He married a modern girl like himself. They didn't go through all the rigor of a traditional courting and wedding arrangements. And he probably didn't think that I would ever meet a girl with prospects."

"Well, you surprised him, didn't you!" Reg scraped the last few vegetables across her plate and finished them off. She was astonished that she had eaten everything. Maybe if Etienne were feeding her all the time, she wouldn't be gaining so much weight. She wouldn't need to be eating fast food crap all the time.

Etienne made a snuffle of agreement and, when he was ready, prepared himself for his morning ablutions.

CHAPTER THIRTY

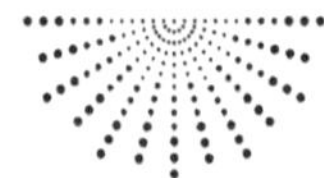

As Reg had predicted, the day passed by quickly. It seemed like they were either waiting for something that was taking forever or working feverishly on the arrangements. There didn't seem to be any happy medium.

Eventually, they were on their way to the dock. Reg ordered an Uber van, deciding she wasn't going to try fitting two Bigfoots into her little car. Even if they could be squeezed in, she was sure they would wreck the suspension.

"You can sit closer to me. No one is going to notice you," Reg encouraged. Probably no one would take a second look at him, even if they did see him beyond the reflection in the window.

"I am more comfortable back here," Etienne assured her. They had reconfigured the seating so that he was sitting by himself. After they picked up their charge, the two lovebirds could sit together and chat. Not exactly out of earshot of Reg and the Uber driver, but at least they would be able to talk. Etienne didn't seem to want to be alone with Ilka anyway. Reg didn't know if that was because he was afraid of her or because of Sasquatch courting traditions. She supposed that any old human culture would expect the prospective couple to be properly chaperoned as well.

"You're sure?"

Reg had helped get Etienne buckled into the seat without catching his fur in the mechanism. The Uber driver had not taken a good look at him, just glancing in the rear-view mirror as Reg got him settled. She supposed the driver thought he was just a hairy man or someone in an ape costume. Or maybe he picked up Sasquatches regularly.

"Yes." Etienne patted at his hair and face. "Do you think I look presentable? I do not want her thinking that I have not taken care of my appearance the first time we meet."

"You look good to me. And I'm sure she is used to men of all different sorts. She won't judge so much from your appearance. The two of you have been writing for how long?"

Etienne nodded but didn't answer the question. "She would not be that shallow."

"Right? I mean, you're not going to judge her by her appearance either, are you? She's been traveling for days; you don't know what kind of accommodations she might have on the boat. Whether she has her own room or has to share steerage with someone. If she's being treated as a guest or as… cargo. If she is dirty and matted, you're not going to assume that she doesn't care for you, are you?"

"No. I would not do that."

"And you know her. She won't either."

Etienne nodded. "Thank you. That is very wise."

"Good. Now just take long, deep breaths. Relax your muscles. Look forward to finally getting to meet your sweetheart face to face instead of getting anxious about what she is going to say. You'll have a wonderful time together."

Reg buckled herself in and confirmed the address at the docks with the Uber driver.

Etienne was quiet for the drive. Reg could hear him occasionally shifting around or rattling his last letter from Ilka again, making sure that he had every last detail right. It wouldn't do for him to show up on the wrong date or at the wrong place on the dock. Reg tried to send comforting, calming feelings Etienne's way. She wanted things to go as smoothly as possible for him. She didn't have anything invested in their relationship, but she wanted them to like each other and for

Etienne to be happy. Etienne was a nice guy and he had helped her out when she had been in a very bad place. He deserved his happiness in the cabin in the Everglades. Raising Sasquatch pups whose coats turned white in the winter.

They arrived well before the time specified in the letter, but Reg still looked around carefully to see if they were the only ones there waiting for the boat. She didn't see anyone else who seemed to be looking for it. And it hadn't arrived early. There was no disappointed female Bigfoot standing around waiting for them.

Etienne blew his breath out in relief. He looked around for a place to sit down, but rested on the bench for only a moment before getting up to pace back and forth, working off his restless energy.

Reg sat down with her phone and pulled up her email to see if there were anything she should be responding to. She was terrible at keeping up with her email, which was funny when she considered how much time she spent with the phone in her hand, looking for a way to entertain herself. But the tiny letters in the emails were difficult to read and she avoided them when she could. She needed to keep track of whether anyone registered for a psychic session through email. Sarah wasn't going to do that. And if people waited too long for a confirmation email, they would just go on to the next person on their lists. They wouldn't continue to wait for Reg, holding out for her return reply.

"I think that is it," Etienne said in a hushed voice.

Reg looked up from her phone and followed Etienne's gaze. There was a boat on the horizon. Not a little sailboat, but a cargo ship. Reg stood and walked up beside Etienne. The breeze was blowing the salty smell of the ocean into her face, sharpening her sense of smell. Reg tried to keep from reacting to it. She was just there with a friend, not to hunt. And the slightly musky, clean-fur smell of Etienne didn't attract her like that of Corvin or Davyn.

She squinted at the boat in the distance. "That could be it."

"The name matches the letter," Etienne told her, indicating the paper in his hands.

"You can read a name on that? I can barely see the boat!"

He looked at her, raising his brows. "Really? Humans do have weak eyes."

"Well… yeah, if you can see the writing on a boat when I can barely see what kind of craft it is!"

They both stood in anxious silence as they watched its sedate approach.

"Regina? What are you doing here?"

CHAPTER THIRTY-ONE

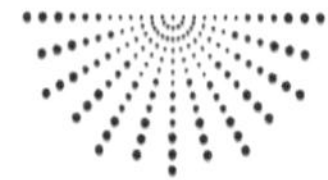

Reg turned around at the familiar voice. She glanced at Etienne anxiously, and then at the man who had addressed her. Corvin Hunter, of course. It figured that he would be there when she didn't want to be seen. Or when she didn't want her companion to be seen. She broke away from Etienne and walked toward Corvin, knowing that Etienne would stay glued in place where he was until the boat docked.

"Corvin."

He smiled, his intense eyes meeting hers, a thrill going through her just at his presence. She reminded herself that it was just a physical reaction to his charms. A biological function. It didn't mean anything. She tried to stay far enough away from him that she wouldn't catch his scent.

"What's going on?" Corvin looked at Etienne's back. "Who is with you?"

"A friend. Look, this is kind of private. I'll call you later and we can chat, okay?" She made a shooing motion to make him step back.

"Private?" It didn't seem to dissuade him, but to encourage his inquiry more. "I didn't imagine you would be out and about in public today, after seeing your picture in the newspaper."

"Yeah." Reg sighed. "But what am I going to do? I can't go underground every time someone thinks I had something to do with a crime. I didn't do anything, and sooner or later, they will figure that out."

She could feel Corvin probing at the edges of her mind, wondering how much of what she said was really how she felt. Reg tried to resist him, but the telepathic pathways between the two of them were too well-developed for her to keep him completely out.

"What's going on? Something has happened."

"I don't know. Stuff happens. We'll just let it all get sorted out. Everyone I talk to says it is nothing to be worried about. I just need to settle down and relax, and everything else will be fine."

"I haven't known you to be particularly predisposed to hysteria. If something is wrong, why don't you tell me about it?"

"Nothing is wrong. Now, like I said, this is a private thing," Reg motioned to Etienne. "If you could just go on your way, you and I can discuss my life later."

"What kind of private thing?" Corvin was looking curiously at Etienne's back.

"A family thing. He's just meeting someone off the boat."

Corvin gazed out to sea. "It's a cargo boat, not a passenger ship. I don't think that's the one his family member is going to be on."

"It could be. Sometimes… people arrive in this country in unconventional ways."

"If you're caught up in some kind of human smuggling, you could end up in considerable trouble."

"I'm not. It's nothing like that."

"Is that what this dead guy in the paper was all about? Human trafficking?"

"No. That was nothing to do with this. That was just… I don't know. I just happened to be there. It wasn't to do with Etienne or anyone else here in Black Sands."

"It was something to do with *someone* here in Black Sands," Corvin pointed out.

"Fine. Yes. With someone in Black Sands. But not me. I'm just helping out a friend. That body had nothing to do with it."

"It could be that you just don't know what the connection is."

Reg gave him her best glare.

Corvin backed down, holding up his hands and taking a step back. "Okay, okay."

He took another step back, trying to get a good angle on Etienne to see who he was. The wind from the sea shifted, and Etienne's cloak billowed out, revealing more of Etienne's body type and shape. Corvin's eyes popped.

"Is he a…? No, he couldn't be. Here? On the dock?"

"Just don't make a big deal, okay? He came here to meet someone. He doesn't want strangers hanging around while they meet."

"Who is he meeting?"

"Corvin, can you just go home? Or go do whatever you came here for? I need to be here to support a friend. It isn't any of your business and it isn't anything illegal." Though, of course, Reg had no idea if that were true. She didn't know whether Ilka was a stowaway, a paying passenger, or in a shipping container. But she didn't want Corvin there when Ilka got off.

Corvin hesitated. "I'd like to talk to you. I think there's something going on, and maybe we could talk, get it sorted out." He gazed into her eyes, and she could feel him again probing into her mind, trying to make sense of things. "Something just feels… off. Are you okay?"

"I don't want to talk about it. With everyone else who is already involved, I don't need to have someone else in on it."

"Who else is involved?" he prompted.

"No one. The police are on my case. I asked Sarah for some help. Other people are on the fringes… I'd rather not have to share it with anyone else."

"You know I am discreet. And I've been able to help you other times."

"This is different. Just go take care of whatever you are here for."

He sighed, but after a moment, he moved away from her. "Call me. Later, when you can talk."

Reg rolled her eyes and shook her head at his persistence. It was hard to know how to feel about his offer to help. There was always a danger in dealing with Corvin about anything. And too often, his offers to help came with strings attached. He had been useful in the past, it was true, and they had helped each other through difficult situations. But what she had said was true too; she didn't need the whole world knowing about her problems and felt like the story was already getting away from her. Jessup and Sarah both knew about her memory blanks. Corvin already knew something about her sporadic loss of powers, though of course she hadn't told him that it had happened again. Several of them knew about her strange new obsession with snakes.

When she'd had dreams about spiders, there had been a reason for it. They had represented the eight ghosts that were attached to a client. So did the snakes represent something? Or were they literal? If a snake had bitten the troll, and he was known to be a snake handler, then they were just something conjured up by her overactive imagination.

Reg rubbed the space between her eyebrows. She was thinking too hard, making herself tense and headachy. She needed to just relax and be there for Etienne. This was his moment.

CHAPTER THIRTY-TWO

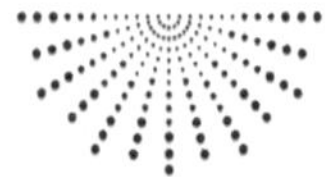

The boat was getting closer. Reg still couldn't see the writing on it as Etienne could, but it did appear to be coming directly toward them. Reg tried to quiet her mind as it approached. She sent calming waves of thought toward Etienne. He looked over his shoulder at her but did not motion her to stand with him. So Reg stayed back where she was. She tried to imagine what it would be like to meet her mate for the first time like this. They had been writing, they thought they were compatible, and Etienne fully expected to go on and marry Ilka, provided both of their families agreed.

Maybe part of the reason she couldn't fathom what that would be like was that she didn't have any family, let alone any traditions that would require them to be involved in her life in that way.

She could feel Etienne's excitement and anxiety as the boat drew close. She walked up and stood next to him. The boat was finally close enough for Reg to confirm that the name on the prow matched the name in Etienne's letter. There were shouts back and forth between the crew as the boat drew up to the dock. Lots of activity before it actually bumped up against the edge and was secured. Etienne practically vibrated next to her. He pulled his cloak around him so that his nature would not be as obvious to the crew of the boat. He watched the deck for any sign of Ilka.

They put down a gangplank and started unloading crates and pallets. Etienne and Reg moved to the side to give them space, watching anxiously for the passenger.

As the crew unloaded the cargo, a figure made its way across the deck. Like Etienne, she was wrapped in a cloak, but it was apparent even from the dock that she was very tall and broad. Etienne took a sharp intake of breath. Reg felt herself holding her breath as well, even though she didn't have anything at risk.

The crew pretended not to notice the tall figure, but it was obvious from the drop-off in their conversation and sideways glances that they were perfectly aware of her. They kept working at unloading the cargo. Ilka made her way behind one of them down the gangplank. Her hooded face was turned toward Etienne. When she reached them, she put out both hands to take his.

Her hands and wrists were covered with golden brown fur. Her hands were similar in size to Etienne's, the fingers only slightly slimmer. Their heights were almost exactly the same. Ilka leaned forward so that they got a better look at her face, though she kept the hood up to hide it from the workers. It was almost as hairy as Etienne's, though trimmed shorter, closer to her face. But she had not attempted to shave it off. It was fine, lighter in color than Etienne's red-brown, almost translucent around her eyes.

"Etienne," she whispered. Reg could detect the Russian accent in even just that one word. "I am Ilka. I am here."

Etienne squeezed her hands and said something to her that Reg could not understand. She wondered if she should walk away and let them talk to each other in private. She looked at Etienne and took a little step to the side. Etienne shook his head. "You will tell my brother we were not alone."

"I can still do that and give you a little room."

"I do not care," Ilka declared, "I do not need anyone's approval to choose a mate. I don't care about traditions. I am here," she pointed out, "I do not wait for anyone's permission."

"I know," Etienne agreed, sounding a little chagrined. "You are very… independent."

"If my father does not like the match, too bad. He is not here.

What is he going to do about it? And your brothers… they have not been a part of your life for many years. So why does it matter what they say? You and I know each other. We know it is a good match. We don't need anyone to tell us that."

Etienne nodded. He continued to hold her hands. "You are even more beautiful than your picture, *ma chéri*."

Ilka turned her face to the side demurely. If she were blushing, Reg could not see it through the fur.

"Do you have luggage to get off of the boat?" Reg asked, thinking that if they didn't need to wait, they could continue the conversation in the van, where both Bigfoots could lower their hoods and be more free with each other.

Ilka looked back toward the boat. "A trunk," she agreed.

On cue, a crew member wheeled a very large trunk toward them. Reg eyed it, wondering if it were actually going to fit in the van. She motioned the crewman toward the vehicle, and he nodded. When he got to the van, the Uber driver jumped out and started reconfiguring the seats and storage area once more, talking rapidly to the crewman, who gave no indication that he understood English.

Once he had the cargo area configured the way he wanted it, the two men tipped the trunk down flat and attempted to lift it into the van. Their muscles strained as they tried to get it up off the ground. Etienne and Ilka stepped forward to help. Ilka swept the two men aside with one swipe of her arm, picked up the trunk, and slid it into the van. The Uber driver stared with his mouth hanging open. The crewman from the boat pulled a handkerchief out of his pocket and mopped his sweaty face. He shrugged at the driver and headed back toward the boat with his wheeled cart.

The two Sasquatches got into the van and took their seats. Reg returned to her seat in the front. The Uber driver looked at her and looked like he had something to say. He made a couple of starting noises, but couldn't seem to get the words out.

"Did you have a hotel booked?" Reg asked Ilka. "I don't know what arrangements you have or haven't made."

Ilka looked at Etienne to see what he would offer. Since he was staying with Reg and already knew that she didn't have space for one Sasquatch, let alone two, he didn't offer to take her in.

"There are some acceptable hotels," he said, "if you don't have someone to stay with already."

"I guess so. I was hoping… we could go to your place."

Etienne stammered for the first time since Reg had met him. "Uh, m-my place is quite a distance away. You have probably had enough of travel today. We can get you settled in a local hotel and then call our families to see if we can come to an agreement."

Ilka made a growling sound deep in her throat. "That could take months. I am not willing to wait until they negotiate an agreement."

"We can at least give them a chance, see if they can come to a landing in the next day or two. Things will go much more smoothly if they think it was their idea."

Ilka cocked her head slightly as she considered this, then she nodded. "I suppose they will be easier to deal with if they can. But I am not going to wait more than a few days. If they will not talk, we can go to your house and wait until they break down."

Etienne rubbed the back of his neck anxiously. Ilka was obviously much more progressive than he was, and the suggestion that she could just move in with him without their family's approving the match obviously made him uncomfortable. Reg suspected that the arrangement had never been discussed in their letters.

"Do you have a preference for a chain?" Reg asked. She had no idea if Ilka or Etienne would be familiar with any of the American hotel chains. "Holiday Inn? Motel 6?"

"Whatever you think is appropriate," Etienne said with a shrug.

"I don't know, uh…" Reg looked at Ilka. She'd had the money to book passage to Florida, but had that exhausted her resources? Or did she have loads of cash? Would she be insulted if Reg put her in a lodging that was not up to her standards? Reg hated to imagine how Ilka would react if they insulted her. "Um…" Reg made a covert "money" gesture rubbing her thumb across her fingers, hoping Etienne would understand.

Etienne looked at her for a minute, frowning. "Oh." He turned to Ilka. "Do you have money?"

Reg laughed. Etienne was so old fashioned and careful to do and say things just the right way that she hadn't expected the bluntness.

Ilka nodded. "Of course. I wouldn't come here without anything."

Reg blew out her breath in relief. "Do you have a budget? A certain amount to spend on hotels?"

"Whatever is necessary. Nothing fancy, I will not be there long. We will need somewhere we can get food brought to the room."

"Sure. Somewhere with room service and a good restaurant. Or we can order something delivered."

Reg picked a midrange hotel and gave the name to the driver. He nodded his agreement and pulled out.

It was only a short drive. When they drove over the speed bumps in the parking lot, the van scraped bottom. Reg winced. Having two Bigfoots and one massive trunk in the van was probably not good for its suspension.

"Sorry," she said to the driver.

He just shook his head and looked in the rear-view mirror at his furry passengers. "Are they going to book the reservation?"

Reg looked at them. "I'll go in and get it done," she offered. "Just… I don't know if you have cash or a credit card…?"

Ilka reached into the capacious pockets of her cloak and came up with a minimalist wallet. She handed Reg a black credit card and what Reg assumed was the Russian version of an AAA card.

"Okay… I'll get you a room." She hoped that the hotel would take whatever the credit card and club card were. She didn't much feel like explaining to the desk clerk that she had a Yeti in the car and would they please at least try to process the strange credit card?

CHAPTER THIRTY-THREE

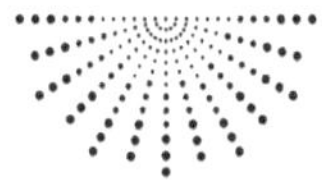

uckily, the desk clerk didn't seem the least bit surprised or puzzled by Ilka's foreign cards, and they went through on the first attempt. The clerk read through the messages that popped up on her screen.

"You qualify for free breakfast, concierge services, massage, and… a list of other services. If you need anything, please just ask. We would be happy to help."

"I'm actually not the guest; I'm just setting it up for her," Reg explained, her cheeks warm with embarrassment. She didn't want them treating her like she was something special and then being surprised by the sight and bulk of Ilka. "She'll be in in just a moment."

"Of course. Well, if she does need anything, she has only to ask."

Nice. Reg wouldn't mind treatment like that when she booked herself in at a hotel. Her experiences with hotels had been the opposite—having to prove that she would actually be able to pay for her stay. Enduring the owner of some shabby motel looking down his nose at her and grimacing like she smelled like an old, sick dog.

The woman quickly put together a folder with all the details Ilka would need, including the room key in the form of a proximity card. Reg went back out to the van to pass the folder on to Ilka.

"Is it all arranged?" Ilka asked.

"Yes." Reg reached out with the folder, but Ilka didn't take it. She and Etienne climbed out of the van and Ilka picked up the trunk with one hand as if it were no heavier than an average suitcase.

"Shall we go in, then?"

Reg led the way back into the hotel lobby. She nodded at the clerk, who watched their progress with wide eyes. Reg wasn't at all sure that all three of them would be able to ride the elevator together. They might only be three people, but she was still worried about exceeding the elevator's maximum capacity. And then what would happen? She'd rather not find out.

It made some loud grinding noises moving up the floors, but it didn't stop or plummet to the basement.

The doors opened on what looked like a penthouse suite. Reg opened her mouth to say that they must have gotten it wrong. She was pretty sure she had just booked a single suite with a king bed. Nothing as fancy as all that. But with the way the clerk had been behaving, maybe the credit card and points card had given Ilka an automatic upgrade.

Ilka strode into the suite and looked around, nodding. Etienne followed a few steps behind her, reaching out to take the trunk for her. He looked around with wide, surprised eyes. Reg was glad that she wasn't the only one who had misjudged the situation. Asking whether Ilka had enough money for a motel, when she apparently had enough for the presidential suite. Etienne had to be thinking of his rough little cabin in the Everglades, wondering what she would think when she arrived there. It was cozy, but had no amenities. Well, it did have flush toilets, at least. That was something.

Ilka allowed Etienne to take the trunk from her. He seemed just as capable of hefting it as she was. That was a relief. Reg didn't want Etienne to look like a weakling beside his bride. He was going to have to find some way to impress her. He looked around the suite and found the door to the bedroom, where he deposited her trunk carefully. He returned to the main reception area and sat down on one of the large pieces of furniture. "The, uh, bed is of a good size," he informed Ilka.

They all looked at each other.

"For *you*," Etienne clarified. "You would not want your legs to hang off the end."

"Yes," Ilka agreed, a small smile shifting the fine fur on her face. "Now, shall we get some food?"

"Do you need help?" Reg asked Etienne. "I should probably get back to my house. I'll tell the Uber driver that you won't need him anymore."

"We need a chaperone," Etienne insisted, looking almost panicked. "You cannot leave us here. In this place." His eyes went to the bedroom where he had just deposited the trunk. "It would not be proper."

"Oh. Okay." Reg had been hoping that once Ilka was checked in at the hotel, they would be able to manage on their own. But apparently, that was not going to be the end of it.

A few minutes later, Reg was on her way back down to the main floor of the hotel where the restaurant was, with written instructions from Ilka as to what she wanted prepared. Apparently, she did not understand about ordering off the menu and had insisted on making a special order.

Reg walked into the restaurant, a nice place with dim lights and real candles on the tables. Not the flickering-flame electric lights that many of the places Reg had been to used. Reg immediately felt her own fire calling out to the candles. She tried to tamp it down and to focus on the job at hand. She flushed with embarrassment when she was approached by the hostess to be seated. She handed the paper to the statuesque woman, giving a little grimace. "I'm sorry… I'm assisting one of the guests. She's from Russia, so there's kind of a cultural disconnect… she has made this order and asked me to bring it down to you."

The hostess looked down at the order, looking uncertain. "I'll… talk to the kitchen. What room is this for?"

"The, uh, penthouse suite, I guess?"

"Oh. Yes, we'll see what we can do about this. Do you want to stay here and wait, or would you like someone to bring it up to you?"

"Uh, maybe I'll hang out here for a bit." She needed to send the

Uber driver on his way, and would give Etienne and Ilka a little privacy, even though they didn't want it. No one could complain about them being unsupervised for a few minutes while Reg saw to their food. They had to eat, right?

The hostess nodded and indicated the bar. "Please feel free to have a seat, and whatever drink you like, on the house."

Apparently, there were even more perks associated with having the money to book the best suite in the hotel. Lots of free stuff seemed to come to those who could afford to pay for it all. Why didn't they give free stuff to the poor people and charge the rich people the higher prices they could afford to pay?

Reg sat at the bar and ordered a beer. She didn't need any fancy wine or cocktail. Just something to help relax her while she waited to see what the kitchen had to say about Ilka's special order.

She texted the Uber driver, checked her social networks, and watched a few videos, lost in the world of her little phone screen. Other people sat down to have a drink and then migrated to tables. The restaurant was filling up, getting noisier.

Eventually, Reg was roused by a tap on her shoulder. The hostess hovered there. Beyond her, Reg could see a couple of waiters with a number of covered platters.

"We have everything ready for the empress."

The empress?

Reg blinked in surprise. She looked around to see if the hostess could be talking to someone else. She pointed to herself, mouthing "me?" and the woman nodded impatiently.

"Yes, we have everything she requested."

"Uh, great."

Reg slid off the barstool. She tossed a bill on the counter for the bartender. Even if she was comped the drink, she thought she should still tip the bartender.

Reg led the way to the elevator, with the hostess at her side and the waiters trailing behind them. Reg had expected the hostess to stay behind in the restaurant, but apparently, she was hoping for some glimpse of the VIP's. They all rode up the elevator together in embarrassing silence. Reg thought she should probably make small talk, but had no idea what to say. She hadn't known anything but Ilka's name. Etienne had never told her that Ilka was an empress; she was quite sure of that.

No wonder the match was going to take some negotiating.

What did Etienne and his family have to offer the royal family, other than a little cabin in the swamp? Even though the two had been courting by mail, Reg was no longer quite so sure that it would be a simple matter of the families rubber-stamping their union.

CHAPTER THIRTY-FOUR

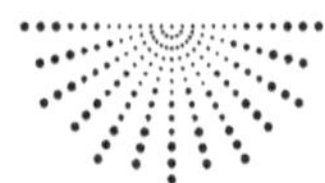

When the elevator doors opened on the suite, it was empty. Etienne and Ilka had apparently withdrawn to one of the other rooms so they would not be on display.

The waiters made their way over to the dining room table and began to lay out the platters and place settings. "How many people?" one of them asked.

"Uh… three."

He raised his brows and nodded, and they efficiently set the table. Reg could see that it was a lot of food for just three people. At least, for people of her size. Ilka and Etienne would eat a lot more than she would. Especially if Ilka had not been eating well on the boat. It wasn't exactly steerage suited for an empress.

They all waited around awkwardly after setting up the food. Reg wasn't sure whether to shoo them out, or whether she was expected to tip each of them. That could get expensive very quickly. But after looking at her expectantly for a moment, they ushered themselves out. Reg watched the light over the elevator for a moment to make sure that they were really gone.

"Everyone is gone again," she called out. "Food is here if you're hungry."

"We will be out in a moment," Ilka called out.

Reg stood by the table, wondering if she should sit down, hold Ilka's chair for her, or serve them. She had no idea what the empress was expecting.

It was a few minutes before Etienne and Ilka appeared. They had both removed their cloaks and looked more comfortable in their fur, with only the necessary minimal coverings. Reg tried not to stare at Ilka's shining golden-brown coat. Nothing had changed. Just because she was an empress—if the hostess had even been right about the title —she was no different from the woman who had hefted her own trunk not even an hour before. She was still the same person Reg had known about: Etienne's long-distance girlfriend, there to visit him and see if she could speed their union along.

But she couldn't help giving a little bow in Ilka's direction.

"I hope they got everything right. They said they had prepared everything you asked for."

Ilka's eyes swept over the table, and she nodded. "Yes, this looks very good."

The smell of the food made Reg hungry, even though she had not thought that she would be able to eat anything. She waited until Ilka and Etienne sat down, then took a third chair, not too close to either of them, but not separating herself down the other end of the table, either.

"It smells great. Did you know that Etienne is a very good cook?"

Ilka looked across at Etienne, giving a smile that showed her sharp teeth. "That is good! It is an important skill, especially when you are living so far from civilization."

At least she knew that the cabin Etienne lived in was remote. But then, Reg didn't know what sort of place Ilka came from. Even though she appeared to be at home in the lavish penthouse suite, that didn't mean it was the kind of place she had grown up in. Perhaps she was used to roughing it. Maybe she had gone away to finishing school to learn how to behave when she was among the rich, even if her home life was not like theirs.

Ilka and Etienne dished up the food. They gave Reg their names for the dishes, in English, French, Russian, or all three, and Reg nodded with interest. They would tell her a little bit about the background or story behind the dish, little folk tales that had been passed down from one generation to the next, or little tidbits about their families, like how James hated anything he declared mushy.

"Are you going to be calling James tonight? Or will you leave that for tomorrow?"

"We will attempt to get things started tonight," Etienne said. "If I can use your phone again."

"Sure, of course. They might have a computer that you could use here. You just have to—" At Etienne's look, she broke off. She wasn't going to teach him how to Skype or Zoom when he knew nothing at all about technology. "I'd be happy to help you."

"My thanks, Reg Rawlins. You have been most accommodating. I have been quite an imposition upon you."

"No, not at all. It's been nice having you here. And you've cooked for me, so how is that imposing? I haven't exactly been a good host."

"A good guest does not make the host feel inadequate."

"Well… I don't think that's on you. That's just me. I'm not used to having people stay over."

"Where are you staying tonight?" Ilka asked Etienne. "Not at her cottage again, surely. It is not appropriate."

"I don't have anything better," Reg said, embarrassed, "Or I would offer. I could ask Sarah whether you could stay in the big house. She has spare rooms. I'm sure she wouldn't mind…"

"No," Ilka said firmly. "It is not your responsibility. He should find somewhere better suited. Like here."

"You could book another room here," Reg suggested. "I could help you with that."

Etienne looked at Ilka uncomfortably. "I think it would be better for me to stay at another inn."

"You can stay here. You don't need to book another room or another hotel. Look at it," Ilka made a gesture. "There is plenty of room."

"But no chaperone," Etienne said. "We cannot ask Reg to stay all night. She needs to sleep. She has a cat."

"Then stay here without a chaperone," Ilka said brazenly.

"I cannot do that. Your honor…"

"My honor is not at risk. I am the same person whether we stay together or not. It does not matter what anyone else says or thinks."

"It matters to our families, to our community."

"They want cubs, do they not?" Ilka demanded. "If they do not want our people to die out, we need families. Large families. What is the point in courting for years and only having a cub or two in the time we have together?"

Etienne looked at Reg, his eyes wide. Reg tried not to smile at his shocked expression. Ilka was certainly an independent girl, quite happy to break their traditional rules if she thought it advisable.

"We are not starting a family tonight," Etienne said, his tone stubborn. "We will not rush into this so quickly. It is not seemly." He ate a couple of bites of his dinner. "I admire your ideas and your spirit, my Ilka, but I will not be hasty in this. We will follow at least some of the expected traditions as we prepare ourselves for a life together." The words seemed to stick in his throat. His brother had not yet approved their marriage, so even just indicating that he was prepared to start a life with Ilka was apparently a difficult step for him.

Ilka considered this, then nodded. "There is no need to rush into anything tonight," she agreed. "But do not think I am going to let our lives be dictated by our family representatives. If they do not agree or think that we are going to court for decades…" She shrugged. "We are old enough to make our own decisions without them."

Etienne gave a little nod as he ate. Reg looked down at her food, which she had nearly forgotten. She took a few more bites. It was very good, but not as good as Etienne's cooking had been. She looked over the various dishes, trying to identify all the vegetables. She had never been big on vegetables and didn't even know what all of them were called. She knew that Etienne did not eat flesh normally, but some of the dishes looked suspiciously meaty to her.

Ilka looked at Reg sharply. "We do not eat creatures," she said, giving a shake of her head. "Unlike you."

Reg swallowed, her cheeks hot. "I just don't know what they all are," she explained. Most of the cultures she had come into contact with while at Black Sands disapproved of mind-reading without the permission of the subject, but Reg remembered that Etienne had sometimes responded to her comments and questions before she voiced them as well. Had they read her mind or just guessed at what she was thinking?

Etienne made a motion toward Ilka to stop her, but Ilka went on.

"You smell like flesh," Ilka said, the fur on her face bristling as she wrinkled her nose. "Like the animals you eat."

Reg was mortified. She remembered the smell that had clung to Tybalt, the scent of putrefying flesh. It had nauseated her. Etienne had still been able to smell it on her the next day. But it had never occurred to her that they would be able to smell the meat that Reg consumed. She supposed it was just like the stronger smells that a human could detect, the garlic, onions, or alcohol that someone had recently eaten. And she remembered kids at school with different ethnic backgrounds who smelled different because of the different foods and spices they ate.

Reg broke into a sweat, which, of course, would only increase how strong her scent was to the Sasquatches.

"I'm sorry. I didn't realize…"

"They can't smell it themselves," Etienne told Ilka. "They don't have proper scent organs."

She waved this away. "They must be taught. I would never allow any of my attendants to eat meat."

"Reg Rawlins is not my attendant. She is a friend who offered to help."

"And she smells like flesh," Ilka maintained. "And snakes."

Etienne's gaze slid sideways to Reg.

"Snakes?" Reg repeated. "Why would I smell like snakes? I haven't touched or eaten any snakes."

Ilka shrugged. "I do not know what you have been doing. But it comes out of your pores."

Reg appealed to Etienne. "I haven't been doing anything with snakes."

"Perhaps from your visit to the cemetery?" Etienne suggested. "There was a snake there, was there not?"

"There was a snake there, but I didn't even see it, let alone touch it. I don't see how you would be able to smell that, especially a day or two later."

"I can smell it," Ilka maintained. "Like you have been handling snakes or their products."

"I haven't. There was a man killed who was a snake handler, but I only saw him; I didn't touch him."

Ilka considered. "Maybe that is why you smell so strongly of death and snakes. But you must have been very close to him for some time if it is true that you did not touch him."

"Well… I practically tripped over the guy. I didn't, but I was close. And they kept me there for a while because we were waiting for the groundskeeper to open the gate. Do you really think that would be enough to make the smell cling to me still?"

"No, I do not," Ilka said flatly. The implication was that Reg was lying and Ilka did not believe her.

There was silence around the table for some time. Reg tried to eat, but everything had turned dry and tasteless and kept sticking in her throat when she tried to swallow. She wanted to get up and leave, but Etienne had asked her to stay to chaperone them and she didn't want to let him down. She surreptitiously tried to build a protective spell around her to keep them from being able to smell her and being able to read her thoughts. She scratched her nose and sniffed her hand to see if she could smell the offending odor on herself. While she didn't smell putrefying flesh like she had on Tybalt, she did smell something sort of musky and wondered if it were snake.

How could she smell like snake when she hadn't had anything to do with them?

CHAPTER THIRTY-FIVE

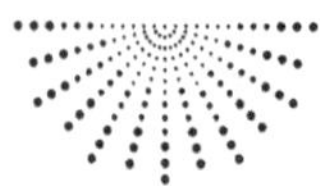

It was one of the most awkward evenings Reg had sat through. Normally, she would not have stayed, particularly after it had been pointed out how much she stank. But every time she made a gesture or looked toward the elevator, Etienne gave her a pleading, puppy-dog look, and she couldn't bring herself to insist that she go home.

She didn't try to visit with them; she just sat in the corner staring at her phone and ignoring their conversations. They didn't do anything that she thought a real chaperone would break them up for. They sat apart and didn't cuddle or kiss, just held hands occasionally or made cow eyes at each other.

Eventually, she was released from her duties to go home. Etienne asked if he might stay with her one more night and then he would find other accommodations if he were not able to go home yet. Reg couldn't bring herself to deny him. He had rescued her when she had been in desperate circumstances, and it wasn't his fault that Ilka had taken it upon herself to sail to America and try to take their relationship to the next level. That had clearly been all her.

"I am sorry to take so much of your time today," Etienne apologized when they were back at the cottage. "And for... any awkwardness."

Reg nodded. She fed Starlight without saying anything to Etienne in response. She hoped that the smell of the fish didn't bother Etienne too much. And she hoped that it did. Just a little. Because she was irritated at Ilka treating her the way she had and Etienne not standing up for her more. Saying that she didn't have a proper scent organ was not precisely the kind of defense she would have expected from a friend.

* * *

The phone rang in the small hours of the morning. Reg was lying in bed because she didn't have anything else to do, not because she was ready to sleep. She had been up too early that morning, so she was tired, but not sleepy. She petted and cuddled with Starlight and binge-watched an old TV series on her phone and wished that the next day was over so that she would have the cottage to herself again and didn't have to worry about Sasquatch mating rituals.

Reg saw it was Corvin. She swiped to answer the call. "Hi, Corvin."

"Regina," he greeted, voice husky and inviting, as always. "Is everything okay? You didn't call me. I've been worried about you."

"There's nothing to be worried about. I told you that I'm fine."

"And yet… I don't get the feeling that is true. Things feel disrupted and unsettled, and I know that you've had a run-in with the police."

"Everyone in town knows I've had a run-in with the police," Reg agreed unhappily.

"I'm sure not everyone read that article."

"No, there was probably one person who didn't."

Corvin chuckled at Reg's dark humor. "So tell me truly. What's going on. Are you well?"

"Just the same old stuff," Reg lied. "Still figuring this whole new world out. Nothing serious, I'll get it sorted out."

"I would be happy to help."

"I don't need help right now. I've got enough people who want to know all about everything that's going on in my life and to fix it. I don't want it all fixed. I want people to leave me alone."

"Perhaps what they think is broken is not."

"Yeah. Maybe that's it." Reg had always resented the authority figures in her life who had labeled her broken. Traumatized. Learning Disabled. Disturbed. Psychotic. Was it any wonder that she resisted people who said they wanted to help? "As if finding out that I was part siren wasn't enough… to suddenly have to deal with all of the stuff that entails… being triggered by water when I'm surrounded by it on three sides. People vandalizing my house and casting spells at me. I didn't need anything else right now."

"What else is going on?"

"Etienne visiting me. The snakes. This body in the cemetery."

"Snakes?"

"Did you know that they can smell snakes?"

"The… err…"

"Forest people is what they call themselves. They can smell snakes," Reg reiterated.

"Well, I suppose they do have a smell, and most creatures have a better sense of smell than humans."

"They say they're human too."

"Well then… our species or sub-species. We're kind of blind as far as smell goes."

"She said that I smelled like snake just from being in the graveyard."

"She…?"

"Ilka," Reg snapped, then realized there was no way for Corvin to know that or anything about Etienne's and Ilka's presence. "Sorry. Etienne's… fiancée."

"Ah, congratulations are in order. The Department for the Preservation of Endangered Species will be happy to hear that."

"Well, we'll have to see whether they actually do the deed first. They're not quite on the same page about everything."

She could see his shrug in her mind's eye. He didn't really care whether the couple got together or not. It was interesting, but it wouldn't have any impact on him personally, and for Corvin, everything was weighed by how it affected him.

Not that Reg could argue that she didn't evaluate most things the same way.

"So… what's this about snakes? In the graveyard? And you smelling like snake?"

"Oh… yeah."

"I'm very interested."

Reg shifted uncomfortably. Starlight stirred beside her, stretched out his paws, yawned, and settled again.

"The guy in the newspaper. He was killed by a snake. I guess they didn't release that detail."

"No. They said the cause of death was still under investigation."

"And I guess it is. Jessup hasn't said anything, and she said she would let me know. When they confirmed the cause of death. But he had a snake bite on him. And diamondbacks can be deadly with just one bite."

"They have the snake?"

"No."

"But you saw it."

"Mmm…" Reg tried to figure out how to say it. "I saw a snake… and thought it might be the same one. Or the same kind."

"I see. And the one you saw was a diamondback."

"Yeah."

"Those are nasty."

"He was supposed to be a snake handler. Someone who was used to snakes. But I guess even someone really familiar with them can make a mistake."

"Snake handlers do get bitten, at least the ones that I have heard of. But the more you get bitten, the more immune you become to the venom."

"As long as it doesn't kill you."

"Exactly," Corvin agreed.

"So he must not have been bitten by a diamondback before."

"I suppose. But it does seem odd. Where was he bitten?"

"The throat." Reg didn't tell him that she had thought of vampires. And thought of Corvin himself.

"Ah. Well, if it hit an artery, that would spread the poison very quickly."

Reg tried not to picture it. She didn't think that the troll's death had been agonizing. His expression had not been contorted. But maybe that didn't mean anything.

"So, how did you come into contact with this snake?" Corvin asked.

"I didn't. I haven't touched any snakes. That's why I was so surprised that Ilka could smell snakes around me. I didn't touch any of them."

"Any of them," Corvin repeated. "How many of them have there been?"

"Just… two real ones."

"And…?"

"Some that I've dreamed of, or had… sort of… visions of."

"Before or after the body in the cemetery?"

"Before."

"Premonitions, then."

"I don't know… maybe… but I didn't actually see anything that happened. I just keep… seeing and dreaming about snakes."

"And now you smell like them."

"Well… according to Ilka, yeah."

"This reminds me somewhat of the spiders."

"I was thinking that too. But I don't know why. If the spiders represented eight ghosts, what does a snake represent?"

CHAPTER THIRTY-SIX

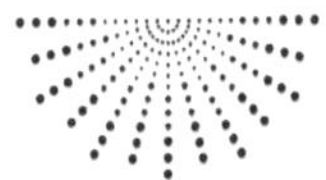

She could hear Corvin's chair squeaking as he settled back into it, considering. "What could snakes symbolize? Well, there is a lot of precedent. Snakes have symbolized many things over the ages, from sin to immortality."

"That's not helpful."

"I'm just warming up. There's a lot to think about."

Reg thought quickly, trying to head him off. Although she wanted to get to sleep, she didn't want to be talked to sleep by Professor Corvin. "What about that medical symbol? The rod with the snake."

"There isn't just one such symbol. The most well-known is probably the caduceus of Hermes, but there is also the Rod of Asclepius, the Staff of Moses, and the serpent Wadjet. If you go back to Sumerian and Mayan mythologies—"

"No. I just meant like the medic alert symbol."

"The Rod of Asclepius."

"So that represents… medical care?"

"Healing or medicine," Corvin agreed.

"So maybe… I don't know. I could be dreaming about snakes because… that guy would need emergency care. Only he didn't get it. So… that sucks."

"I think we need to dig deeper than that. The snake is such a potent symbol. The venom—and other parts of the snake—can be used for healing or for poison. It is both an instrument of death and, many have believed, an elixir of life and immortality."

"Wouldn't we know if it made people immortal?"

"Perhaps not. It would be a carefully-guarded secret. And there may be a special preparation technique or spell that is not widely known. Something to protect the person who uses it from its lethal qualities."

"You think snake venom can make you immortal?"

"No, I'm just speculating… you can't dismiss it out of hand."

"Even if it was… what would that have to do with me?"

"Well, we haven't connected anything up yet. Right now, we're just brainstorming. Thinking about what it might represent. Clearly, this man's death has intersected with you in some way."

"Yeah… I stumbled across his body. I never met him before or had anything to do with him. And he was a troll, Jessup said. Not a human."

"A troll. A snake-handling troll."

"Yeah."

"Why would he be handling snakes and how would that connect to you? Some people handle snakes for spiritual reasons. Sometimes it's for medical experimentation. Or just risk-taking behavior."

"I think Jessup thought it was the first one. A religious thing."

"I would be less likely to jump to that conclusion knowing he was a troll. Most trolls are not Pentecostal. He could be something more ancient; there are African and Asian snake cults. Christians are pretty new on the scene."

"So you think it was one of those? Or a different reason?"

"We'll have to see if we can squeeze it out of Marta. The police will be investigating his background, so they should know if he was a medical professional or frequently participated in risky behaviors."

"I'm not involved in any of that, though. So why would it intersect with me? Why would I be dreaming about snakes just because of some random troll I never heard of before and who I didn't have anything in common with."

"Has there been any pattern to these dreams or other appearances? Is it always when you are in a particular place or around a certain person? Or did they start when someone new came into your life? Like this Etienne."

"They started a few days ago… after the closing of the Games. After the equinox. Before Etienne came."

"But you had met him before."

"Yes. In the… in the Everglades."

"Ah!" Corvin sounded delighted to have made this connection. He had been with her in the Everglades. Though not, of course, when she had met Etienne. "So you had met him, and he came to you for… help with this situation?"

"I guess. Yes. I don't think he knows a lot of people in town. Though it turns out he's met Sarah before."

"I think Sarah has met everyone before," Corvin chuckled. "It's a much smaller world when you've been around as long as she has. I'm just thinking, you already had a connection with Etienne, so you might have started having dreams or visions when he decided to come to see you, even before you knew that he was coming to town. And the fact that his fiancée is the one person who, apparently, can smell snakes around you adds another layer of connection."

"But Etienne doesn't have anything to do with the snake-handler. How could he? He's not from here."

"Perhaps the troll isn't either. They could both share another connection. Have you told him about what happened? About the troll? Maybe he would be able to make the connection if he knew the details."

Reg was reluctant to involve Etienne. The Bigfoot would be leaving the next day. If he were the connection to snakes, then the snakes would stop, and Reg would know that he had been the trigger. If they kept appearing, then she would know that it wasn't anything to do with him. She didn't see how Ilka could have anything to do with a snake-handling troll in Florida. What kind of connection could there be with Russia?

"What about Russia? Do they represent something in Russia?"

"Well… there is the smey, the great Slavic dragon. They are frequently female, sometimes shapeshifters."

"Ooh." Reg wondered whether there could be a connection with Ilka. "What do they shift into? Yetis?"

"No." Corvin laughed. "Snakes. Handsome young shepherds. Not yetis."

"Dang. I thought maybe we had something there. I don't think they could be connected to Etienne, I really don't."

"Well… anyone else who has recently come into your life or asked you for help? Maybe a new client?"

"No. There was Julian, of course. But he was gone before the snake dreams started. Same with Wilson. I don't know why either of them would have anything to do with it. Clients… I really haven't had anyone lately. I've been kind of… not feeling up to par."

"You haven't been doing any readings? Any visions in the crystal?"

"No. Just… hanging around here. Watching TV. Playing with Starlight."

"And what does the cat think about the snakes?"

"He hasn't seen any of the real ones. I played with him with a shoelace…"

"Okay…" Corvin didn't see a connection there. "So, not something to do with the cat."

"No."

"Has anyone else seen them?"

"Forst saw the one in the yard. He chased it away."

"Did it bite him?"

"No. He used his shovel to chase it away. I don't remember—" Reg stopped herself.

"You don't remember what?"

"I don't… know. I forget what I was going to say." She wasn't willing to tell him about her memory blanks. No one else had been able to offer anything helpful concerning the memory lapses, and she didn't want to tell Corvin about them. "What about Adam and Eve?" she asked to divert him. "There was a snake in the story about them."

"Yes, there was," Corvin agreed. "The first deceiver. There are snakes bound up in many creation myths. People throughout the ages must have been quite mystified by them, seeing in them the power of creation out of nothingness."

"But you can't make something out of nothing," Reg said. She remembered something that Julian had said when talking with Harrison. "It's a law or something."

"The law of conservation," Corvin agreed. "But it's a theory rather than a rule—something we have observed but can't exactly explain. We can convert energy into matter, and who knows what other possibilities there are. Does magic ever break the law of conservation? We don't really know since we can't see or measure magic."

"But the whole world? You couldn't create the whole world out of nothing. Something little, maybe, but the whole thing?"

"Then where do you propose it came from?" Corvin asked, a smile in his voice. "Has it always been here? Forever? We can observe the universe expanding and, from that, we extrapolate the birth of the universe."

"And it didn't come from nothing, did it?" Reg challenged.

"No…"

"And a snake didn't make it."

He laughed. "Not as far as I know. But you might have to ask the immortals about that. They are much better at the whole creation myth thing than I am. They might give you a version that actually makes sense."

"I doubt it," Reg disagreed, "They can never answer any other question in a way that makes sense to me."

"Then maybe it is inexplicable."

"Yeah. I guess so. And nothing to do with snakes, so we're getting off topic." But getting him off topic was what she had wanted to do, wasn't it? Reg gave her head a shake. Maybe she was getting tired. Her thought processes were getting muddled.

"Perhaps I can come over tomorrow and we can discuss it some more," Corvin suggested.

Reg yawned. She squeezed her jaws closed again and murmured an apology. "We can talk some more," she said, though she thought better of it. "But don't come over."

"Ah, Reg. You could make things so much easier for yourself."

"For you, you mean."
"Yes, for me too," he agreed with a snort.

CHAPTER THIRTY-SEVEN

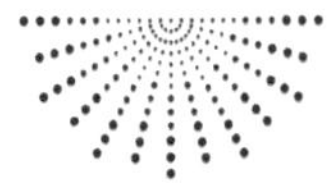

Something spoke to Reg in her dream. Was the whispering in her ear a snake hissing? Or was it a person? Her mind conjured up images like Voldemort in the Harry Potter movies, hissing to his snake Nagini in her own language. Harry could do that too, if she remembered right. But it wasn't as spooky when he did it.

Nagini. What was the name of the troll who died? It was something like that. Nagendra?

She tried to listen closely to the words of the snake in her ear. If she could just understand, it would unlock the door. It would be the last piece of the puzzle she had been trying to put together. Or maybe the first piece of the puzzle, she didn't have a lot of it put together yet. Or maybe none of it.

She listened to the hissing and thought that she had heard it before. Maybe she'd had other dreams about the snake and hadn't remembered. A snake-whisperer. Was that someone who talked to snakes or who could understand them? Or just someone who could make them listen to him. Wasn't there a myth about that, too? The Pied Piper? Or St. Patrick? Someone had called all of the snakes to himself.

She would hate that. She wouldn't do anything that would bring them all closer to her. Surrounded by piles of slithery snakes? No thanks.

"Who are you?" the snake in her ear demanded. "Why have you taken memories from me?"

Memories? Reg was the one who had lost memories, not the snake. She had lost powers and memories and maybe a little bit of her sanity since she had started seeing snakes. And apparently, the snakes were so real she actually smelled like them.

Reg wasn't the one who was crazy. She wasn't the one who could smell the scent of something she'd never even touched coming out of the pores of her skin. That was crazy.

"Who are you?" she returned. "Why do you keep hissing at me?"

She could feel him. Not outside of her, whispering in her ear. He was already in her brain. Coiling around, trying to establish himself and to read her mind. Trying to build a picture out of what she thought so that he could see her. Know who she was.

"I'm not trying to read your mind," Reg told it, "I just want you to go away. Go away and stop bothering me."

"You are here in *my* brain," the hissing voice objected. "You are the one who is where you should not be. You withdraw and leave my mind, and we will forget all about it."

Reg rubbed her head and tried to focus on what the words meant. She had not entered anyone else's mind. The whisperer had invaded her dreams, not the other way around.

"You're wrong," she insisted. "I never came to you. You came to me. And I don't want to see or touch any more snakes. I don't even like snakes. You keep them for yourself."

"You think you can take them away from me?" the whisper demanded, as if Reg had said the opposite. "The snakes are mine. I need them to accomplish my goals. You cannot touch the king of snakes."

"King snake?" Reg wondered. Her mind drifted to Ilka. The empress. Who was her king? Was he a snake? A snake man? A man snake? Her thoughts were slippery and disconnected.

"The king of snakes," the voice said harshly, some power behind the whisper. "The basilisk."

"Basilisk." Reg remembered there was a basilisk in one of the Harry Potter movies. A huge thing. She didn't want anything to do with a monster like that. "Why would I want a basilisk? Ew."

"The basilisk can kill, or it can confer immortality," the voice told her. It was beginning to sound familiar. As if she might know the person behind it. She tried to place it but could not. Who would want snakes? And why did he think that she had invaded his mind?

* * *

When Reg awoke, her sheets were all over the place, wrapped around her body and spilling onto the floor, all damp and soggy with sweat. The sun was shining in her window, heating up the room and making it muggy. Her air conditioning must not be working.

She looked around the room, unsticking her tongue from the roof of her mouth and trying to remember everything that had happened the past few days and the details of her dreams.

The memory blanks were still there. No new ones, she didn't think. If she walked out to the kitchen and found out that it was days or months later than she thought it was, then she would be proven wrong.

She ran her fingers through her braids, then forced herself to get out of bed and head to the bathroom.

She hadn't even bothered to look at her phone, but she had a pretty good idea it was too early for her to be fully awake yet. She had needed to catch up on her sleep and instead had fallen even further behind. She used the facilities and patted cold water onto her face, trying to wake herself up enough to make the decision whether to go back to bed or to have a cup of coffee and try to stay awake. Eventually, the lack of sleep would catch up to her and she would fall deeply asleep instead of having restless, disrupted cycles of wake and sleep.

Reg wandered into the kitchen preparation area, rubbing her eyes. She could hear breathing, and looked around, startled. After dreaming about that snake-like whisper in her ear half the night, she panicked at the idea of another presence in her cottage.

But when she turned and looked, she saw it was just Etienne. He was sitting up in his wooden chair, eyes closed, breath moving in and out very slowly. Asleep? Meditating? Reg didn't know whether to talk to him or sneak back to her room until he was up and around. She should serve her guest if he were awake, but if he were asleep, it wouldn't hurt anything to sneak back into bed.

Reg decided to make coffee. By the time it finished brewing, she should have a better idea of whether Etienne was awake or asleep. She was sure he must be awake. He was one of those early-riser types. But he didn't even twitch, breathing deeply and evenly in and out. A good facsimile of sleep if he wasn't actually in dreamland.

Reg prepared the coffee and watched it drip into the pot. Starlight meowed loudly for his food and Reg looked over at Etienne. Still not a twitch.

She looked through the fridge and found a partial can of cat food that hadn't been used up yet, and spooned some of the gelatinous contents into Starlight's dish amid his meowing demands for her to work faster and give it to him. She looked at the color and sniffed at it uncertainly. How long had it been in the fridge?

She placed it on the floor for him and watched the last few drips from the coffee machine. Good.

"Do you want coffee?" she asked Etienne in a normal voice.

He opened his eyes. "Yes, please."

Reg looked for her largest mug and poured his before hers. Etienne stood up and joined her at the kitchen island. It was dwarfed by his height. He must have had to crouch down to use it when he cooked. Reg hadn't noticed that before. She'd been too focused on her own issues.

"Did you sleep well?" she asked him.

"It was restless," Etienne admitted. He didn't criticize the sleeping accommodations—how could he, when he had known that if he stayed there instead of with Ilka or at another hotel, he would not have a bed to lie down in? "I had much to think about, and my brain did not want to quiet for sleep."

"Been there, done that," Reg said. "Oh boy, have I done that."

Etienne nodded and sipped the coffee.

"How did things go with James last night?" Reg asked. She had given Etienne her phone for a while, but had not asked him at the time how things had turned out. She had been too tired of Bigfoot problems to care anymore. But now that she'd had some sleep and didn't want to share her own issues, she turned back to them.

"James has some concerns," Etienne admitted. "As does Ilka's father. Both families are in favor of a union, but we cannot completely ignore the traditional rites and requirements."

"It seems like you worry a lot about what your families say. What about how the two of you feel? Do you think you're ready? You're compatible?"

"Ilka would like to join our families immediately, without waiting for the usual negotiations and rituals. But I am not in quite as much of a hurry. I would like to spend more time together… but that is difficult when she does not have a place to stay near my home and neither of us has a home here. One cannot stay in a hotel for more than a few days. Especially not… our people. We attract too much unwanted attention."

Reg nodded. She had seen how people watched them, tried to see their faces and get more information about them when they clearly did not want to be seen.

"Ilka… at the hotel, they called her the empress." Reg raised an eyebrow at Etienne. "Is she… royalty?"

Etienne sighed. "Yes. We are not… equals. And she is used to getting her own way. It makes things… challenging."

"Is that why her father is not sure about the two of you getting together?"

"No. He is quite happy to have her join with… a common man. But I think he believes she is too young to know her own mind yet and is worried she will change her mind later. Our people… mate for life. There is no rite for divorce or remarriage, as there is in your culture. If she were to change her mind later… it would bring great shame upon her entire family."

"Do you think she might change her mind?"

"I hope not… but her father knows her well. We have only just met in person for the first time. She has already broken with many of our practices by coming here on her own. That could bring scandal upon her family even without any further breaches." Etienne pondered. "I like her very much, and I think our families will come to terms."

"And you'll go ahead if they say yes?"

He was still for a few long moments, then nodded.

"Even though you think she might change her mind down the line?"

"Perhaps she will only be with me for a short time." Etienne took a long drink of his coffee, draining the mug. "For me, that is better than not at all."

"Even though you wouldn't be able to marry again?"

He nodded. "Yes."

* * *

It was agreed that Reg would go back to the hotel with Etienne so that he and Ilka could talk and the negotiations between their families continue. Reg was walking ahead of Etienne to the front of the house where her car was parked. As soon as she crossed the border between the back yard and the front, she stopped. She could feel a difference between the protected space she had been in and the front sidewalk and yard. She and Sarah had set the wards in the back to block malevolent witches from approaching Reg's cottage to vandalize it or harass her, but they had set them only in the back.

Etienne stopped behind her, waiting. She could hear him sniffing the breeze and wondered what his very sensitive scent organ could detect. She had to rely on her eyes. She saw a car parked close to hers that didn't belong on the street. There were shadowy figures inside. There was no legitimate reason Reg could think of for two people to be sitting on the road in front of the house. It wasn't the kind of place where people just pulled over to take in the view. It wasn't a car she recognized, and no one got out to go to the door of any of the nearby houses. They just sat there.

"Stay here," Reg ordered. "Unless I call you."

Etienne breathed quietly, saying nothing. He was used to hiding from observers and searchers. He knew how to keep quiet and not give himself away. The magical protections would help keep him hidden from outside eyes.

Reg walked closer to the vehicle. She was almost right up to it when the doors popped open and the two occupants stepped out. Reg had seen both of them before. Detective Marta Jessup, who could sometimes be called a friend, and her partner. Devaughn, Reg reminded herself, looking at his name bar.

"What are you two doing here?" Reg asked, not being terribly polite.

"We wanted to talk to you," Jessup said. "We had some more questions for you. Would you mind coming in to the police station, please?"

"Why would I want to go to the police station again? I already told you everything I could, which is nothing. I didn't know the guy. I never met him before. I don't know anything about how he died, other than from what you've told me."

"We would still like to talk with you."

Reg could have tried inviting them to the cottage to talk, but she didn't want to put Etienne into an awkward position. And the other times when she'd had a couple of cops in her house, things had not turned out well. She could refuse to go with them or she could agree. If she refused, there might be consequences. They might come back with a warrant to search her house and they might arrest her. They didn't have enough information to arrest her—she was pretty sure of that—but sometimes cops didn't exactly follow all the rules. Some of them were prone to doing an end-run around procedures if they thought they could get away with it. Devaughn was there to babysit Jessup and make sure she didn't break any rules, but Reg didn't know anything about him. He might be the type who could be talked into things.

"I don't have anything else to tell you," she tried again.

"Maybe we have some things to tell you."

Reg studied Jessup, trying to figure out what she was getting at. What would they have to tell Reg? Police didn't share information. They gathered it and they kept what they gathered close to the chest. Though Jessup had already told Reg several things about the investigation that she probably shouldn't have, to see if Reg could make any connections. No one believed that Reg could have just stumbled over the body by accident. Even if she hadn't known anything about it ahead of time, something had led Reg there.

Only Reg had no idea what it was, and neither did anyone else.

"Why don't you just tell me about it here," Reg suggested.

"We would like you to come to the police station." Jessup raised one eyebrow and looked at Reg intently. Trying to tell her something, to give her a signal, but Reg had no idea what it was. She and Jessup were rarely on the same wavelength. Reading her took a lot of effort, and Reg needed her strength and brainpower to get through the day if she had to go to the police station for questioning.

CHAPTER THIRTY-EIGHT

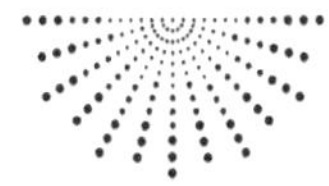

tienne knew Sarah. So he could go to her for help. Reg didn't need to feel guilty about leaving him behind. She was protecting him. By leaving with the police, she made it possible for him to still go and meet with Ilka unmolested. Of course, he might feel differently if he had Sarah drive him to the hotel. He would be taking his life in his hands. Or putting it into Sarah's. He might have preferred facing the police.

Hopefully, he would just get an Uber, having seen how that worked the day before. He didn't have a cell phone of his own, but Sarah could order a car for him. By the time he was ready to leave the hotel, Reg would be finished at the police station and could arrange to pick him up.

"I'll take my own car," Reg said firmly. "I'm not going in yours."

"You'll come to the station?" Jessup asked.

Reg nodded. "Yes… for a little while. But I can leave whenever I want."

"You are not under arrest," Devaughn agreed. He had remained quiet, letting Jessup make the request.

"I'll come in my car," Reg reiterated.

Jessup nodded. "We'll see you there, then."

They climbed back into their car, but they didn't pull out. They stayed behind Reg's car until she pulled away from the curb, then followed. They stayed right on her tail all the way to the police station. It was a good thing Reg didn't need to stop for gas. They might have rear-ended her.

Jessup escorted Reg into the building, standing very close to her, friendly and helpful. Reg looked sideways at her. "You mind giving me some space?"

Jessup moved a few inches away. "Sorry. We'll just go over here to one of the conference rooms and see if we can work anything out." She pointed to the hallway Reg had been down before.

"You said you have some things to tell me," Reg reminded her. This was to be an information session, not an interrogation.

"Yes, yes, we'll cover that once we sit down."

Reg went warily into the interview room Jessup pointed out. She took an uncomfortable chair and looked around the cold, cheerless room. Like most of the interview rooms she had been in, it was not a happy place. Sometimes, nicer rooms were used to talk to families, witnesses, and victims, but Reg didn't usually get one of those. She folded her arms across her chest and looked at Jessup.

"Okay, what's new?"

"First, I wanted to know if you have remembered anything or if anything came to mind that you might want to share with us."

Reg pressed her lips together, reminding herself not to say anything stupid. "No."

"No to both?"

Reg stared at her, waiting for her to move on.

"Okay. I told you a little bit about the victim. We still only have his street name..." Jessup gave Reg a significant look, warning her that Devaughn and the police department clearly were not in on the fact that Nagendra was a troll. "The postmortem has been completed and the ME has given her opinion that he died of a snakebite."

"Diamondback?" Reg asked, then bit her lip, wishing she could take the query back. It had flown out of her mouth too fast for her to stop herself. Devaughn looked surprised at her question. She probably wasn't supposed to know that part.

"Uh, surprisingly, no," Jessup said. She spoke slowly. "We thought from the circumstances that a diamondback was probably the most likely scenario, but the ME says not. She has some other possibilities to check still, but so far, the kind of snake is unknown."

"Unknown?" Reg frowned. Was it that hard to identify what kind of snake had bitten someone? She had thought that each snake would have a different kind of venom, and it would be easy for the scientists to put some on a slide, stick it in a machine like the ones on TV, and it would come back with a spectro-something analysis showing certain peaks that would tell them which kind of snake it had come from. But apparently, it wasn't quite that easy. Maybe all rattlesnakes had the same type of venom. Or there were only certain kinds entered into the database and they were missing more rare species of snakes. Or they couldn't get a good enough sample of the venom from the troll's bite mark. Who knew? Science didn't always work the way it was shown on TV.

"Unknown," Jessup agreed, nodding. "She'll send the test results around to a few snake people and see if they can be of any help, but she said it didn't match anything she had in her reference materials. Not something widely known."

"Do you think… it's a new kind of snake they've never seen before? They talk about there being all of these new species of animals around us, like frogs and insects, and we don't even know it."

Jessup's shoulders lifted and fell. "She'll do some more checking."

Reg nodded. She waited for more information or questions.

"I have a request for you, Reg," Jessup said, using a friendly, encouraging tone.

Reg was immediately on alert. Jessup normally wouldn't dare call her Reg in front of her coworkers. Nothing to indicate that they had a close relationship. Jessup calling her Reg now could only mean that Devaughn would approve of her treating Reg like she was an ally, asking for favors.

"I've told you everything I can."

"I know. What I'm wondering is… would you look at Mr. Nagendra, see if maybe his face triggers anything for you…?"

"You already showed me his picture. I don't know him, and it didn't make me think of anything."

"I don't mean his picture. I mean him."

Jessup wanted her to look at the body. *Ew.* Reg started to shake her head. Why would looking at the body be any better than the pictures Jessup had already shown her? It wasn't like Nagendra would look more lifelike in person than he had in the pictures. Reg would have to deal with any postmortem bloat, the smell, and who knew what other indignities at the morgue. They didn't take civilians to the morgue, she knew. That was just a dramatic TV thing. In real life, they showed pictures or a TV screen. Not face-to-face.

Jessup waited for Reg to finish working it through. Reg took it a step further. Why would it make a difference for her to see Nagendra's body in person?

Reg *did* communicate with the dead. That was kind of her thing. And one thing that would be different attending in person instead of looking at a picture would be how strong his spiritual presence was. There was no guarantee that Reg would be able to see or hear his ghost. But if she could, it would be strongest where his body was, until he was buried.

CHAPTER THIRTY-NINE

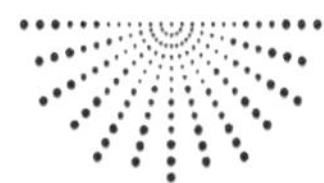

Reg wasn't keen on seeing the body. She heard enough ghostly voices without intentionally putting herself into the path of another. But Jessup was right; it was the one thing that she could do for them. No one else could ask Nagendra what had happened to him, just Reg.

The medical examiner's office was in the same building as the police station, so they didn't have to go anywhere else. Just a walk down the hall to take the elevator to the basement. Why were morgues always in the basement? Because it was easier to keep them cold? Because nobody wanted to see them by accident?

To keep the ghosts away from everyone else?

Reg waited in an undecorated lobby area with Devaughn while Jessup went in to talk to the medical examiner and get things prepped for her. Reg was a little nervous about how it was all supposed to go. She couldn't very well have a conversation with a ghost with nonbelievers watching. Not if Jessup wanted her to give them something usable as if she were just a regular witness who happened to remember something when she saw the victim's face in person. She wasn't sure how they were going to swing it.

Eventually, Jessup returned, nodding at Reg and motioning her to enter. Devaughn stayed in the waiting area.

It wasn't a dark place like Reg had imagined. It looked pretty much like an operating room. Brightly-lit, everything white or brushed steel, lots of cruel-looking implements. Like they were going to do surgery on a live person instead of a body. Reg didn't see any drawers full of people in refrigeration. She looked away from the table with a sheet pulled over a lumpy form.

A woman in scrubs stood in the room, looking Reg over. Her arms were crossed in front of her. "I repeat my objection. This is highly unusual."

"The witness insisted," Jessup said. "This is the only way she would identify the body. Said she couldn't do it from a picture or a video."

The medical examiner shook her head.

"If you could leave us alone for a couple of minutes," Jessup suggested. "We won't be long."

Reg was already getting a headache. She should have known better than to go somewhere a bunch of ghosts would be hanging out. When she had gone to the ghost village, at least Corvin had given her extra strength and helped her hold a protection spell around her to keep the ghosts from swarming her, fighting to use her for their own purposes. She pressed her fingers against her forehead, trying to stay in control of herself.

The medical examiner looked at Reg for a minute, opening her mouth as if she would object again. Then she just shook her head and walked out. Jessup waited until the door clicked behind her, then turned to Reg.

"Okay. I don't know how long we will have, so make it quick." Jessup walked to the table and folded the sheet back from the troll's face. She placed herself between Reg and the nearby camera so that Reg could appear to be looking at the body even if she were doing something else. Reg turned her back to the camera and looked down.

"You don't actually have to look at him, if that helps," Jessup whispered. "Do you need me to do anything?"

Reg wished that Jessup *could* do something. "Look," she said, rubbing her head painfully. "This place is full of ghosts. This wasn't a good idea."

"Can't you see him? Do you need help with knowing which one is him?" Jessup clearly didn't understand the problem.

"They all want to talk," she said, forcing the words out. "Imagine everyone in Disneyland trying to get on the rides at the same time."

"Uh, okay. So how can I help with that?"

"You can't. You don't have any gifts. It didn't occur to you that this wouldn't be easy?"

"Sorry, no. I just thought… his body is here, so maybe you'd be able to see his ghost and figure out what was going on here… give me a tip or two that might help solve the case."

"Well, no trouble seeing the ghosts."

"Sorry."

Reg looked down at the body, hoping that it would help her focus all her energy on the one ghost and shut the others out. One, in particular, a little girl, was niggling at her. Standing off to the side, crying, asking for help. Reg didn't know how to ignore her. Kids were always the worst. How could Reg explain to her why her life had been cut short and that she wasn't going to be able to do any of those things that she'd wanted to do when she grew up? It was over. She didn't get to be with her family, grow up, date, work, travel the world, or try new foods. She was stuck until she was able to accept it and move on with her next life, whatever form that took.

Nagendra's face was puffy and doughy looking. Gray. Like a developing bruise. The smell was powerful, making her want to back away and just get out of there before she threw up. She could see the bite mark on his neck. It was bigger than it had seemed in the picture. She had pictured a small snake, but now she was thinking of something larger. She didn't know how big rattlesnakes could get. She knew they could open their mouths really wide, and that would make the bite look like it came from a larger animal, but what came to mind was a huge python. The kind that could swallow an alligator.

Reg took a deep breath in and gagged, nearly losing her lunch—or her morning coffee—right there. She forced it back down and tried to slow the beating of her heart.

"I am here for you," she murmured. It would be safer to talk to him in her mind, but with the distraction of the other ghosts, it helped her to hear the words aloud. She grasped the sound of the words and tried to hold them, to keep them from slipping away from her.

"You are the vessel," came the mournful response.

Reg focused on the ghost on the other side of the table. Nagendra's ghost resolved, looking more solid. Reg hoped that he didn't grow solid enough for Jessup to see him or to show up on the camera feed. She would have a hard time explaining that. Though people usually came up with their own explanations when what their senses told them was in opposition to their beliefs about what was true.

"Nagendra," Reg said, rolling his name around her mouth. It was a strange name, but it didn't seem foreign to her. It seemed completely appropriate, with him standing and lying there in front of her.

"You are the vessel," the ghost repeated.

Reg tried to process the words and to understand what they meant. She cocked her head and looked at him.

"The vessel. What does that mean?"

"He said there was another. Someone who was sharing consciousness with him. He was unable to complete the spell because he was tainted."

"Who? Who are you talking about? What was the spell?"

"I told him he needed to be pure for it to have a chance of working. He thought that because of his great power, he could work the spell himself, that it wouldn't matter."

"What spell? What was he trying to do?"

"The basilisk." The ghost touched his throat where the snake bite was on his corpse. "He was angry when it didn't work."

"What is a basilisk?" But even as Reg said it, she remembered the basilisk in Harry Potter and her discussion with Corvin. Had it appeared in her dream? A snake. A big snake. Bigger than the python she had imagined.

Nagendra was shaking his head. "Not like that. That is... imaginary."

Reg shrugged, feeling herself blush. "I know that. What is the basilisk?"

"It is… a great snake. Powerful. The venom confers longevity. Perhaps immortality."

"Oh. Then… Corvin was right." She shook her head. "But what does that have to do with me? Why am I involved?"

"You are the vessel. Your blood ties you together."

Reg immediately thought of Calliopia and Ruan. The blood of three races on Calliopia's blade had been powerful magic that had bound them together. Did this have something to do with Ruan? She couldn't imagine why he would be trying to put a spell on her or trying to achieve immortality. He wanted to be with Calliopia, and if he was immortal and she was not, then the day would come when they had to be parted. She couldn't see Ruan choosing that.

Whose blood, then? Reg had been referred to as Weston's blood. But he was already an immortal. He didn't need any snake for that.

The 'he' that Nagendra spoke of had to be someone else. She couldn't quite tie it all together. She was missing a piece.

"Who? Who are you talking about?"

The ghost looked at her. "The great wizard."

"The great wizard. Do you mean Wilson? Is that who?"

The name didn't seem to mean anything to him. Maybe Wilson had never introduced himself by name, only by his qualifications. Or maybe he had paid Nagendra for his services and the payment itself had been identification enough. Like a drug dealer who didn't need to know his customers' names, as long as they were able to pay.

"The great wizard," Nagendra repeated. "He who you share blood with. I told him it would not work as long as he was tainted, but he did not believe."

"How did he get tainted with my blood?"

"You put a spell on him," the ghost said. "Without his knowledge."

Reg thought back to their few interactions. She had never done anything to Wilson until he had drunk the tea and his memory had returned to him. Until then, he had been a nice old man, but when he remembered himself, things were completely different. And Reg had felt obliged to protect herself and the others by using a protection spell to counter Wilson's power. Was that what Nagendra meant?

But there had been no exchange of blood, literal or figurative, in that spell. They hadn't touched each other physically. It had just been mind against mind, power against power. And eventually, Wilson had conceded. Reg had not seen him since.

CHAPTER FORTY

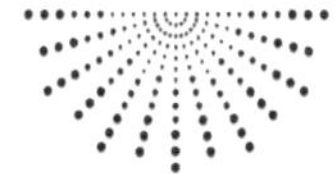

"Reg? Reg, are you okay?"

Reg was woozy, but she pushed any assisting hands away. She didn't want help. She didn't want anyone to touch her. She braced herself against the cool steel of the table, trying to get her bearings back.

"This is why we don't do in-person identifications," a woman's voice snapped. "Besides the fact that there could be contamination of the body. No one needs to see the person they knew face to face."

"She'll be okay in a minute," another voice said defensively. "Let's get her out of here and back into the other room. It will be fine."

Again, the hands tried to help her. Reg blinked, trying to look around her and take in what she was seeing. The shift had been rockier than usual. Probably because she had been trying to maintain a protection spell at the same time. It was easier during sleep. She rubbed her eyes with one hand and stared down at Nagendra's bloated corpse on the table.

It served him right. Nagendra had failed. He had promised results and then he had gone back on his word, saying that it wasn't his fault. Then whose fault was it?

"Let's just go this way," the policewoman said, trying to direct Reg to the door. "You'll feel better once you get a bit of fresh air."

It was strange seeing through Reg's eyes. The room, which physically contained only the body and the three women, was filled with ghosts of all description. Faint ones that looked like skinny, strung-out junkies. Bums. An old, well-cared-for woman who seemed to be confused as to why she was there. And Nagendra's ghost, hovering over the table as if he could do something by hanging around. Bring his inanimate corpse back to life.

Of course, it could be done, but not with the power that Nagendra took with him as a spirit. Too little power to take his body, or any body, back. Ghosts were weak by their very natures. Just another reason Reg never wanted to die.

Reg walked toward the door, feeling at first like she couldn't remember where to put her feet, but getting gradually steadier so that both women didn't look like they were going to have to dive in to save her if she fainted.

She walked out of the door and saw the other policeman waiting there. She didn't remember the names of either one and looked at their name bars to refresh her memory. The woman was Jessup, and the man was Devaughn. The woman in scrubs didn't have a name tag. Reg supposed she was a lab worker who would put the body away when they were done.

"Sit down over here," Jessup instructed, motioning toward a couple of unoccupied chairs.

"I don't need to sit down."

"I would feel better about it if you did. Just for a few minutes until I'm sure you're okay."

"There's nothing wrong with me."

"Did you have breakfast this morning?"

"I don't remember. Probably not."

"That's maybe not the best idea when you're going to be coming over to the police station to identify a body."

Reg just looked at her. Jessup shrugged. "Yes, okay, I didn't exactly have a chance to warn you that's what we were going to be doing today. Maybe I should have brought some pastries or muffins so that you could have had something before going in there."

"And ended up with her barfing all over the morgue floor," Devaughn suggested.

Jessup sighed. She looked at her partner. "Would you mind seeing if you could find some ginger ale? Something sugary to make sure that Reg isn't going to faint on me here."

"I'm fine," Reg repeated.

Devaughn nodded to acknowledge his partner's request and retreated through the door that led to the hallway and the elevator. It would take him a few minutes to get up to the nearest vending machine or corner store and back again. Jessup spoke in a low, urgent tone. "What did you see, Reg? What can you tell me about what the ghost said? I could only hear what you were saying, and that wasn't particularly enlightening."

"He didn't know what he was talking about. I don't think he had any idea who killed him or why. It was probably just an accident. People who handle snakes… They all end up getting bitten sooner or later."

Jessup gave Reg a puzzled look. "What did he say about a basilisk?"

"He didn't know anything about it."

"He's the one who brought it up; you said you didn't know what it was."

"It's a kind of snake. Very rare."

"I know what a basilisk is. What does it have to do with this case?"

"Nothing at all. It was misdirection."

"Reg. What are you hiding from me? What's going on?"

"I've done everything you asked me to do, but I can't help you like you hoped. Sorry."

They looked at each other, Jessup's eyes pleading for more. Reg could feel her frustration over the way things had ended up. She had figured that there was at least a shot that Reg would be able to get some vital information out of the ghost. The troll had to know how he had died, didn't he? But Reg's non-cooperation or lack of results stymied her. Which was fine because Reg didn't actually want Jessup to make any progress on the case. Dead guy in the cemetery. Bitten by a snake. The end. Nothing further to investigate.

Reg didn't know what Jessup could see when she looked into her eyes. Could she see the difference in her witness between the time she had entered the morgue and the time she broke off contact with the ghost? Or were the cop's gifts so weak that she couldn't even guess at what was happening?

Devaughn returned with a soft drink. He handed it to the woman, who popped the tab and handed it over to Reg. "It would make me feel a lot better if you could get some of that down. I don't want you to be sick or to have an accident driving home."

Reg sipped at the cloyingly sweet drink, holding her breath so that she didn't have to taste it. She'd had so many soft drinks when she had been in the Everglades that she never wanted to drink another one again. What vile stuff. Highway robbery to even charge anything for the sickly sweet, flavored water. Bubbles didn't make it any more appealing.

* * *

It was some time before Jessup agreed to let Reg go on her way. She had done her best to keep Reg there under the guise of being worried that she was too sick to drive but, eventually, she had to give up on that and let her go anyway. She could follow in her own car if she were that worried about it. See that Reg got home safely. But she didn't. She had reports to file, even if she hadn't found out what she wanted to.

When Reg reached home, there was a white compact car parked in front of the house. Someone visiting Sarah? She reached out with her powers. They were a little unwieldy; Reg wasn't familiar enough with how her mind worked to handle them dexterously, but she managed to figure it out. The visitor had not gone into the house, but was somewhere close by. Waiting. Reg got out of the car and looked around warily. She didn't want anyone ambushing her.

She was warm and the air seemed thick and sweet and scented with flowers.

Nothing but a warm spring day. Just perceived through someone else's senses.

But as Reg took the pathway toward the back yard, she saw a male form waiting in the shadow of a tree. She stopped abruptly, raising her hand to cast a protection spell before he could get the drop on her. The man stepped forward, smiling, his manner reassuring.

"Regina," he crooned, "it's just me."

He was one of the men who had accompanied Reg when she was in the Everglades. One of the men who had helped remove Wilson from that place and bring him to Black Sands for the Spring Games. But he had not been there when Wilson had reawakened. She fished for the name. They knew each other well; it wouldn't do to get the name wrong. Corwin? Corvid?

"What are you doing here?" she demanded.

"I'm concerned about you, Regina. The way you've been behaving for the last few days. Your… lapses. I can feel shifts in your consciousness, back and forth. At first, I thought I just imagined it." He took a step toward her, smiling reassuringly, the scent of roses growing stronger. Someone should tell the guy he was using way too much cologne. "Tell me what's going on."

"Stay back," Reg ordered, feeling a wave of warmth and giddiness as he got closer. She strengthened the protection spell she had started to build, trying to protect herself from his influence. But he was powerful.

Where had he gotten so much power? As a seeker of power herself, Reg was interested in the answer to that question. Most witches found it difficult to add to their powers. They exercised the gifts they already had, learned, and practiced in their areas, but they rarely built more power.

"Reg. What's going on?" He leaned forward.

Corvin. The name came to her suddenly. Corvin the Hunter. And he *was* on the hunt, but pretending to be concerned with Reg's well-being. *A power-drinker.* He was trying to get inside of Reg's mind to figure out what was going on, and that couldn't be allowed.

"Get out, witch!" Reg pushed back, the force of her mental power so strong that Corvin went stumbling several steps backward before catching himself and looking at her in surprise.

His eyes were dark and piercing, staring into her eyes. "You are not Regina."

CHAPTER FORTY-ONE

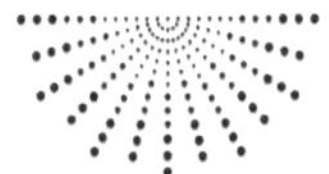

eg flashed him a confused smile. "What do you mean I'm not Regina? I'm standing right here in front of you; you can see that."

"I can see the form you've taken. But you are not her."

"I am."

Corvin reached out to take Reg's hand. She pulled back. Touching would give him a stronger connection to her. He was already too close to the truth.

"If it's you, you'll let me touch you, verify it."

"No. Nice try. I know what you are, and I do not consent to your terms."

Corvin cocked an eyebrow. He looked slightly amused at this. "You know what I am."

"Yes."

"You have known that for a long time. It isn't something new."

Reg shrugged. "Nevertheless. You will not take my powers."

"You are not Regina," he repeated.

"Stop saying that. You can see who I am. Now get off my property, or I'll call the police."

"This is not your property."

Reg looked around her. "Yes, it is."

"It belongs to Sarah."

"It does not belong to you. I live here, and I'm telling you that you're trespassing. So go away."

He didn't move. "Who are you going to call? Jessup?"

Reg's lips tightened. "I don't need Jessup. I can just call 9-1-1. They'll remove you from the property."

"Go ahead." He leaned forward again, smiling wolfishly.

Reg considered her options. The police would come. They would remove Corvin from the property. But what effect would that have on her? She would have to deal with the police again. What if Corvin decided to tell them that Regina was not really Regina? He wouldn't be able to prove it, of course; everything that the police could see and measure would tell them that she was Reg Rawlins. But did she want that complication on top of everything else she had to deal with that day?

"Just go away and then I won't have to," she told him.

Reg eyed the gate. Once she got past there, she was pretty sure that he would be barred by the protective wards from following her to the door of her cottage. She would be safe. She stepped toward the gate. Just a few steps and she would be safe.

"Come on, Reg," Corvin coaxed. "We're partners. Working together again, just like in the Everglades. Just like in the dwarf mountain."

It was clearly a test, but Reg was at a loss as to how to respond to it. Had they been partners on those ventures, and she should agree and would feel warmly toward him for those occasions? Or was it something that she was supposed to argue with because he would know that she was lying if she agreed?

"That's not the way I remember it," she tried, hazarding a guess.

His eyes were calm, studious. "I helped you when you fought Weston. When we all fought the Witch Doctor. Are you forgetting that? Everything we've been through together?"

Reg made a dash for the gate. Corvin moved lightning fast to grab her arm, which had the dual effects of stopping her from being able to make an escape and making the two of them practically light up like a Christmas tree when skin met skin. The electrical shock sent Reg reeling. Corvin looked similarly surprised and stunned.

"See? It is me," Reg said, inching toward the gate. "Or that wouldn't have happened."

He was still holding on to her, despite the current of electricity that ran between them. Corvin was still trying to keep eye contact with her and to force his way into her mind.

"Who are you?" he demanded, voice low and forceful.

"You know who I am."

"How did you get possession of Reg's body? What kind of sorcery is this? Are you a ghost? A demon?"

"Let me go."

"No. I'm not letting go. I am holding on to you, and you have to answer me."

"I have her powers. Do you know how strong she is?"

"Do you know how strong I am?"

That gave Reg pause. She could tell he was powerful. But he couldn't force his will upon her. Or he hadn't yet, if he had that ability.

"Not strong enough," she speculated.

"Oh, no?" He tightened his grip on her arm, the power buzzing between them. "Do you really want to make this a battle of wills?"

"Are you willing to risk her body?"

There was a slight hesitance on his part, a withdrawal of his force. So there was more between them than just his desire for her gifts. He cared something about her as a person as well. Enough that he didn't want to risk hurting her.

"What are you?"

"Just a human. Like you."

"No. You couldn't possess her like this as a human. What else?"

She looked around, waiting for something to happen to distract Corvin. Or she could cause a distraction. Anything from a bird flying past him close enough to startle him to a car accident on the street beside them.

Or she could pretend this had all been planned and pull him in further by pretending to cooperate.

"You could have her," Reg suggested. "We could make a deal and I could leave her in your hands. You could take her powers. It wouldn't hurt her. She wouldn't know what had happened."

Corvin's eyes glinted as he considered the idea. So much for his caring about Reg as a person. The first hint that he could get what he had been after all along, and he was ready to take it.

"Come into the cottage. We'll talk there."

Reg took a step toward the back. Corvin followed, still holding her arm. She took another step, sliding through the open gate that divided the front yard from the back. Corvin followed behind her. He wasn't barred from the back yard. Reg looked around, worried. How could it be, with all the wards Reg had set up? She wouldn't have let this creature past the protective wards.

Corvin kept walking, not giving Reg time to think. She was struggling to remain present. The other soul was trying to reassert itself. Corvin kept pushing or dragging her along. At the door, she stopped again, knowing that he would not be allowed inside. She opened her purse to look for her key, but as she did, she heard the click of the lock and then the doorknob turned. The door swung silently open.

"You can't do that," Reg snarled. "You cannot enter without a key! The protections!"

He stepped through the door with her. She had been sure he would be left behind, unable to enter.

"I don't need a key. I have an invitation."

"No! The wards. The protections. You cannot enter here."

"Reg would have known better than to invite me in."

"This is my home. There are rules. If you don't want to be judged, you must obey them!"

"I've stood trial before. I'm willing to take my chances."

One hand still holding her arm so tightly that her fingers were tingling with loss of circulation, Corvin raised the other to touch her face. Too close. Too intimate a connection. Reg smelled the flowers, felt the cloying sweetness overwhelming her.

He would drain her powers. He would take them all. But Reg could no longer fight him. She no longer wanted to. She wanted him to pull her into an embrace. To complete the merging of their spirits, making her whole at last.

CHAPTER FORTY-TWO

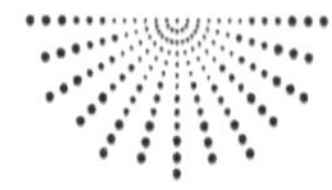

*R*eg's head spun. She tried to make her way through the layers of confusion and protective spells to reach the surface. It was a long way and took a lot of effort, and she wasn't sure whether it was worth it. She stopped to rest and gather her strength, then tried again. Then, like breaking through a thick membrane, she was out of the water and into the air, able to breathe again.

"That's right," he murmured. "Breathe. Take a minute. Are you okay? Reg?"

Despite telling her to take a break and rest, he was demanding immediate answers. Reg tried to compose an answer, but she wasn't sure where she was or what she was doing, so how could she know if she were okay or not?

"He's gone," Corvin said. "But I don't know how long. I'm sure it won't take him long to get his strength back and make another attempt. He's very strong."

"Who?" Reg kept her eyes closed, not wanting any outside stimuli. It was like she had a migraine or fever and any extra light or sound hurt her brain.

"Do you know who it was? Who it is that keeps taking over your body?"

"Taking over my...? What?" Reg tried to push his hands away, but he held on to her, which was probably a good thing, because she wasn't sure whether her legs were solid or jelly and if they could hold her up without help.

"The spirit taking over your body? Who was it?"

"Was it Nagendra?"

"Who is Nagendra?"

"The troll."

"No, I don't think so. You don't know who it is?"

Reg was starting to remember the conversation in the morgue with Nagendra's ghost. *You are the vessel. He was not pure.*

"No… he has… my blood. But I don't know how."

"Your blood. This was accomplished with a blood spell?"

Reg nodded, her head heavy. "Yes. But… I don't know how."

"Did you give him your blood willingly?"

"I don't know. I don't know how it happened."

"Reg." He gave her a little shake. "Regina. Please open your eyes and look at me. This will be much easier if I can see you."

Reg tried to pry her tired eyes open. Was she still asleep? Was that why it was so hard to come to the surface? She'd had dreams like that before. Where she knew she was asleep but couldn't pry off the levels of sleep to bring herself out of it.

Finally, she managed to get them open a crack. She squinted and saw that she was in her cottage. Not at the morgue anymore. And the man with her was Corvin.

Corvin. In her house.

"No! No, you can't be here," she told him, trying to push him away from her. "Get out. Leave this place and don't bother me again."

He wasn't just in the cottage. His arms were around her, holding her close. The smell of roses was overpowering. She didn't know how she had allowed herself to be ensorcelled by him again.

"No!"

"It's okay, Reg. I *had* to. To get him out. I couldn't think of any other way. His hold on you was very strong."

"Who?"

"I was hoping you could tell me. Why didn't you tell me the rest of the details? How you were missing time? How many times has he taken over?"

"I don't know. What happened? How did you… get me free?"

"I drained as much of *his* powers as I could. Eventually, he fled. Can you tell me who it was? Where he would go?"

Reg closed her eyes again, concentrating on the questions. She started to drift again, and Corvin gave her another shake to keep her awake.

"The cemetery. That's where he was before."

"Okay. Can you walk? Let's go to the cemetery."

"Don't want to walk to the cemetery." Reg sagged in his arms, just thinking how much energy that would take.

"No. I just meant walk to the car. From here to the front of the house."

Reg blinked a few times to remind herself where she was and pondered the distance to the front sidewalk. She didn't have much strength.

Corvin turned her and started her walking toward the door, still holding on to her. Like dancing or a three-legged race, trying to move naturally when they were pasted together.

Starlight was there, barring the door, hissing and yowling at Corvin for holding Reg or trying to take her out of the cottage. Corvin tried to negotiate with the cat or get past him.

"Cat, get out of there. I'm helping her. Get out of my way. Cat!"

"He has a name," Reg murmured.

"I'm not treating him like a person."

"He's more than a person." Reg hadn't told him about what she had discovered about Starlight, but he should have known. He was the one who had studied about creatures and immortality and mythology. With everything that he knew, he should have known that Starlight was more than a cat. Corvin could at least call him by the name he had chosen. "Starlight. It's okay," she told him, blinking sleepily and slipping down in Corvin's arms for a minute. "We're just going out. He's going to help."

Starlight hissed and spat. When Corvin moved forward anyway,

Reg felt him attack their feet, nipping and clawing, trying to get them apart.

"Ow! Ow! Starlight! Stop!" Reg reached her hand toward him and tried to impart calming feelings to him, to make him see what they were doing. "Let us go."

Corvin pushed his way past the cat and the door, carrying Reg along with him. Her feet barely touched the floor and she certainly wasn't helping him in any way. Reg looked around, panicking.

"Don't let him outside. I don't want him to get lost."

"He won't get lost. Come on. We have to worry about you. About catching this… hitchhiker… before he grows in strength. Another possession and he may own you completely. We can't take the chance."

"Starlight!"

Corvin didn't waste his breath arguing with her. Starlight continued to attack their legs all the way to the car. Reg's feet and ankles felt like the skin had been stripped off. They stung and tingled, and she could feel blood running down. Corvin managed to shove her into the car's passenger seat, then picked up her feet and pushed them in as well, pushing the door shut to secure her.

He went around to his own side, and Reg could hear him fighting with Starlight again, cussing the cat out royally for continuing to cause him trouble. There was a yowling and hissing like a dozen male cats trying to establish their territory, and a ball of fur and claws landed in Reg's lap.

Corvin slid into his seat, shut his door, and started the engine, muttering to himself.

"Starlight. Shh." Reg tried to gather the fighting fur and fangs into a ball and to cuddle him close. "It's okay. Settle down."

By the time they got to the cemetery, Starlight was starting to settle down. He wasn't curled up into a ball purring, but he had stopped attacking, much to Reg's relief.

The cemetery was not yet closed. The gates stood open. Corvin drove in. He looked around for any visitors.

"Do you know where he is? Can you show me where the body was found?"

Reg looked around. It didn't look the same as it did at night. She could see farther, and everything looked normal and natural, not creepy and supernatural like the night she had arrived to find the body. "I think… that way…"

She heard something. A whispering. Snakeskin slithering through the grass and leaves? Hissing in her ear? Warning her what was going to happen if she let herself be caught. Corvin had said that if she were possessed again, he might own her completely. What did that mean? Would she be gone? Would she be dead? Worse than dead?

"I memorized some of the markers. Slow down, let me see the headstones."

Corvin's car crawled along. Reg tried to find the tombstones she had seen that night.

"To the right. Up there."

She remembered holding the phone in her hand, trying to find something. Had she been looking for the victim or the snake?

"Here, I think."

Corvin stopped the car. Reg slipped Starlight from her lap into the footwell and opened the door. "Is he here? I don't see anyone. Maybe I was wrong."

Corvin was around the car to help her out in a few seconds. He took quick glances up and down all the nearby aisles.

"Where exactly?"

A yowl from Starlight. They turned toward him to quiet him again, and Reg saw the cloaked figure. Was it him? Was there one person who had been causing all her problems?

CHAPTER FORTY-THREE

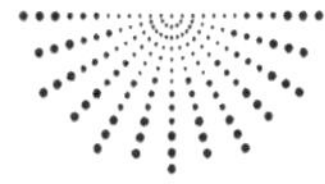

Reg blinked and squinted, trying to bring him into focus. A cloaked man. A warlock.

No, a wizard.

A powerful wizard who had sworn on his powers to do her no harm.

Jeffrey Wilson.

"Why?" Reg asked, shaking her head.

She was weak and disoriented, but that was no excuse for not realizing it was him or for not understanding why he had done what he had. But what had he done? And why?

"I helped you. I made you the tea that helped you to remember. So why... why would you harm me like this when you said that you wouldn't do anything to hurt me?"

"It was your own fault," Wilson snarled. His face contorted when he spoke to her, taking on different expressions as if he couldn't control it. "At first, I didn't know why. Why I kept taking on your powers and memories and losing mine. You must have been aware of it. Entering my body as I entered yours."

Reg shook her head. She couldn't remember anything other than some weird dreams. She hadn't switched places with him. She had stayed in her own body while he tried to control her.

"The troll said that the potion wouldn't work because I was not pure. I had prepared myself. I prepared myself for years before I became lost. When you reawakened me, it was to continue my life's mission. My pursuit of perfection. Of immortality. Advancing not just beyond what any other mortal has achieved, but beyond the immortals as well."

And that, maybe, was why the immortals had taken away his memory and dropped him in the Everglades, where he had remained lost for fifty years. Because he'd had the hubris to think that he could be better even than they were.

"What does that have to do with me? You said you wouldn't do anything to harm me or my friends. You swore it on your powers."

"*I* did nothing. It was you. You were the one who prepared the bitter cup."

Reg knew she had put too much lemon juice into his tea. She had apologized at the time.

"How did you grind the leaves?" Wilson challenged.

They had been tough. Reg had been surprised at how hard and sharp they had been. They had pricked her fingers when she had broken them up. She'd been too lazy to go to Sarah's to ask for a mortar and pestle. It was too much work, and she had done well enough breaking up the leaves by hand.

"Just…" Reg made a motion to demonstrate. "I just crushed them up by hand."

"Stupid!" Wilson howled. He swallowed his other invectives, shaking his head at her, eyes blazing. "How could you be so stupid! You were the one who found me. You were the one who figured out how to restore my memory. How could you be stupid enough to mix a drop of your own blood into the tea?"

"Is that… what happened? That was what I did?"

"You stupid witch. No research. Not bothering to get proper equipment. No recipe or spell to follow. Just whatever you thought was right. You wrecked everything!"

"I'm… sorry…?"

She again heard scales slithering through the grass. Reg looked around, trying to pinpoint the noise.

No one else seemed to be able to hear it. But Reg did see one thing. She saw a black tail with a white tip disappear behind a gravestone. Starlight stalking. She wanted to call out to him and warn him that it could be dangerous. A snake in this graveyard had killed the troll. A troll who was used to handling snakes. How was an inexperienced cat going to fare?

Wilson was still going on about how Reg had ruined his life and destroyed any chance he had to achieve his goal of immortality. He started ranting to Corvin about how he had destroyed Wilson's other chance by not letting him subsume Reg. If he couldn't use his own body, then he could use hers. It was her blood. She had considerable powers, and if he added his own to the mix and finished the transition, he could try again.

The basilisk was still there, after all. It hadn't gone far. Wilson could try again. Could complete the spell without the troll's help, now that he had seen how to handle the snake properly.

Reg watched the white tip of tail as Starlight stalked between and around graves.

Corvin was watching Reg thoughtfully. How much of what she was thinking could he read? He had been joined with her, the conduit between them open so that he could sense the difference between her consciousness and Wilson's.

"So it's everyone's fault but your own," he said to Wilson. "You just can't take responsibility for your own actions. You are the type who always has to find someone else to blame."

"It *is* her fault," Wilson shouted, furious. "I did not choose for her to contaminate the tea. That was her mistake. She should have known that blood would taint it. She should have known to use the proper equipment. What kind of a witch can't even make tea?"

"I'm just a psychic," Reg said. "That's all I've ever claimed to be."

CHAPTER FORTY-FOUR

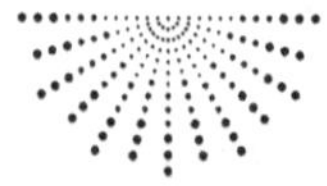

Starlight pounced.

Reg jumped, startled by his sudden movement. He struck as quickly as any snake could have, maybe faster. She could hear the body of the basilisk as it struggled to free itself, coiling and uncoiling and trying to wriggle away. Starlight growled, anger in his voice.

"No!" Wilson realized that the cat had the snake and ran toward them. "What are you doing bringing a cat here? This is… you can't do this!"

He reached out to take the snake from Starlight and got his hand slashed for his trouble. Starlight let out another warning growl.

"Let it go! Give it to me!" Wilson raged. "A dead basilisk is no good to me! It must be alive. It must be milked at midnight. You can't…!"

Starlight wrestled with the snake. Reg couldn't see him very well and moved closer, going around the headstones, until she could see that he had the snake behind the neck, so it would be unable to strike. His muscular body braced against the ground and sometimes twisted and turned with the writhing of the snake but, eventually, the writhing stopped and the snake slowly uncoiled, its body limp on the ground.

"No!"

Wilson turned back toward Reg. "How could you do this to me? I had one more chance. You let the warlock drain my powers and the cat kill the snake! That isn't a coincidence. You pretend to be innocent, but you know exactly what you're doing! This will not be tolerated! I will not be satisfied until you are dead and your spirit banished to the void. To nothingness! Death alone will not do!"

Reg looked over at Corvin to see what he thought of the wizard's rantings. Corvin raised one eyebrow in amusement. Nothing for Reg to be worried about. Yes, he had been a powerful wizard at one time —perhaps the most powerful. But Reg and Corvin had broken him down. His threats were pointless. Toothless.

Wilson bent down and picked up the basilisk's body, furious. Starlight protested the removal of his prize, but didn't attack Wilson. Wilson brandished it at Reg.

"Do you know what I can do with this? Do you know how valuable basilisks are? How many uses there are for basilisk venom or parts? You think this is just garbage? You let your cat drag it around until he's tired of it and then throw it in the trash?"

Reg didn't bother to tell him that she hadn't said any of that. He was on another tear, again putting everybody else down to elevate himself.

"You should be careful with that," Corvin warned. "The head can—"

"I should be careful? Do you know who I am? Do you not realize that for hundreds of years, I have—"

Reg wasn't sure what it was that Corvin had been about to say. That a basilisk could still bite after it was dead? That the venom was still deadly, even if it couldn't be used to make Wilson immortal?

It didn't really matter what he had been about to say, because Wilson hadn't listened. He had chosen to ignore everyone else's advice, believing that he was the smartest and strongest.

As he ranted, he waved the snake around, holding it by the middle, not the back of the head like Starlight had. He wasn't even looking at it when the head end swung against his body, and the jaws suddenly snapped shut somewhere around his armpit.

Wilson let out a yelp. He looked down in astonishment at the body of the basilisk.

"You have to be careful of those," Corvin said.

Wilson stared back at him.

"Unfortunately, it's not quite midnight," Corvin went on, looking down at his watch. Though he had no need to check the time; it was still light out and the cemetery still open.

"No!" Wilson said. He yanked the body of the snake, jerking it away from himself. Reg winced at the thought of the needle-sharp teeth ripping through his flesh. That had to hurt. But Wilson didn't show any sign of pain. Maybe it had already been numbed by the basilisk venom. "No, this can't be happening!"

The head of the basilisk drooped down to the same level as the tail. The jaw snapped again, fastening onto the end of the tail. And then, bizarrely, dead though it was, the basilisk began to swallow itself, shrinking into a smaller and smaller loop until there was nothing left of it.

"I am a powerful wizard!" Wilson protested. He felt the area that the snake had bitten, trying to discern how seriously he was wounded. Reg had no idea how fast basilisk venom worked, but she suspected it was too late to do anything about it. They were a mythical creature, so even if they were to get Wilson to the hospital, the doctors wouldn't know what to do for him. They could treat him for snakebite if he were still alive, but they wouldn't have the antivenin, if there even was one.

"Help me!"

Wilson's knees buckled and he held on to one of the headstones to keep himself on his feet. Corvin moved closer to help him. Reg didn't have any desire to help. And she didn't want her fingerprints or any kind of evidence on this man when the police found him in the cemetery.

Corvin held Wilson's arm as he slowly sank to the ground, breaking his fall. He slid his hand under Wilson's jaw to feel for a pulse, keeping it there as if he were counting. Reg realized too late that Corvin didn't have any interest in helping Wilson either. He wasn't trying to stop the flow of the poison. He didn't call for an ambulance or start CPR. He was taking what he could of Wilson's powers before he died. Like a carrion bird watching a sick animal circle the drain. Her stomach turned at the thought of what he was doing.

"Corvin, you shouldn't—"

"I shouldn't?" Corvin demanded. "I should just let his power dissipate? Waste it?"

"Well… I don't know. I thought the rule was that you had to have his permission."

"You heard him ask for my help."

"That's not what he meant. He meant… save him. Take him to a doctor or something."

"He knew that it was a mortal wound. There is no treatment for a basilisk bite. No chance at recovery."

Reg watched Corvin's face take on a flush, his eyes bright. She could feel the growth of his power through their always-on connection. Maybe she ought to get out of there before he decided to turn on her.

And someone should probably call the police and tell them there was another dead body in the cemetery. Reg didn't want to be the one to do that. She didn't want to be called back in to testify about what she had seen there. What would she say? This time she had seen the snake bite, but who was going to believe the details? A sanitized version wouldn't sound much more believable. She'd already found one snakebite victim. The body of the snake had disappeared. She didn't know if a basilisk was one of those mythical animals that could regenerate itself after death, like a phoenix. If it could consume itself after it was dead, anything was possible. How was she even going to explain her presence at the cemetery?

Reg turned and started to walk back toward the car. She was halfway there when she remembered that she hadn't brought her own car, Corvin had driven her there. And not just her, but Starlight.

She turned back. "Starlight? Where are you? Let's go home."

With all the headstones, there were a million places to hide. She tried to see if he were lurking behind one of them. Or was he still hunting? Maybe there was another snake, or the basilisk had regenerated. She didn't want him to push his luck and get bitten. She remembered how awful it had been when he had been sick. And cats faced lots of other dangers outside too, with traffic and bigger animals. She didn't even know if Starlight would be able to find his way home when they had driven to the cemetery in the car.

"Starlight?" She reached out with all her senses, trying to feel him. He was still close by, so it shouldn't be too hard to find him. Unless he didn't want to be found.

There was a meow nearby. Reg looked around and saw him sitting on top of a flat headstone, washing.

"There are you are. You're okay, right? It didn't bite you?"

Starlight stopped washing for a moment to look at her. She knew that he hadn't been bitten. If he had, he would have been in worse shape than Wilson. He had gotten rid of a dangerous predator and had prevented Wilson from being able to finish his spell. Reg wasn't sure how Wilson had planned to purify himself of her blood, but it probably wasn't something she would have appreciated.

"Come on, let's get out of here," she told Starlight. She made a kissy noise to call him after her and took a few steps away. He stayed where he was, washing.

"We need to go. I don't want to stay around here."

He was not to be deterred. Reg imagined she would probably want a bath after wrestling a basilisk too. In fact, a bath sounded like a pretty great idea right about then.

There was a movement among the graves, and Reg saw Corvin coming toward her. She was tired, but quickly wove a protection spell around herself. He would be stronger than ever. Wilson had been a powerful wizard, and if Corvin had been able to absorb any of his powers before he died, he would be stronger than ever.

"Regina." His eyes were glassy like he was high. "We should go."

"Yeah. That's what I was just thinking. You want me to drive?"

He gave a vague smile. "Why would I want you to drive?"

"You look… intoxicated. If we get pulled over, they're going to think you're DUI."

Corvin considered this as they walked toward the car. Reg looked back at Starlight, who finally decided he'd better move his furry butt and followed them. Corvin wove a little as he walked toward the car.

"I'm driving," Reg insisted when they reached it.

He blinked at her slowly, his pupils wide pools of darkness. "Are we going to your house?"

"Well… I have to get Starlight home. Then I can drive you to your house."

"I'll just stay at yours for a while."

"You can't."

"I was there earlier today, in case you don't remember."

"Well… I can't help that. I wasn't exactly… in charge then."

"I behaved myself."

"Did you?"

He gave a slow smile. "I got him out of you, didn't I?"

"Apparently, but I'm not sure about your methods."

Corvin opened the passenger door to slide into the seat. "I'm not holding your cat."

Reg called Starlight as she opened the driver's side door. "He can sit in the back. He doesn't need to be in anyone's lap."

"Good. Of course, I'll have to get it cleaned."

"He's not dirty. And it's not like you're allergic."

"I don't want cat hair in my car."

Reg rolled her eyes. They had just witnessed the demise of a powerful wizard who had been trying to possess Reg, and Corvin was worried about a little cat fur. Starlight smelled the car, then finally jumped in and settled himself on the back seat.

CHAPTER FORTY-FIVE

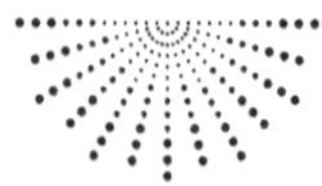

Reg picked Starlight up from the back seat and carried him into the cottage. She could have just asked him to follow her, but cats were ridiculously unpredictable and he might just as easily decide to run away to see his old friend Nicole or a stray he had spotted out the window. Or to go hunting for the diamondback rattler that Reg had seen.

"Reg! Oh, Reg!"

Reg turned as Sarah came out the back door of the big house. "Hi."

"Oh," Sarah noticed Starlight in Reg's arms. "Did he get away?"

"No… not exactly. He was… helping on a case."

"Oh." Sarah frowned, looking doubtful about this. Although she tolerated Starlight, Sarah didn't like cats, and she didn't want them out in her yard chasing birds or wrecking the garden. And she worried that Starlight would attract other cats from the neighborhood. She knew that Starlight was Reg's familiar and worked with her, but Reg didn't usually take Starlight with her except on longer trips. "Okay. Well, let's get him inside first, so you don't have to worry about him getting away."

Reg agreed. Sarah's eyes turned toward Corvin, who had followed

Reg into the yard, and her frown deepened. "How did he get past the wards?"

"Uh…" Reg tried to come up with an explanation that Sarah would understand. Something that would not make her want to throw Reg out. "Well… that's sort of a long story, and I'm not sure I can tell you all of the details."

"You let him in?"

"Sort of."

"Either you did or you didn't," Sarah said severely. Reg unlocked the door and let herself in. She put Starlight down on the floor and he trotted away as if going out on an excursion to kill a basilisk were routine.

"I didn't," Reg said. "But I did."

"You did," Sarah repeated.

"But I didn't."

Corvin followed them into the house. Sarah studied him.

"What's wrong with him?"

"There's nothing wrong with me," Corvin said, giving Sarah a sloppy grin.

"He's acting kind of drunk," Reg said. "I don't know if that's normal or not."

"Normal for what?" Sarah asked. Then her eyes widened. "Has he been feeding?"

Reg nodded. Sarah blinked at her. "Who?"

"You remember Jeffrey Wilson?"

"The wizard? Of course. But how could—he would never let Corvin…"

"He wasn't exactly in a position to object. He was…"

"He was dying," Corvin said baldly. "What would you expect me to do? Allow those powers to be dispersed?"

"Dying. What happened to him? He was very powerful."

"Powerful apparently doesn't mean smart," Corvin said with a smirk. "Would you have let yourself be bitten by a basilisk?"

"Bitten… heavens, no. Not another one?"

"The same one that bit the troll," Reg said. "But… it's dead now.

Actually, it was dead when it bit Wilson. Actually, I don't know if it is dead now."

"Looked pretty dead," Corvin contributed. "Well… until it bit Wilson and swallowed its own tail. What happens after that is anyone's guess."

"I don't know," Reg repeated. "I don't know if that means it's dead or alive."

"Well. You've had an eventful afternoon. But he can't stay here," Sarah look pointedly at Corvin.

"I was thinking of driving him home. I don't think he's safe to drive himself."

"I've been driving myself after feeding for many years," Corvin informed her. "It has never been a problem."

"Well, maybe he was on some drug that is affecting you. I don't know."

Corvin rolled his eyes. "It isn't like I have consumed his body. I don't take in anything of his physical form."

"What is it then?"

Corvin considered the question. "Perhaps the basilisk," he said eventually. "Maybe it conferred on him with some extra powers after all. I feel very… well."

Sarah nodded slowly, her brow wrinkled. "Maybe so. There are old texts that speak of… divine intoxication conferred by the basilisk. It is the result of drinking the elixir of life. The essence present in the snake's venom."

"I don't know what it is," Corvin said slowly, "but it feels very, very good."

Sarah looked at Reg worriedly. "Maybe we'd better keep an eye on him. If he's drunk on the basilisk's essence, there could be negative effects too. And we would do well to find out now what powers he was able to consume before Wizard Wilson's death." She shook her head and dropped her voice. "I don't like it. It would have been better if the wizard's power had been spread out."

* * *

They eventually persuaded Corvin to sit on the couch to watch TV and, eventually, he fell asleep there. Sarah asked questions at length and did some witchy stuff that Reg didn't understand, mumbling spells or prayers, walking around Corvin several times, laying out herbs and touching the various wards around the cottage. Even Starlight, who was very interested in these activities initially, eventually tired of watching Sarah and curled up on Reg's bed to go to sleep.

"I'm kind of tired too," Reg confessed to Sarah. "Do you mind if I go lay down for a while? You can wake me up if Corvin wakes up or if you need anything."

"Of course, Reg. I don't imagine you got much sleep last night with a restless Bigfoot on your hands. You were up pretty early this morning. For you, I mean."

"Oh!" Reg rubbed her eyes, trying to focus on this. "I forgot all about… is Etienne okay? Did he come to see you this morning?"

"Yes. I drove him to the hotel where his lady friend is staying." She paused and shrugged. "The poor boy has a bit of a weak stomach. But I suppose that's what happens when they vary from their natural diet to eat things like Hershey's bars and… whatever happened to be in your fridge."

Reg felt sorry for Etienne. He had already been anxious about Ilka and Sarah's driving had clearly not helped. She hoped he'd felt better once he got to her suite.

"When is he coming back? Is he coming here before he goes home?"

"He took his things with him. I don't think he was planning to come back here, but he did say he would be in touch and let us know what he was doing."

"And you haven't heard anything back?"

"I haven't. He doesn't have a phone, does he?"

"No, he would probably just come back here. Or get someone to make the call for him. I feel so bad about abandoning him this morning… but things got very strange."

"Yes," Sarah cocked her head to the side. "They certainly did. But I'm sure he understood. He would be much happier being left to his own devices than having to deal with police and snakes and the rest of it. They are a very quiet people. They would much rather be left to themselves."

CHAPTER FORTY-SIX

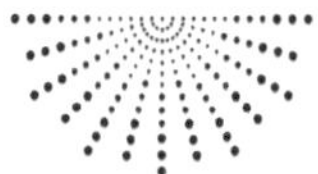

*W*hen Corvin awoke, he seemed much steadier. Sarah proclaimed him recovered and able to get himself home rather than Reg having to take care of him. Reg sat on the couch watching Corvin get ready to go. He seemed to be okay.

"If you want, I could stay longer," Corvin teased.

"No, no. I just want to make sure that you are back to normal. I don't want you getting in an accident on the way home."

"Nice to know that you care."

"I just think I've spent enough time at the police station, morgue, and cemetery this week. I'd rather not have to do it all again."

"You just don't want to admit that you like me."

"No, I don't," Reg agreed.

His mouth twisted into a grimace at her ambiguous answer. He decided not to push it any further. Reg turned to Sarah after Corvin was gone. "So do you think… he's dangerous?"

"He's always been dangerous, dear. Now… even more so."

"I know…" Reg sighed. "*Be careful. Don't let him into the house. But it wasn't really my fault; I wasn't in control.*"

"You certainly do attract the interest of powerful creatures, don't you?"

"It's just a coincidence." Reg didn't want to think that something about her personally or about the choices she made had something to do with it. It was just bad luck.

Starlight rubbed against Reg's legs, and she scratched his ears.

"Maybe if I want better luck, I should get rid of the black cat," she teased.

He looked at her with big, unblinking eyes.

Sarah laughed. "Yes, maybe you should," she agreed. But Reg knew she had a soft spot for Starlight. She wouldn't tell Reg to get rid of him if she actually thought Reg would do it.

* * *

Reg felt more caught up on sleep and decided it was time to get herself something good to eat. Not just something grabbed in a hurry from the cupboard or the fridge, but a good meal. And The Crystal Bowl was always her restaurant of choice.

When she got out to the street, she was distracted from her own vehicle by a long black limousine. She watched in surprise as it pulled over in front of her car. Maybe Sarah had visitors?

But she knew the cloaked figure who climbed out of the car. Etienne straightened up, then gave a brief bow in Reg's direction.

"Reg Rawlins. I am returning home."

"In style," Reg observed.

Etienne looked through the door into the car's interior. "More legroom," he commented. "It will be better for the trip."

"Is Ilka...?"

Etienne indicated that she was in the car, which didn't surprise Reg. The limousine was more like something the empress would rent than Etienne. "She is going to go to Miami. There is a family there that will take her in so that we can continue to see each other and court... and maybe in time..."

"You're not rushing things."

"No." He sounded relieved about that. "Our families are both in agreement that this should not be rushed. We need to take the time to get to know each other well before any irreversible steps are taken."

"Yeah. That sounds smart. Is she okay with that?"

"We will find out. She has agreed to a trial, but I know she is impatient to move things forward." He smiled his shy, embarrassed smile, his teeth showing slightly behind his full beard. "The women of our species are very strong-minded."

"So I have noticed. Well, good luck. I hope it will all work out. You have my address; you can write and let me know how you are doing anytime."

"I shall. Bruce takes my mail into town once a month."

Reg nodded, familiar with the procedure. "The last Tuesday of the month. I look forward to hearing how it goes."

And surprisingly, it was true. Reg had never looked forward to having to read anything, but she hoped that all would go well for Etienne and Ilka, and they would find happiness together. She looked forward to finding out how they fared.

Did you enjoy this book? Reviews and recommendations are vital to making a book successful.

Please leave a review at your favorite book store or review site and share it with your friends.

Don't miss the following bonus material:
Sign up for mailing list to get a free ebook
Read a sneak preview chapter
Other books by P.D. Workman
Learn more about the author

STEP DEEPER INTO BLACK SANDS

Step deeper with Reg Rawlins into the mystical town of Black Sands

Reg Rawlins never thought she'd stay in Black Sands.

What started as a simple con turned into something else—strange cases, impossible choices, and a town where the usual rules don't apply.

If you want more, you can explore Reg's cases in a different way:

🔮 Ask the Crystal Ball

Find out which case you should read next

🐢 Draw a Card

Discover strange people, impossible situations, and dangerous choices

Get Exclusive Access

Special content, new releases, and reader-only extras

Welcome to Reg Rawlins's World

CAREFUL OF THY WISHES

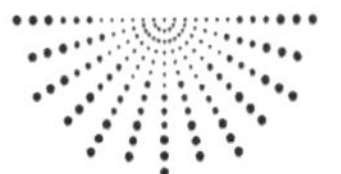

REG RAWLINS, PSYCHIC INVESTIGATOR #13

CHAPTER ONE

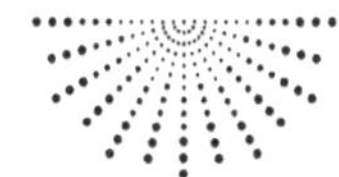

Reg had been putting it off for too long. She had been spending more, knowing that she had the gems to fall back on, so, although she had been doing okay with her psychic services business, she had been spending more than she was making, which wasn't a great way to keep her bank balance in the black.

She kept putting off cashing in a couple of the gems because of the work involved. She hadn't ever done it before, for one thing. She had used pawnshops in the past to get a bit of cash for jewelry she had acquired through one means or another, but she knew that she didn't get anywhere near what they were worth. And she couldn't take cut, unset gemstones to a pawnshop. They weren't jewelers. They wouldn't know how much they were worth or give her a fair price.

That meant that she had to figure out where to go to sell the gems. She found several gemstone buyers in nearby cities; that was an easy enough internet search. The problem was finding one that would not only give her a fair price, but would look the other way on gems that might not have come through *regular channels.*

The stores in Black Sands would be more understanding about how she had acquired the gems, but she didn't think it was a good idea for anyone in Black Sands to know about the fact that she had a small chest of cut gems in her possession. She hadn't yet rented a safe deposit box like Sarah, her landlord, had suggested, which meant that the box of gems was in Reg's closet. Or under the bed. Or whatever other place she had chosen to hide it in temporarily. She moved it around regularly because she knew it wasn't safe. There wasn't anywhere secure to hide it within the guest cottage she rented from the older woman. If word got out that she had the gems, she could have a problem.

Of course, the cottage was protected with magical wards and charms, but Reg knew that there were still ways for less-honorable thieves to find their way around the wards, or for powerful beings to break them. She knew because it had happened before. Sarah had helped her to set new wards several times. She always rolled her eyes and gave Reg a stern lecture on not allowing herself to be talked into releasing the wards, allowing a pixie into the house, or surrendering by any other means to which the wards were vulnerable.

So Reg knew that she couldn't liquidate any of the jewels in Black Sands. It was too risky. She would have to go into one of the bigger cities where she was unknown and where she would not be required to explain how the stones had come into her possession. And those kinds of places didn't advertise the fact on public websites.

But she couldn't afford to wait any longer.

There were a few interesting listings on Craigslist and eBay. Reg made screenshots of them and looked up the addresses on the maps app on her phone.

"What do you think?" she mused aloud.

Starlight looked at her, blinking first his blue eye and then his green. She didn't know how much of commerce or the internet he understood. His psychic powers might not extend that far.

"I need money if I'm going to get you food and kitty litter. So you want to help me with that, right?"

He blinked again, both eyes together this time. Reg focused on the white mark in the third eye position on his forehead. The star that gave him his name. She squinted her eyes slightly and let them go out of focus, thinking about the listings that she had just found on her phone, trying to sort out which of them was the best bet. She brought up the first one in her mind, a David Price of Rite Price Gem

Exchange and immediately felt a sense of foreboding. Her stomach tied itself in a tight, heavy knot that nearly made her physically sick.

She didn't know what the danger was in going to Price, but she knew it was not a good idea. She mentally struck that one off her list.

"Okay…"

She opened her eyes for a couple of seconds to check out the next listing. *Dreame Jewelry. Achieve your highest dreams.* That one sounded even sleazier than the first. But she focused her eyes on Starlight's white star again and thought about it.

She had never dreamed that she would come into possession of such a fortune. There had been plenty of times in the past when she had dreamed of somewhere safe and sheltered to live and a bowl of warm soup in her hands. Reg had found that and more in Black Sands, a little Florida community that had seemed ripe for all kinds of paranormal cons. But, as she had soon discovered, there was more to Black Sands than just a high percentage of practicing psychics and retirees with thick wallets that needed unburdening. Instead, she had found a community that had not only accepted her as a bona fide psychic, but had opened up to her a whole new world of paranormal practitioners and experiences that were often difficult for her to believe existed.

She still woke up some mornings wondering if the past year had all been a dream and she didn't really possess any unusual psychic or paranormal abilities. Maybe there were no witches, fairies, sirens, or immortals. Maybe it was all just a very detailed and involved hallucination.

And then she talked to her cat and pulled out the little chest of gems and looked out the window at Sarah's backyard garden, flourishing under the care of Forst, the garden gnome. And she knew that it was all real.

"Do you think they would give me what the gems are worth?"

Not what they were worth, of course, but at least enough that she wouldn't have to worry about her bank account again for a few months.

She had a good feeling about Dreame Jewelry. Maybe it was the right place to go.

There were still more places on her list, but she didn't want to go over all of them with Starlight. Using her psychic powers, even with Starlight, was tiring, and she couldn't maintain her focus for that long.

Besides, it was nearly noon, and she was ready for some breakfast.

CHAPTER TWO

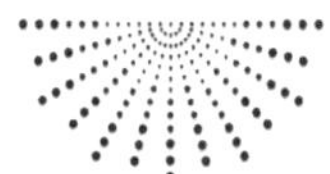

It had taken Reg a couple of hours to get to the city and locate the little store front that Dreame Jewelry worked out of. When she saw the dingy front window with dusty displays of what clearly was not real jewelry, she nearly changed her mind. There were several other jewelers on her list. Dreame really did not live up to its name.

But she was there. She might as well at least check it out. She'd had a good feeling about the place initially. Maybe it was a diamond in the rough. So to speak.

Reg pushed open the door. A bell tinkled, announcing her arrival. The interior was dim after the bright Florida sunlight outside. She couldn't see much at first. She closed her eyes, then opened them again and squinted around.

There were a few display cases with much the same kind of product as she had seen in the window. Maybe a few real pieces, but even the ones that appeared to be real weren't spectacular. They needed a good cleaning, to begin with. The store smelled dusty and old and sort of oily. A jewelry store shouldn't smell oily, should it?

Reg browsed through the displays. When she looked up, she saw a man standing behind the one that had been on her right when she had pushed her way through the door. She was sure that he hadn't been there, standing in the dim recesses of the room, when she had arrived. But he had either appeared out of nowhere or had crept in from the back of the store so quietly that she had not heard him or been aware of his presence.

"Oh. Hi there. I didn't see you."

The man was dark-skinned and had a short black beard that was not properly trimmed. Or maybe it was just a few days' growth of whiskers that didn't count as a beard. His face was round and his body wide.

"Good afternoon," he greeted in a resonant, surprisingly reassuring voice. "Jean Beaugrand at your service. How can I help you today?"

"Well, I was just looking…" Reg indicated the display cases, not yet showing her hand. Maybe she was just a tourist who had wandered in off the street.

The man's eyes traveled over Reg, from the multicolored headscarf around her head, to her red box braids, to her flowing peasant shirt and skirt. Maybe she didn't look like a tourist. But Beaugrand would have no way of knowing who she was. She didn't know anyone in the area and she wouldn't tell him that she had come from Black Sands.

"Are you here to buy or to sell?" he asked, getting immediately to the crux of the matter.

Reg pursed her lips, thinking about what to say. Admit that she was there looking for a buyer? Or continue to look at his wares and feel him out before revealing the fact?

She didn't say anything at first. She ignored his question as if she hadn't heard or understood it and browsed through the display case that he was standing behind, getting closer to him, reaching out with all of her senses to examine him, to read and classify him. She was good at cold-reading people. Or what she had always thought of as cold reading but might actually have been using her psychic powers before she knew she had them.

"Like what you see?" the man inquired mildly.

There was more to Beaugrand than met the eye. Few people showed their true selves to the world, but she sensed that he was hiding more than most. While his face and voice suggested that he was open and honest, there was a cloak of mystery and secrecy around him. Something stopped her from being able to probe him further.

"Well, there are a couple of pieces," Reg said, turning her attention back to the jewelry and pretending that was what he had been asking. She indicated a necklace that was almost directly in front of him. The ruby in the pendant was real. She could feel that. After having handled her own gems regularly, she could sense the power of a real stone. "This one…"

The man smiled, showing two rows of white, even teeth. "That is a very nice piece," he agreed. "Are you interested in buying?"

There was no price tag on it. Reg studied his face. He did not appear to be sarcastic or judging her as being too poor to afford it. It was a simple question about her interest in it.

"No," Reg admitted. She pulled a small velvet pouch out of her pocket. "I saw on Craigslist that you purchase gemstones. I don't see any out, so I was just wondering…"

"I do not display them," Beaugrand agreed. "I sell them privately to silver- and goldsmiths. People don't generally walk in off the street looking for unset stones."

Reg hesitated for another instant, reaching out to assess his feelings and intentions again. Either he was very good at blocking her, or he was an honest man. She loosened the strings on the pouch and spilled the gems she had brought with her onto her palm. She didn't know if he would be interested in everything, or whether he only bought certain gems. Or perhaps only what he knew his smiths were currently looking for.

The man leaned forward to look at them. He opened a drawer and put a shallow tray on top of the display case. "You can put them in there, and I will have a look."

He pulled a loupe from a pocket and picked up a ruby. He looked at it for a few moments, then put it back and picked up a blue gem, a sapphire, Reg assumed. He studied it for only an instant before putting it back.

He shook his head slowly. The opening move of his negotiation. Reg was familiar with negotiation, and he wasn't going to scare her away by declaring that her gems were worth very little or nothing.

She could be hard-nosed and get a fair price. She'd had a lot of practice when she had been a lot more desperate than she was now.

"They are real," Reg asserted, looking him in the eye.

Beaugrand nodded. "Oh, yes. They are real. And good quality."

She was surprised to hear him concede that. But maybe it was part of his strategy. A little carrot to tempt her.

"Then what is the problem? They're good stones, you purchase stones for your smithies. Why wouldn't you be interested?"

"Do you know anything about the provenance of these stones?"

She had sold enough family heirlooms to know that provenance referred to being able to prove where the goods had come from and what hands they had passed through. She hadn't bothered to doctor any papers to give the gems fake histories.

"I understood from what I read that you… will purchase gems without provenance," Reg said delicately. She didn't want to imply that he was doing something against the law, or even unethical. But she'd done her research. She knew that Dreame dealt in… shadier areas.

"This is true," he tilted his head in a slight nod. "However, I wondered if you know *anything* about these gems. How did they come into your hands?"

"They are not stolen."

"That is good, but does not answer the question." The man pulled a stool over and sat down, resting his meaty forearms on the top of the case.

"They were given to me as a gift."

She doubted he would believe that, but he didn't give any sign of disbelief. "And did you accept them? Or did you say that you would check them out first?" He looked down at the gems in the tray.

"They are mine. I can sell them or do whatever I like with them."

"So, you accepted the gift."

Reg nodded impatiently. "Yes. Of course. Who wouldn't?"

Beaugrand smiled, showing his teeth again. "Perhaps someone who is not as rash as you."

Reg's stomach knotted. This did not sound good. Why should it be a problem that she had accepted the stones that were given to her as a gift? Unless they were stolen property, she couldn't see what was wrong with her owning them. The police couldn't do anything about that.

"Why? What do you mean?"

"I cannot buy these stones from you. You will need to find another avenue to rid yourself of them."

Reg stared at him, frowning.

* * *

Careful of Thy wishes, Book #13 of the *Reg Rawlins, Psychic Investigator* series by P.D. Workman
can be purchased at pdworkman.com

* * *

ABOUT THE AUTHOR

P.D. Workman is a USA Today Bestselling author and multi-award winner, renowned for her prolific output of over 100 published works that span various genres. With a knack for crafting page-turners, Workman captivates readers with everything from cozy mysteries like the Auntie Clem's Bakery series to gripping young adult and suspense novels.

A prolific reader and writer since childhood, P.D. Workman crafts emotionally powerful stories that don't shy away from hard topics. Her books tackle mental illness, addiction, abuse, and trauma with raw honesty and compassion, giving voice to the often unheard. If you crave authentic, character-driven page-turners that hit deep and stay with you long after the final page, you're in the right place.

With each new release, fans eagerly anticipate another thrilling blend of thought-provoking storytelling and relatable characters that define P.D. Workman's brand as an author of unforgettable page-turners— gripping tales that leave a lasting impact long after the last page is turned.

> P. D. Workman, does not shy from probing the deep psychological scars of childhood trauma, mental illness, and addiction. Also characteristic of this author, these extremely sensitive issues are explored with extensive empathy, described with incredible clarity, and portrayed with profound insight.
>
> ——KIM, GOODREADS REVIEWER

Some of Workman's titles have been translated into Spanish, French, Portuguese, German, and Italian.

Workman began writing at an early age and is a prolific reader as well as writer. She is also passionate about teaching and learning, expresses her creativity through art and cooking, and loves exploring the Calgary parks and green spaces where the Parks Pat Mysteries are set. She was a legal assistant for many years and has done extensive charitable work.

Workman was born and raised in Alberta, Canada, and is married with one adult son.

* * *

Please visit P.D. Workman at pdworkman.com to see what else she is working on, to join her mailing list, and to link to her social networks.

* * *

If you enjoyed this book, please take the time to recommend it to other purchasers with a review or star rating and share it with your friends!

tiktok.com/@pdworkmanauthor

facebook.com/pdworkmanauthor

x.com/pdworkmanauthor

instagram.com/pdworkmanauthor

amazon.com/author/pdworkman

bookbub.com/authors/p-d-workman

goodreads.com/pdworkman

linkedin.com/in/pdworkman

pinterest.com/pdworkmanauthor

youtube.com/pdworkman

Find P.D. Workman's books at

PDWORKMAN.COM

Scan the QR code below

www.ingramcontent.com/pod-product-compliance
Lightning Source LLC
Chambersburg PA
CBHW021305190726

48288CB00003B/693